———————— ★ ————————

THE SICKLY SWEET ODOR GREW STRONGER AS THEY SNAKED PAST SHELVES TOWARD A ROW OF DOORS.

Reluctantly Sheila followed as Capeletti inserted his key and pulled open the door.

The odor that had invaded the stack rolled out to greet them. Simultaneously, Capeletti and Yusuf went rigid. The older man held out one hand to ward Sheila off, but she had already seen what they were seeing.

Covering her mouth with one hand, she backed one step. But the scene was engraved somewhere just in front of her eyes: a room empty except for one rolled rug. And protruding from one end of that rug, a woman's blue boot.

———————— ★ ————————

"The hallowed academic community provides an ideal backdrop for sleuthing and skullduggery."

—*Booklist*

D0017545

Forthcoming Worldwide Mystery novels by
PATRICIA HOUCK SPRINKLE

MURDER IN THE CHARLESTON MANNER
MURDER ON PEACHTREE STREET
SOMEBODY'S DEAD IN SNELLVILLE

MURDER
at Markham

PATRICIA
HOUCK
SPRINKLE

WORLDWIDE.

TORONTO • NEW YORK • LONDON
AMSTERDAM • PARIS • SYDNEY • HAMBURG
STOCKHOLM • ATHENS • TOKYO • MILAN
MADRID • WARSAW • BUDAPEST • AUCKLAND

MURDER AT MARKHAM

A Worldwide Mystery/November 1992

First published by St. Martin's Press Incorporated.

ISBN 0-373-26108-X

Printed in U.S.A.

MURDER

at Markham

ONE

THIS SIDE OF THE STREET was still clinging to winter, piles of grimy snow oozing down the sidewalk. Sheila Travis anchored her purse more firmly on her shoulder and strode to the other side, where a small green wooden shed glowed in sunlight and a grizzled old man with a grin sold papers.

Chicago in February was nothing like she had been warned. She had come armed with coats and heavy suits against sub-zero temperatures. Instead, ever since her Monday arrival, capricious Gulf breezes had startled the city with blue skies, sunshine, and balmy air. Children trooped to parks for muddy games of tag. Teenagers shot baskets on improvised courts. In the Loop, sweatered shoppers exchanged grins as they hurried between Marshall Field's and lesser establishments. Even bus drivers smiled.

Here in the Hyde Park neighborhood—enclave of liberal thinking dominated by the University of Chicago and her somber satellites—Sheila dodged a red Frisbee and stepped aside to let a student in shorts jog virtuously past. Overhead the Rockefeller Chapel chimes tolled eleven. Another hour of winter reprieve.

"Paper, lady?" All but two of the old man's teeth had long since departed, leaving him an enchanting jack-o'-lantern smile as he peered up at her over his counter.

She could never resist a newspaper, especially these past weeks. But she hesitated, considering her choices.

"What you looking for?" he quavered, gnarled hands poised above his wares.

"I may need to find a job." Her eyes scanned his counter.

He reached for the largest paper. "Then it's the *Tribune* you want. Best classified in the nation."

She fumbled in her purse for American coins, brought out a Japanese one by mistake.

"You from somewhere else?" he inquired, one busy brow cocked.

She nodded. "I was. I've lived in Japan most of my life, but I've come home now. My husband died last November." Why, she wondered, was she saying this to a stranger? Was she going to become like other women who lived alone, women who bared their souls on buses for lack of someone at home to talk to?

The old man didn't seem to mind. "Seems like it happens to everybody sooner or later, don't it?" he said in candid sympathy.

She nodded, her smile returning. He was so delightful, with his red-veined cheeks and faded blue eyes, that she was tempted to linger—almost.

"Not now," she told herself firmly, tucking the paper under one arm and giving him a nod in farewell, "you've got an interview."

As she climbed the worn stone steps of a university building, she warned herself not to pin too many hopes on Dr. Wilcox. He'd been very helpful in launching Tyler into diplomatic circles, but what could he have to offer a widow with a sixteen-year-old degree in history whose only accomplishments were dressing well, listening well, and running a complicated embassy household with a modicum of grace and ease? By the time she entered his office, an office stuffy with years of wool jackets, stale pipes, and prestige, she was trembling slightly, braced for rejection.

Dr. Wilcox, however, leaned back in his huge leather chair and heard her out. Then he puffed a couple of times on his meerschaum pipe and considered the green ceiling above his head. "You don't want to return to Japan?" He carefully matched his buffed nails to form the skeleton of a ball. "With all the uncertainty about trade agreements these days, we badly need people with your social skills. I know it would be hard at first, but to abandon fifteen years of work..."

"Tyler's work, Dr. Wilcox," she interrupted.

He sighed deeply. "Such a loss. Few men possess that vision and charisma. Tyler Travis was a legend in his own time."

Sheila suppressed a wry smile. Was it *Time*, or *Newsweek*, that had first used that cliché in Tyler's obituary? It always reminded her of an after-shave that Tyler would have despised.

Firmly she brought the subject back. "But Tyler was the diplomat—I was basically a housewife. Except for entertaining, I was seldom involved in what he was doing. And I'd prefer to remain in America for the time being—Chicago, if possible. I have the loan of an apartment in Hyde Park this semester, and I'd really like to find something..." She bogged down. "Interesting" and "challenging" were inadequate words to convey the yearning she'd felt for a couple of years. "Something that's *mine*," she wanted to scream, "something I accomplish as myself, not as somebody else's wife!" Dr. Wilcox would probably dive beneath his desk in dismay.

He misinterpreted her silence. "Surely Tyler's pension is adequate. Would he want... I mean, do you really need to work?"

"It's *precisely* what I need," she said, more forcefully than she'd intended. "Not for the money, but to keep busy," she added. "Tyler's dead, Dr. Wilcox. The question now isn't Tyler, it's me."

That had come off well. Her voice hadn't even trembled through those oft-rehearsed sentences, and they brought a flicker of compassion to the man's eyes. He ran one manicured hand over his thick gray hair and stood. "Excuse me for a moment. I've just remembered something..." He strode out of his office and returned in a moment with a scrap of paper in his hand.

"Markham's looking for someone. You've heard of Markham?"

Sheila nodded. Who hadn't? Markham was to diplomatic circles what Juilliard was to music.

"And Eleanor Quincy? I think you knew her several years ago?"

"Yes, she was in Japan for a couple of years. We played tennis together sometimes."

"Well, after Jake died, Eleanor was Administrative Assistant to the President at Markham for five years, until she went to work on the White House staff last November. They haven't replaced her, and I heard last week at the Quadrangle Club that they are looking. I don't know what the job entails, exactly, but it might be right up your alley."

Meaning, Sheila thought wryly, that it's been filled by embassy widows for the past hundred years. She kept her eyes on her lap so he couldn't see her eyes. "It sounds interesting. Whom should I see?"

In less than ten minutes she was on her way.

The building she sought was so plain, so nondescript, that she almost missed it. The only sign of prestige was a heavy door, probably oak under its years of weather and student palms, beside which a brass rectangle said, simply: MARKHAM.

She checked her watch. Thirty minutes before her interview to fortify herself with coffee and a peek at the newspaper she still carried. As she retraced her steps toward a coffee shop she remembered, a sudden gust off Lake Michigan made her hug her elbows across her chest and wish she'd worn a coat over her suit. She thought longingly of her folks in Montgomery, and Aunt Mary in St. Petersburg. Could she really stand Chicago's cold?

As suddenly as it had come, the wind died and the sun bathed her again. With it returned her resolve. She would *not* give up, until she had spent some time proving Sheila Travis could take care of herself. And Hyde Park, where she had the offer of an apartment until June, was as good a place as any to try.

Passing a plate-glass window, she wrinkled her nose at the gawky woman loping along in reflection beside her. "Giraffe," she mocked herself gently, "the only giraffe in captivity with frizzy black hair."

Ten minutes later, chewing a bagel and sipping muddy coffee, she opened her paper. "Only a peek at the front page," she promised herself. But her hunger for American news made her read every word, turn inside to continue the predictable stories of bribes in high places, battles between the mayor and city council, whines from the school board that it could never meet payroll all year, and violent crime.

Crime? How horrified Dr. Wilcox had been to read that one item in her folder when he consulted it. Almost as horrified as Tyler had been each time it had happened.

"You have been involved with the Japanese police?" The professor's voice had been hushed on the last word, like a small boy voicing a forbidden obscenity. She'd been torn between vexation and an almost irresistible urge to laugh.

"Not as a criminal, Dr. Wilcox. Surely it must say somewhere there that I was called in to help once or twice because I knew the people involved and was fluent in Japanese."

"Three times." His finger had actually marked the place. Remembering, Sheila smiled.

"What you finding so funny?" She looked up from her paper to meet the rheumy gray eyes of a man at the next table. "Same old stuff," he muttered. "Can't tell what year it is anymore by reading the paper." His gray-stubbled jowls hung over his collar, his middle hung over his belt, and his bottom hung over his chair. Sheila found him endearing, extended her smile to include him.

Encouraged, he expanded his theme. "And look at the ads." He jerked his doughnut at the paper. "Get-away Florida vacations, luggage, and furniture. You know why they sell them together? Luggage to take on your trip and furniture to replace what gets ripped off while you're gone." He grunted, heaving himself out of his seat. "Good talking to you." He lumbered off, fumbling in his pocket for change.

Sheila smiled at his back. Hello, America, she thought fondly. Resolutely she stood and headed back to Markham.

The president's secretary had a thin yellow face and black almond eyes behind round spectacles. Sheila spoke automatically. *"Gomennasai."*

The woman's eyes rounded like her glasses. "Was that Japanese?" Her accent was thoroughly American.

Sheila flushed. "Sorry, it was habit. I've lived in Japan most of my life. Both my parents and my husband worked there."

The skin around the woman's eyes crinkled with delight. "Really? I'm third-generation American. Just think!

Anyone would think you were American and I was Japanese, when it is almost the other way around!'' As she took in Sheila's long body, white skin, and very curly black hair, her eyes sparkled so merrily that Sheila found herself smiling back.

"You are Mrs. Travis? Your husband was Tyler Travis?'' She scarcely waited for Sheila's nod before she went on. "My name is Yoshiko Furutani. The president will see you in just a minute. Please have a chair.''

When Sheila was seated, Yoshiko typed for a moment, then turned to ask, "Did you know Eleanor Quincy?''

"Yes, she and her husband were in Japan several years ago.''

The tiny woman beamed. "And now you are considering coming to us. Isn't that wonderful! Eleanor did a marvelous job—hosting visiting dignitaries, coordinating special events, that kind of thing. She was also a sort of liaison between our president and the students. He's away a lot, and...'' She lowered her voice confidentially. "Eleanor was a sort of aunt to them.''

Sheila repressed a shudder. Aunt to a horde of students was not precisely what she had been looking for in a job. The little woman was still chattering on. "In two weeks we are beginning a very important lecture series to commemorate our one hundredth year. I've been wondering who was going to make sure things run smoothly—finalize travel arrangements and meet planes, arrange for hospitality, coordinate the secretaries who'll have to type the manuscripts...and now, here you are!'' She almost bounced in her chair.

"I don't have the job yet,'' Sheila reminded her. "I don't know much about academic institutions.''

"Oh, don't worry about that. We're not really an institution, we're like a great big family. And President Dehaviland will be delighted to add you to the family."

"Dehaviland?" Sheila spoke involuntarily. "John Dehaviland?"

Yoshiko nodded. "Yes. Do you know him, too?"

Years of experience kept a mask of pleasant surprise on Sheila's face, but mentally she wrinkled her nose. "Just slightly." Only mentally did she add, *by personal choice.*

TWO

THE FOLLOWING Tuesday afternoon Sheila pushed open the door to Markham's second-floor coffee room. The smoldering fire and pungent odor of coffee were so welcome she almost staggered in.

Bertha, Markham's plump brown maid, was alone, bending over a table in the far corner. When she saw Sheila, she beamed. "I just made the coffee fresh. Come get a cup while it's hot." She tugged her skirt down over her hips and bustled toward the door. "And remember, now, you come down to the basement for soup one day." Her laugh rumbled behind her as she hurried downstairs.

"Joyousness!" Sheila kicked off her shoes and padded across the silky Oriental rug to a table holding brass samovars, china mugs, and crisp, expensive cookies. "Who would have thought starting a job could be so complicated?" She drew a mug of steaming coffee. "Or so exhausting? Only two days, and I'm beat." Yoshiko's blithe job description had omitted facing three grim, suspicious board members. ("Do you have a security clearance, Mrs. Travis?" "Do you feel you have the, *harrumph*, credentials for this position?") Yoshiko had also neglected to mention that she'd have to do her work with the cheerful assistance of Markham's business manager, Nick Capeletti.

She cupped her hands around the mug for warmth and paused by a window. Last week's sunshine and balmy breezes seemed memories from a remote past. Today, the University of Chicago rose gaunt and gray against a leaden

February sky. Only one ray of sunshine pierced the gloom, streaming through Markham's leaded casements to pool around a big old leather chair. Sheila followed it. She shifted the chair to more nearly face the window and sank down—tucking her long legs beneath her, closing her eyes, and giving herself up to what she had privately dubbed Markham Mystique.

Outside, Markham might be merely another three-storied granite building dwarfed by the Gothic vastness of the university. But its plain exterior deceived. For one hundred years this institute had trained young men in the complex business of running the world. Presidents, senators, and ambassadors can be made in acting schools, on peanut farms, in spaceships, or behind pulpits. But Presidents, senators, and ambassadors come and go. Markham trained the men (so far, *only* men) who remain to advise new Presidents, school new senators, instruct new ambassadors. Loftily above party, Markham fellows offered wisdom and expertise wherever required. In a nation of plebeians, Markham men belonged to the one true elite.

And when the nation needed a place for important conferences away from the Argus-eyed journalists of the East, planes landed at Midway Airport and limousines purred south along Lake Shore Drive, carrying gray-clad somber men or white-robed sheikhs (once, even, a familiar stocky figure in green fatigues smoking an excellent cigar) to Markham's elegant seclusion.

Its reception hall, vaulted like a cathedral, had red velvet cushions to soften stone benches for those who must wait. The library, which occupied most of the second floor, was furnished with heavy oak tables and butter-soft leather chairs. A third-floor conference room and two parlors—Wentworth, off the reception hall, and this upstairs coffee room—fostered intelligent conversation between gentlemen. The coffee was always fresh and, in Chicago's windy winter, fires burned in every grate. The president's office was furnished with a quiet contemporary taste that immediately set Sheila speculating about expense.

This afternoon, however, she did not intend to speculate about Markham's finances. She intended to savor what she had promised herself for hours; a cup of really hot coffee and fifteen minutes of absolute, peopleless quiet.

Her quiet was short-lived. Suddenly the door was flung open. A backpack crashed to the table near the door and heavy steps strode to the baby grand in the far corner. Someone struck a loud minor chord. Sheila twisted to peer across the back of the chair. All she could see was a fiery head bent over the keyboard. The initial chord was followed by a rapid, practiced arpeggio, then, with one final chord, the young man dropped his hands and glared at her across the empty music rack.

"Hello." Sheila spoke with as much grace as she could muster in her awkward position. He did not reply, but continued to glare at her with huge dark eyes. Above them his eyebrows and hair were a deep mahogany. His face was very pale, as if all the color of his body had been sapped by eyebrows, hair, and eyes.

"Are you one of the students here?" Sheila scudded her chair around to face him as she spoke.

"One of the *few*." His voice was deep and bitter. Striking another minor chord, he demanded, "Did you know that Markham used to enroll nearly a hundred students? This year's freshman class is barely thirty. Guys are doing their graduate work at state universities." He spat as if it were a dirty word.

Sheila tried to think of a reply, and failed. But the student at the piano didn't seem to expect a reply. With the same suddenness that had marked his entrance, he breathed out his anger in one long sigh. "Sorry. I didn't mean to take it all out on you. I've been talking to some other guys, and..." He left the sentence unfinished and gently began to play a Chopin prelude. "Yoshiko said you're the president's new right-hand woman?"

She nodded. "I'm Sheila Travis. I don't think we've met, but I've met so many—" She was interrupted by the arrival of another student, a slender man with skin the color of café au lait. He flung his parka over a chair and, ignoring the young man at the piano, ambled over to the coffee table and picked up the trailing end of Sheila's sentence as he swung a tea bag into a mug of hot water.

"We may seem like a lot at first, but we really aren't." He added sugar and picked up a handful of cookies. "You'll soon get to know everybody, especially those of us who stayed an extra year to take Cal Williams' seminar. There's me—I'm Todd Walte, by the way—and Brad D'Arcy, who lives with Jen and me in a community house. Then there's Yusuf Jaffari, from Saudi Arabia. Stan Frieze, the proctor, and Peter there—they live in Pres-Res, so they practically live here. Oh, and Quint, who's out of town just now. He lived in Pres-Res last year, but this year he's got a place of his own." He munched a cookie reflectively. "That's most of who you need to know. Undergrads take a lot of classes at the university, so they aren't around much, but we six are in and out all day, every day. You'll get heartily sick of having us underfoot."

He crossed to the couch nearest her chair and sprawled across it. Balancing his mug precariously on one overstuffed arm, he crammed two more cookies into his mouth and brushed crumbs from his short beard with the sleeve of his drab flannel shirt. Sheila pulled her gaze with difficulty from the teetering mug and considered him instead.

Of medium height, with eyes that twinkled gently, he wore a short Afro through which a round patch of soft brown skull peeped like a monk's tonsure. His clothes were regulation dress for Hyde Park men: drab plaid flannel shirt, faded corduroy jeans, and scuffed shoes. Nowhere near the university had Sheila seen a pair of shoes that looked as if they had ever been introduced to polish—nowhere except at Markham.

Markham men, however, dressed like the successes they intended to become. Slacks, white or blue shirts, power ties, and wool jackets were standard; she'd even seen a couple of three-piece suits. She tested a theory about Todd. "Yoshiko said some of you were in the Peace Corps."

He nodded. "I was in Thailand—that's where I met Jenny. She's the librarian."

"I met her yesterday." Sheila was putting names to reputations. Todd's father must be the senior congressman from one of the eastern states, his mother a leader in women's-rights issues. Where did Todd plan to go after Markham? She asked him.

He brushed the question away with crumbs he flicked off his brown cord thigh. "Somewhere in Africa, probably. For now, Jen and I are the poor man's advocates at Markham. And what's your name again?"

He seemed to file it for future reference. "We're all on first-name basis here, Sheila, except for Dr. Dehaviland and two of the Fellows. Even Calvin Williams lets us call him Cal." His voice was reverent, awe well-earned by an adviser on Latin American affairs for two Presidents. Sheila wouldn't mind sitting in on some of Dr. Williams' seminars herself, if she ever got a free afternoon. Just now she needed information.

"Which Fellows prefer not to be called by first names?"

Todd munched his cookie before answering. "Mr. Rareby and Mr. Southard. They're from the old school, the *very* old school. Came to Markham on the *Mayflower*." Within its beard, his gentle smile extracted most of the barb from the remark. Sheila found him restful after the first student, who had resumed his pursuit of the perfect minor chord.

Todd loped over to the table and brought back another handful of cookies. How on earth did he stay so slim? "Has Nick Capeletti given you the Markham Grand Tour?" he asked.

The term was singularly apropos. "I think I've seen every inch of the place," she admitted, "including the fuse box—although I doubt I could find it again in the dark."

Todd snorted gently. "Our business manager is almost as famed for his thoroughness as for his devotion to Markham."

Across the room the piano chords were becoming increasingly restrained, so restrained they seemed about to swell and burst. Todd seemed not to notice.

"Are you married?" he asked conversationally.

Sheila's eyes fell to the white circle on her finger where her rings used to be. "My husband was killed last November. He was mountain climbing and he—fell."

"Oh." Todd seemed to search his memory. "Travis? Hey, was that Tyler Travis?" At her nod his face brightened. "I heard him speak once, at a Far Eastern conference. He was great. I didn't know he was married, though."

Sheila smiled with a shrug. "It wasn't a very important part of his dossier—last line at the bottom."

Todd seemed at a loss for more conversation. "Can't you give us a little more cheer, Peter?" he called over his shoulder. The pianist's hands came down in a crash of discord. Todd shook his head in dismay. "You'll have to forgive Peter's manners today—he's mourning the old Markham."

The pianist shoved back the bench and leapt to his feet. "Unlike some people I could name!"

He was tall, taller than Sheila had realized, and so thin he appeared gaunt. For the first time she saw his face clearly—handsome and tormented. He looked much younger than he probably was, his skin beneath the mahogany hair smooth and almost transparent across wide cheekbones. But what she still saw most clearly were his eyes. They were such a rich brown they looked maroon, and they smoldered in his pale face as if fired from within.

Meeting the full force of those eyes as he towered above the piano, Sheila felt an urge to chant.

> Tiger, tiger, burning bright
> In the forest of the night . . .

What was that line about eyes? Something like "In what distant place, or skies, burnt the fires of thine eyes"? No, that wasn't quite right. She'd have to look it up. Blake could have had this young man in mind.

As he left the piano and moved to the coffee table, he even walked with feline grace. Definitely a tiger—a long, nervous tiger who hadn't eaten well recently, to judge by the way his bones stuck out. Yet at the table he passed over the cookies and took his coffee black. He sipped it as he glided over to glare down at Todd. "Don't you think Markham could do with a bit more respect?"

Todd spoke mildly. "You've enough for us both today, Pete."

"Give them a chance," Peter insisted, apparently continuing a former conversation. "You can't judge before you've heard them."

Todd brushed his hands together to get rid of crumbs. "I can judge that whole class schedules have been arbitrarily thrown off. And if what Brad says is true . . ."

"What does he know?" Peter seared him with his eyes.

Todd shrugged. "He's heard the first guy. If he's as dull as Brad says, we'll not only be wasting our time, but we'll bore the whole university community. Markham's coasting on the past, and you know it, Peter. If we're ever going to move into the future, Dehaviland's going to have to spend less on pomp and circumstance and more on top-quality speakers."

Peter continued to glare down at him. Todd spread his hands in a gesture of defeat. "Okay, I'll give him a chance. What choice do I have, anyway?" He heaved himself up from the couch and nodded to Sheila. "Good to get to know you a bit, Sheila. Be seeing you." He tossed a couple of logs on the fire, then, without any farewell to Peter, gathered his books and left.

Peter dropped to the edge of the couch. His free hand clutched the front of one cushion as if he would crush it. "Someday I may strangle the lot of them with my bare hands." He swallowed hard. "What the heck?" he asked in one of those swings of mood she was not yet accustomed to. "It isn't your fault."

It certainly wasn't, and she didn't want to get involved. But fifteen years as an embassy wife had formed habits that were hard to break. It was always the waiting that did it—prompted people to pour out their angers, fears, and tedious love affairs. By habit, Sheila waited.

Yet, in spite of his simmering fury, this young man was curiously reticent. He held her gaze for a moment longer, then rose and collected his books. At the door he turned. "Sorry to dump on you. It just gets to be a bit much sometimes. And although you didn't ask, I'm Peter Lucas. Be seeing you."

SHEILA GLANCED AT her watch. It was time to get back to her desk. As she reached the landing, Nicholas Capeletti bustled out of a door at the foot of the stairs.

"Hello, Sheila!" The business manager was so round and short he resembled a rubber ball, and his sentences usually bounced. "I was checking Wentworth for the alumni meeting this evening. You're welcome to attend— did we tell you?" As he looked up for her nod and waited for her to descend, he automatically reached behind him to be sure the ornately carved door was locked.

That door guarded Wentworth, Markham's formal parlor. Sacred to the memory of Eusebius Wentworth, Markham's second president, it was kept locked except for special occasions. On her first day's tour Sheila had been ushered in by Mr. Capeletti and permitted briefly to view the maroon velvet draperies, stiff formal furniture, and black marble fireplace. The only note of discord was an Oriental rug that covered only half the floor. It looked as if a matching one was out for cleaning.

"That's Dr. Wentworth himself." Mr. Capeletti's voice had been hushed to a husky whisper. Sheila moved closer to look up at the portrait over the fireplace. Eusebius Wentworth, surrounded by gilt, had met her gaze with grim gray eyes. He was obviously not impressed by what he saw—he wore the expression of one who has just bitten into an exceedingly sour persimmon.

"Dr. Wentworth furnished this room personally, exactly as it is today." Sheila believed it. Only a man like the one in the portrait would create a room at once so lavish and so funereal.

Today, Mr. Capeletti's only concern for the room was that it was locked. As Sheila reached the bottom step she entered the cloud of tobacco smoke and English Leather that would forever call him to mind. He walked beside her to the door of the attractive front office Eleanor Quincy had furnished in soft blues and greens. Had Eleanor also seen it as a refuge from the demands of students, faculty, and Mr. Capeletti himself? Had she had the courage, which Sheila still lacked, to close the top of the Dutch door between her and the rest of the school?

Nick still stood by her door. "Everything in order for next week?" he said jovially. "You've got someone to meet the plane?"

Sheila nodded. "I'm going to meet it myself. But that reminds me, I want to ask Yoshiko about ordering the limousine."

"Did I hear my name?" The tiny secretary's voice floated from the far end of the hall. "I'm putting out mail." Making a quick excuse to the business manager, Sheila loped past his office on the front, Yoshiko's and the president's on the quieter rear, to where the hall widened into a mirror image of the reception hall.

Perhaps in earlier, safer days, this lobby had once served as a second entrance. Now its heavy outside doors were locked and plastered with FOR FIRE USE ONLY signs. Its corners had been filled with cupboards for staff coats, audiovisuals, and extra office supplies. A long row of pigeonholes attested to the truth of Peter's claim that Markham once had enrolled nearly a hundred students. Beyond them, stairs went down to the basement. In the end wall an ornate door, twin to Wentworth's, led (Sheila presumed) to the library stacks.

When she and Yoshiko had finished their business together, the secretary's face screwed into a wicked grin. "Capeletti will do your job if you let him." Her eyes sparkled.

They both laughed. Yoshiko's habit of gently mocking everyone at Markham gave a much-needed balance to the business manager's awe. But her habit of dropping the title from names was proving contagious. "What happens when I call the president 'Dehaviland' to his face?" Sheila asked.

Yoshiko's chuckle rippled as she shoved an electronics catalog into a box marked "Lucas." "Just tell him it's an honorable Japanese custom. You don't have to tell him which Japanese."

The odor of pipe tobacco was the first warning they had that they were not alone. Turning, Sheila saw someone behind them in the dim light, an expression on his face that could only be called a gloat. He more slid than walked toward them.

Yoshiko turned, and jumped. "Stan Frieze, you nearly scared me to death! Where did you come from?"

He puffed on his pipe before he said, "I was studying in the basement and heard you sorting the mail." He reached one thin pale hand past Sheila into a larger box than the others and extracted several letters and a large manila envelope. "Business," he said loftily. "Keep the noise down, will you?" He padded down the stairs.

Yoshiko waited until he was gone, then "That weasel!" she hissed. "As senior proctor he needs to know what's going on, but his curiosity goes beyond what's proper. You never know when you'll find him listening at doors. What he puts into his daily reports to Dehaviland heaven only knows. Keep your eye out for that one, Sheila. He's a bit of a sneak."

THREE

THE REST OF the first week passed quickly, but by the following Tuesday Sheila was still glad to drive through Chicago's twilight gloom to her own (for a time) apartment and a long soak at the end of each day. Longingly she thought of Japanese hot tubs and wished her brick tenement had thought to install one in its grimy basement. She found a place a block from her door and slid out from under the wheel.

"Sheila?"

The voice, so near and unexpected, startled her. She whirled, slipping on a chunk of ice. A hand reached out and caught her elbow to steady her.

"Yusuf Jaffari, you nearly scared me silly!" She felt cross with relief.

In a gray parka and fur-lined hood, he looked more Eskimo than Arabian, but his smile could have been cut from an Omar Sharif poster. "I am sorry. I live just there"—he pointed to a building down the block—"and I was out walking Wolf when you arrived."

For the first time, Sheila saw a huge white German shepherd nosing the tire of the next car. She drew back.

Yusuf laughed aloud. "He won't hurt you. Not unless you try to hurt me. Then, of course..." This time his laugh was short and unpleasant. "Then he would kill you with pleasure."

"Wonderful," Sheila murmured, her eyes glued to the dog. "What if he makes an irreversible mistake?"

Yusuf's smile flashed again in the near darkness. "Do not be alarmed. 'Wolf, heel!'" The huge animal lumbered behind him.

Sheila gave him a smile of real gratitude. Before she could move on, Yusuf caught her arm. "Wait, I would ask a favor of you."

She shivered. "Sure, but ask me quick, before I freeze."

"It is Cal's paper, the big one. It's not going well. We have a new baby, and he cries very much."

Sheila was surprised. "I didn't know you were married."

"I do not tell all my business at school," he said stiffly. "My wife speaks very little English. It is better she stay at home with my son." His voice was deep with pride, but anxiety rippled under his next words. "The baby, though, he does not sleep well at night. I must have quiet, and a place to spread my papers." He spread his hands expressively.

Sheila was puzzled. "But how can I help you?"

"In the basement of the stacks there are five small rooms, used for storage. I ask Jack—you know Jack?"

Sheila nodded. Markham's lanky custodian draped himself over her door to chat at least four times a day.

"Jack says the rooms hold books and papers, but some are not too full. If I can have one to use, I will clear it myself." His offer was clearly meant to be magnanimous.

"But why ask me, Yusuf? Ask your adviser, or Mr. Capaletti."

He sighed. "Mr. Rareby is my adviser. But he is—how do you say it?—head in the sky. He has promised to check on it, but he forgets. Nick will do nothing unless the president says so, and the president gives no special privileges to forcign students."

"So you want me to ask?" He nodded solemnly. "I can try. But I'd rather ask Mr. Rareby for a written request."

He gave her another dazzling smile that even a recent widow couldn't be faulted for enjoying. "The very thing! You are kind and wise, Sheila. I hope nobody wants to get rid of you, like they did the other one."

She had been idly wondering how soon she could get in from this bone-chilling cold, but that brought her up short. "What other one?"

He shrugged as if imparting common knowledge. "Evelyn Parsons. Dr. Dehaviland's secretary, until December, and Yoshiko worked for Mr. Southard. But a clock was stolen and they accused Evelyn of taking it. She left, of course. Me, I believe she was bordered."

"Bordered?" Now Sheila was definitely confused.

"Like a picture." He made a square with his heavy gloves.

"Framed?" she suggested.

He nodded. "Same thing, no? The next weekend a carpet was missed. Evelyn could not have taken that, for by then she had turned in her keys. But no one said so, and no one brought her back."

He rapidly scanned the sidewalk, and when he next spoke, Sheila's shiver had little to do with the cold. "I give you a warning, kind Sheila," he said, leaning close. "Watch your feet."

FOUR

SHEILA CERTAINLY watched her step the next morning as she maneuvered around the grimy piles of frozen snow between her car and Markham. As she clutched her collar tightly around her neck, she wished for the hundredth time that week that she'd made the trek to find knee-length thermals to wear under her skirts. She was astonished to see a young man sitting on Markham's steps wearing only a light jacket and slacks. "Hello," she greeted him. "Are we the first here?"

He unfolded himself, a long, gawky youth she had not yet met. Or had she? The red hair, white face, and big brown eyes were vaguely familiar. His bony face lit with a smile. "I'm Jim Lucas." He held out one ungloved hand, red with cold.

"You're very like Peter! Are you brothers?"

He shook his head. "Cousins. But Peter's the substance and I'm the shadow."

His analogy was apt. He had the same lanky body and the same look of very vulnerable youth. Instead of deep mahogany, however, his hair was pale copper. Instead of eyes like a burning tiger's, his had the warmth of a friendly spaniel's. And in Jim, the force of Peter's clear profile was softened almost to effeminacy. (Only almost, of course—Markham was harder to get into than West Point, and had similar prejudices, she was sure.)

"Have a step," he offered. "I've warmed it for you. Unless you have a key?"

"Alas, no." She dashed his hopes. "Aren't you frozen? Where's your coat?"

He blew on his hands and rubbed them together. "I just came over from Pres-Res, and didn't plan on waiting." Her bewilderment must have been obvious, for he jerked his thumb toward the granite mansion across the street. "The old president's house. It's been a dorm since Dr. Dehaviland came—he wanted to live out in Glen Ellyn. Five of us rattle around in there this year—two freshmen, Stan Frieze, Peter, and me. Oh, and Mr. Southard. But we hardly notice him. He's always gone, or reading."

Sheila was beginning to shiver herself. Through chattering teeth she asked, "Do you do your own cooking, or what?"

He was shivering so hard that his smile looked more like a grimace. "Mostly 'or what.' We live on yogurt and peanut butter. That's why we're the skinniest guys in the place, and why Mr. Southard's such a wraith. I don't think he ever eats, except when his sister has him over."

He stepped out onto the sidewalk to peer down the street. "Wonder where Nick is today?" He retreated back into the shelter of the entrance. "I have a paper to do, and want to get some books before someone else needs them."

Sheila regarded him curiously. Another student would have said " . . . before someone else gets them."

"What made both you and Peter come to Markham?" She asked the question primarily to warm her neck in her scarf with her own breath, but Jim's eyes lit as if she'd given him a gift.

"It's a Lucas tradition—at least two sons of each generation have come here since Markham was founded. Pete's dad and Uncle Henry are both in diplomatic service, and Great-Uncle James just retired."

"Of course! I knew him ten, maybe twelve years ago. I should have recognized the hair. But did you *want* to come?"

"Oh, yes. All my life. It's not as big as it used to be, of course, but that doesn't bother me the way it does... some."

She appreciated the loyalty that had ended his sentence.

Yoshiko bustled up the sidewalk to join them. "Where's Capeletti?" she asked, her voice breathless from hurry and cold.

"Late," Jim told her.

"I hope he's all right." Between her wool cap and scarf the little secretary's face was a maze of concern. "He has a weak heart," she confided. "That's what made him leave his old job and take this one. He used to be a factory foreman."

No wonder Capeletti was so caught up in Markham's mystique. After years in a factory, coming here must seem like dying and going to heaven.

Before Yoshiko could worry further, Capeletti bustled up, full of apologies, old cigarettes, and English Leather triumphing over the wind.

As Jim began to mount the stairs to the library, he called the ubiquitous Markham farewell, "Be seeing you."

Mr. Rareby tiptoed in soon after nine. The gray fur cap he wore and his scraggly salt-and-pepper beard made him look like a goat—a very shy, gentle goat. When Sheila explained Yusuf's request, he grew pink. "I should have done this before." He scribbled a few lines on the paper Sheila held out to him. "He'll have to get a heater." Shyness made his voice little more than a whisper. "There's no heat at all in the stacks. Very hard on books"—he shook his head sorrowfully—"very hard." As he headed toward his third-floor office laden with papers and his briefcase, one of his shoes clicked against a stone step. She realized with surprise that he wore a leg brace. In what pain and inconvenience did he drag himself up and down three flights several times a day? Why had no one given him a more accessible office?

John Dehaviland strolled in three-quarters of an hour after opening time, wearing a black cashmere overcoat and felt hat. Seldom had Sheila seen anyone with the president's sense of authority. Only slightly above middle height, he carried himself with such military exactness that he appeared taller, and from his immaculate silver hair to the tips of his well-shined shoes he exuded that aura of prominence that expects and invariably gets attention merely by entering a room. Sheila considered waiting until he had had his coffee before broaching her subject, but he greeted her with such a genial "Good morning, Sheila!" that she decided to speak at once.

He considered the issue, drumming the top of her door lightly. At last he nodded. "Since Mr. Rareby himself made the request, I will grant it. But Yusuf will have to observe regular institute hours. We can't be handing out keys." He turned to go, then pivoted. "Tell Nicholas to choose a room and have Jack clear it out." He strolled toward his own office. As he passed his secretary's door, Sheila heard, curtly, "Coffee, Yoshiko."

By the time Yusuf arrived, Sheila and Capeletti were poring over a large basement plan spread on her desk. "Come in, come in." Capeletti waved. "We're finding you a place to work." He ran one pudgy finger over the row of five small storerooms located in one end of the stacks. "I've never been in these rooms myself," he confessed. "Jack says they have been used to store old books and records so long that nobody goes in them anymore. Let's just have a look."

"Do you really need me?" Sheila looked despairingly at the work on her desk.

"You never can tell when you might need to find Yusuf for a phone call," the business manager told her. If he thought she was going to traipse all over the building for student calls, he could think again. Only curiosity and good manners made her follow him.

In his office he made a great show of extracting keys from his middle drawer while concealing their hiding place behind his round torso. "He guards those keys like a CIA secret," Yoshiko had told Sheila on Monday, "but everyone in the building knows where to find them."

To Sheila's surprise, Capeletti then led them back toward the reception hall stairs. As they passed Yoshiko's door he called, "Please take all calls, Yoshiko."

Her head swiveled from her typing. "Where are you three off to so merrily?"

Capeletti gave a raspy chuckle. "To explore the closets."

"You be careful," she warned them, shaking her finger, "or you may find a skeleton."

As they mounted the stairs toward the library, Sheila asked curiously, "Why don't we use the door in the unused lobby?"

Capeletti paused to catch his breath. "It's a fake. I made the same mistake when I first came—spent nearly an hour trying every key I had before Jack found me. It was just put there to match the door to Wentworth. Imagine that!"

Sheila found such waste hard to imagine, but knew he meant to impress her.

"There's another entrance through the basement workroom," he continued when he could breathe normally, "but it's kept locked. I'm certain Dr. Dehaviland would prefer for Yusuf to use this one."

As they passed through the library Sheila saw Jim, surrounded by a tall stack of books. He flicked one hand in greeting, and as they entered the stacks she saw his eyes still followed them.

Sheila's initial visit to the stacks had been only a brief glance through the door. Now, as she followed Capeletti and Yusuf across an iron-grate floor to a narrow bridge that led to an iron spiral staircase, they seemed huge—and gloomy. The stacks occupied this entire end of the institute, from basement to third floor, and were basically one huge space divided by seven tiers of shelves, arranged on balconies around the edges of the enormous room. Each tier was reached from the staircase by an iron bridge identical to the one they were now crossing.

Their footsteps rang off the iron in hollow booms. "It's awfully dark," she murmured to Yusuf, looking over the railing into the abyss where the staircase coiled.

"The windows are covered with books," he pointed out.

Looking where he pointed, Sheila saw that once again Markham's architect had opted for symmetry rather than practicality. Windows corresponded not with the tiers of shelves, but with windows at the other end of the building. Since many were therefore covered with shelves, the only lighting in the vast space came from four fixtures swinging near the rafters.

"Each tier has its own lights," Capeletti called from below. His tone implied rebuke. Sheila hurried down after him, vowing to keep future criticisms of the institute to herself.

But as the chill of the room penetrated her light sweater, she abandoned her vow. "Brr! Mr. Rareby was right, Yusuf. If you work in this icebox, you will certainly need a heater."

"If there is a plug," he agreed over his shoulder. "If not, I shall dress warmly."

"Dress like an Eskimo," she retorted between chattering teeth. She hugged her arms to keep warmer and thought longingly of the wool blazer she'd left on the back of her chair.

As they rounded the next-to-last turn she nearly tripped. "Careful," Capeletti called up. "We don't want that skeleton we find to be yours." Because the room was so cold and dark, and smelled so dismally of damp and old books, they all laughed louder than the joke deserved.

There was another odor, too, and it was getting stronger. Sheila wrinkled her nose. Almost simultaneously, Yusuf said, "It does not smell pleasant down here."

Capaletti was panting hard from exertion, but his voice rasped up from the abyss. "Jenny said last week...a rat must have...died down here." He took a deep breath. "It probably started decomposing during the thaw."

"Didn't the students complain?" Sheila called down.

"They aren't in here much. Usually Jenny gets what they need." The business manager had finally reached the ground. He flicked on a light, creating an inviting pool of yellow.

Sheila and Yusuf joined him. The sickly sweet odor grew stronger as they snaked past shelves toward a row of doors at the end of the stacks that Sheila surmised must face the streetside.

"That leads into the supplies storeroom, just off the workroom." Capeletti indicated an inconspicuous door in the side wall. "It's always locked unless Jack is working in here." From the thick coating of dust on the floor, Sheila concluded that Jack seldom did.

They faced five identical doors. Capeletti headed for the second one from the inside wall. "The first is full of kitchen supplies, Jack tells me. Let's try this one.'' He tried two keys unsuccessfully, swung the door open on his third try. The room was filled from floor to the small window with dusty boxes labeled ''President Warren's files.''

''President Warren died in 1948,'' Capeletti informed them. ''He obviously didn't take it with him.''

Sheila smiled faintly, but she was beginning to feel a little queasy. Yusuf had already moved restlessly on.

The next room was empty except for a few dusty cartons labeled ''Historical Photographs.'' ''A good possibility,'' Capeletti admitted, ''but let's just see what's in number five. Number four is full of Jenny Walte's personal books. Library of the librarian.'' He seemed to be making jokes from habit rather than intent, and no one even smiled.

As they approached the door to the last room, Sheila was shivering so violently she hoped it was full to the brim. Two outside walls would make it a virtual freezer, impossible for even a dedicated student to use for any length of time. Reluctantly she followed as Capeletti inserted his key and pulled open the door.

The odor that had invaded the stacks rolled out to greet them. Simultaneously, Capeletti and Yusuf went rigid. The older man held out one hand to ward Sheila off, but she had already seen what they were seeing.

Covering her mouth with one hand, she backed one step. But the scene was engraved somewhere just in front of her eyes: a room empty except for one rolled rug. And protruding from one end of that rug, a woman's blue boot.

FIVE

Yusuf staggered into the stacks and retched violently. Sheila felt as if any moment she would slide gratefully to the dusty concrete floor and lie there forever. Before she could, however, another concern forced its way into her giddy head.

Nick Capeletti was at her elbow, trying to speak reassuringly. But his face was gray, his black eyes filled with panic. She knew he must be gotten out of that close, stinking space, and quickly.

"Can you walk upstairs?" she asked, taking his arm.

He nodded, fumbled for his keys, and managed to unlock the storeroom door with trembling hands. They assisted one another down the hall and up the stairs. So intent was Sheila on getting Mr. Capeletti upstairs before he collapsed that she forgot Yusuf, and was surprised when he spoke from behind them at Yoshiko's door.

"Call the police!" He now looked more green than olive.

Yoshiko's eyes widened as she pulled out her earphones. "What's the matter? You look as if you had seen a ghost."

Sheila's lips were trembling so hard she could hardly speak. "A corpse. But before you call, Mr. Capeletti needs a chair."

The business manager fluttered his hands in protest. "No, no, no," he gasped, "not the police. Tell the president."

Yoshiko was pouring him a glass of water from a carafe on her desk. "He's out to lunch," she whispered. Horror was draining the color from her face. "One o'clock, he said, he'll be back."

Capeletti was beginning to get his own color back and, with it, some tatters of authority. "Then we must wait for him."

Sheila and Yusuf spoke in unison. "What?"

He spoke ponderously, pulling himself up to his full five feet seven and giving weight to each word: "Dr. Dehaviland prefers to handle emergencies himself."

Sheila couldn't believe what she was hearing. "We're not talking about some infringement of Markham rules, Mr. Capeletti. There's a body in the basement! If Yoshiko doesn't call, I will."

Yoshiko looked from Nick to Sheila, something not quite recognizable in her eyes behind their round lenses. "We must try to locate Dr. Dehaviland," she murmured.

"I agree with Sheila," Yusuf said stoutly. "Call the police."

Capeletti held up his hand to forestall what Sheila was about to say. "This is not a new, uh, situation. A couple hours' delay should not make much difference. I will take full responsibility."

Sheila hesitated, but he looked so shaky she yielded. "Okay. But if you can't find the president, you will call?"

Capeletti nodded. "Of course. Would you like to go to lunch now, to catch your breath?"

She shuddered. She might never eat again. He gave her a weak smile. "No, perhaps not. Yoshiko, why don't you go early and let me look for the president?" He lumbered over to his own door, then turned. "Please, don't let's talk about this beyond ourselves."

Sheila watched him go. "There, but for the grace of God," she silently quoted Churchill, "goes a rabbit."

Yusuf shrugged himself deep into his coat. "I think I shall go home for a while, to collect my thoughts. If you need me, call."

Sheila's knees were showing a tendency to buckle. Yoshiko reached one hand up to steady her, led her to her own office, and shoved a chair behind her just as she fell. "You look white as a sheet," she hissed. "That man should have sent you home. All he ever thinks about is Markham, Markham, Markham." She put her hand firmly on Sheila's crown. "Put your head down in your lap. I'm going to get you a cup of tea, very sweet. Don't move!"

"I'll be..." Sheila began, but Yoshiko had already gone.

For several minutes she remained there, head in her lap, taking great gulps of air and trembling all over.

"I say, are you all right?"

She raised her head to meet a pair of wide-spaced gray eyes full of concern. Their owner was leaning against the door. He entered, giving off a clean odor of soap, wool, and pipe tobacco that Sheila found oddly comforting.

"You're alive, then?" His voice was a musical burr. "Are you needing assistance?"

She shook her head. "Yoshiko's gone for tea. I'll be fine."

He did not ask what was the matter, which she also found comforting. Instead he propped himself against her desk and began to fiddle with his pipe. "Then I'll just stick around until she returns."

She straightened, swallowing hard and breathing through her nose to stave off the nausea that still heaved in her abdomen. "I haven't heard anyone say 'retairns' since my husband's Scottish grandmother died." She gave him a weak smile.

He gave her a broad grin. "Aye, few people know how to speak the language properly." He sucked on his pipe, which refused to stay lit. While he worked on the problem, Sheila let her eyes rest on him. She liked what she saw: a man of about her own age, slight in build and not much more than her own five feet nine. He had a high forehead beneath wavy brown hair that dangled in one curl "right in the middle of his forehead," she thought. His face was pleasant rather than handsome—wide cheekbones and pointed chin making a triangle beneath those large gray eyes.

He made no attempt at conversation, but merely leaned on the desk and nursed his pipe until Yoshiko returned.

"Are you staying with her?" he asked. Yoshiko nodded. "Then I'll be pushing off." He rested one hand briefly on Sheila's shoulder and left.

"Who is he?" Sheila asked as the slim tweed back disappeared out the door. Her hands were still trembling so hard she had to clasp the cup with both hands, like a small child. She sipped it gratefully, but with distaste. It was strong, hot, and very sweet.

"That's David MacLean. He's a professor at the University of Aberdeen, but this year he's doing special research. Something to do with Scots who came to America a long time ago, I believe."

"The Highland clearances?" Sheila suggested.

Yoshiko shrugged. "Could be. He's also taking Mr. Southard's Wednesday-morning forum on nineteenth-century diplomacy."

Sheila drank the tea and dismissed the stranger from her mind. She was far more concerned with another matter. "Yoshiko, why won't Mr. Capeletti call the police?"

Yoshiko's face closed like a blind. "He has to do what he feels is right." She went to the door to make sure they were not overheard, then leaned close, like a small tan owl. "Could you tell me what happened, what you saw?"

As Sheila told her, nausea rose again—but weaker this time. Perhaps in a hundred years or so it would completely disappear.

Yoshiko clicked her tongue. "Jenny *said* something had died down there."

Sheila groaned. "How could she have mistaken it for a rat?"

"She had a horrible cold. She could scarcely breathe. And nobody went to check, of course. That Jack is about as useless . . ."

She broke off as Bertha bustled up the stairs. "We having a meeting?" she asked cheerfully, resting her plump brown arms on the top of the door. Bertha was, as she herself put it, hot-natured. Her arms were perpetually bare below the elbow.

Yoshiko tiptoed over to the door and hissed, "There's a body in the stacks. Sheila and Capeletti just found it!"

Bertha's voice rose on successive sentences. "What you say? A body? A *dead* body? In *my basement*? When did it get there?"

Yoshiko waved her hands. "Shhh—don't let Capeletti hear us."

But Yoshiko wanted an answer to Bertha's question, too. Sheila shrugged. "How long has the carpet been missing?"

Yoshiko and Bertha exchanged horrified looks. "You mean the Wentworth Ori-*en*-tal?" Bertha's voice rose again.

Sheila nodded. "The body is wrapped in it."

Yoshiko was counting on her fingers. "It must be five, no—six weeks."

Bertha nodded. "It was the Monday before Christmas I found it missing, when I went in to set up for the staff party. How come nobody found this body before?" She sounded aggrieved, personally sinned against.

Sheila shook her head. "With no insulation and little heat, that room must be a freezer this time of year." She felt very tired, worn out with the strain of not doing what every nerve in her body screamed to do: call the police.

As if on cue, Yoshiko looked at her watch. "I'd better be going on to lunch. Furutani likes his meals on time." She gave Sheila a grin that faded slowly back to concern. "Are you sure you'll be all right?"

"I'll keep checking on her," Bertha rumbled. "You go feed that husband of yours. Philosophers got to keep up their strength."

An hour later, Sheila went home. She looked forward to one hour alone. True to her word, Bertha had spent most of the last hour "checking on" (i.e., chatting with) her. But her stomach was still queasy and a foot sticking out of a carpet seemed to hover just in front of her eyes.

As she entered the foyer of her building and unlocked the door to the stairs, however, she was distracted. Honeysuckle? She wrinkled her nose. In Chicago, in February? Brows puckered, she hurried up the three flights and unlocked her own front door.

"So there you are, dear. I had begun to worry about you!"

The voice seemed far too deep to emanate from the petite elderly woman settled into one corner of Sheila's couch. The jacket to her expensive tweed suit was neatly folded beside her, and, Sheila noticed, the amethysts on her fingers and in her ears exactly picked up the suit's heather tones. Small leather shoes rested empty on the floor, for the woman had both feet tucked beneath her, as if she had been there for some time.

"Aunt Mary, how did you get in here?"

If the woman was aware of Sheila's stare, she gave no sign. From the top of her shining silver curls to the tips of her shell-pink nails, Mary Beaufort was a lady—bred in a world where ladies took no official note of rudeness. Through a tanned network of wrinkles she smiled a gracious welcome. "I've made some iced tea, dear," she said, holding aloft a glass brimming with ice cubes. Remembering the temperature outside, Sheila shivered.

"No, thanks. I'll put on some coffee."

"You drink too much coffee, dear."

It was such an old battle that Sheila didn't bother to reply. Instead, she returned to her original question. "Aunt Mary, how did you get in here?" She flung her coat and bag onto a chair.

"If you hang that coat up now, Sheila, you won't have to do it later," her aunt suggested gently.

Sheila stifled a sigh and did as she was told. Mary Beaufort had that effect on people. Then she returned to the living room.

"You still haven't told me how you got in." In fond exasperation she bent to give the upturned cheek a peck of welcome.

Aunt Mary flung up her hands in a gesture that reduced the question to unimportance. The effect was of fluttering tan birds with shell-pink beaks. "Oh, I just found that sweet Mr. Stovoski who manages the building. He was *such* a love. He not only unlocked your door, he carried all my bags up to your spare room."

Sheila narrowed her eyes. It had taken her nearly a week to persuade sweet Mr. Stovoski to carry up one small trunk. "And how did you convince him you weren't some burglar planning to remove all my worldly goods?"

Under mascaraed lashes Aunt Mary's brown eyes grew very wide. "Why, Sheila, what a suspicious mind you have! I told him the truth, that I'm your father's only sister, come to take care of you until you get settled in. He was delighted I was here."

Sheila tried to picture the surly building manager delighted about anything—and failed. The closest she had ever seen him to joy was when he informed her that the downstairs tenants had roaches. She did not doubt, however, that Aunt Mary had charmed him. She had seen it happen with far harder subjects than Stefan Stovoski. Still, she thought grimly, she would have words with the manager before the day was out. She didn't want to come home to any more surprises.

While the coffee brewed, she flopped into a chair across from her aunt. "I thought you were in St. Petersburg."

Aunt Mary nodded. "I was, dear. Didn't I get a lovely tan?" She held out one arm and pushed up the sleeve of her cashmere sweater for inspection. "I had the sweetest little apartment, right on Tampa Bay. The one I usually take, if you remember. But you can't imagine how that city is changing, Sheila. The pace!" She shook her head in dismay. "No one is content any longer just to sit in the sun and enjoy the view. Everyone is running around all the time. Even the churches aren't restful anymore." Her sigh conveyed the depths of this betrayal. "Between bus trips, bazaars, luncheons, and lectures—I tell you, I was plumb worn out."

"You did all those things?" Sheila was flabbergasted.

"Of course not, dear. But turning down invitations tactfully can be just as exhausting. As you well know, I don't mind a little excitement in my life. But I can't buzz about like a bee every minute. My heart can't stand it."

"Is it giving you trouble?" To hide her smile, Sheila went for her coffee. Aunt Mary's good health was legendary in the family.

Aunt Mary's husky voice followed her. "No, thank God. But it would have been, I'm sure, if I had stayed one day longer. I was worn out, Sheila, purely worn out."

Sheila returned. "So you decided to come see me to rest?"

Aunt Mary shook her silver curls. "That wasn't my original intention. I first thought of going to your folks in Montgomery for a little visit. But when I called, your mother was running her church rummage sale and your daddy was putting in his garden. Of course, they insisted that I come anyway—Tommy said I could help him in the garden. But then he mentioned that you'd settled in up here, so I thought I'd just run up and surprise you instead. I wanted to see for myself how you were doing. And I must say that while the decor is not what I myself would choose"—her eyes roved around the bare white walls, mismatched overstuffed furniture, and bare windows hung with plants—"you seem to be comfortable here."

"I am," Sheila assured her. "The apartment belongs to the daughter of friends, a graduate student who's away for a semester. I stored almost all my own things in Montgomery..."

Aunt Mary nodded in quick comprehension. "A few months of impersonal living is good for all of us now and then."

Sheila smiled in rueful appreciation. "You always understand, don't you?"

"A few years' experience helps. Now I'm not going to stay long enough to make a nuisance of myself, but I hadn't seen you since Tyler's death. You're looking a little peaky, dear. Are you well?"

"I'm glad you're here." Sheila got up to give her aunt's thin shoulders a squeeze. "Something terrible happened this morning, and I don't know anyone I'd rather see right now. But I can't stay long." She mentally surveyed her larder and checked her watch. "I need to be back in about forty minutes. Let me fix some tomato soup, cheese and crackers—not elegant, but the best I can do on short notice—then we can talk."

"Thank you, dear, that will be fine." Aunt Mary settled back into the couch and reached for a mystery lying open beside her.

As Sheila was heating the soup, she called, "Did Daddy tell you I'm working? Dr. Wilcox helped me find the job."

She could almost see Aunt Mary wince—talking between rooms was one of the things she abhorred, and she scarcely raised her voice loud enough for Sheila to hear her reply. "I hope he didn't insist that you needed one, dear. Government people can be so difficult to get rid of."

Sheila, putting crackers into a basket, answered without thinking. "No, it was my own idea. I really needed to work."

There was a long silence from the next room, then Aunt Mary said in a stilted tone, "I hope you know, Sheila, that if you are in financial need . . ."

Sheila left what she was doing to go to the door and stare. Was Aunt Mary actually about to break her code and discuss personal finances? The old woman looked so stoic that Sheila took pity on her. "Thanks, Aunt Mary, but I've got enough money. It's just that I couldn't bear the thought of doing nothing the rest of my life."

Aunt Mary picked up her book. "Well, don't let them wear you out. You are looking peaky, as I mentioned earlier."

A blue boot flooded unbidden into Sheila's thoughts. Resolutely she reached for the cheese and a knife. "I'm almost ready, Aunt Mary. Let's eat—and talk." Her voice, she noted with relief, held only a slight tremor. And she must be a ghoul—she was ravenous!

She carried steaming mugs of soup and a plate of cheese and crackers to a small table under the living room window where she took her meals. Aunt Mary took the place farthest from the kitchen. "Not until after grace, dear," she said firmly.

"As you know," she continued after a short blessing, "I don't normally discuss unpleasant subjects with meals. But since you are pressed for time tell me what upset you this morning."

Sheila explained. Death in the stacks didn't seem to impair her appetite. "She must have been murdered," she mused, taking a dainty bite of cheese with cracker. "Why else would someone roll her in a rug?"

Sheila nodded. "They will have to call the police, of course, whether Dehaviland agrees or not."

Aunt Mary gave her a reproachful look. "Don't be too hard on Mr. Capeletti, dear. He may have his reasons."

They ate in silence for a few minutes. Aunt Mary broke it with an approving nod. "I like the sound of this institute for you just now, Sheila. Something going on, and plenty of men about."

Sheila's eyes narrowed. "I'm not interested in men, Aunt Mary."

"Oh, I didn't mean to marry. But for friendships, loosen you up a bit." Aunt Mary sipped her iced tea and added, almost to herself, "Some widows might rush into remarriage, but fifteen years of Tyler Travis would make any woman rethink the institution."

"Now, Aunt Mary," Sheila started.

Aunt Mary gave a genteel snort and set her glass down with a clink. "You don't have to pretend with me, dear. When I first met that man at your engagement party, I thought to myself, he doesn't want a wife, he wants a lackey. You stuck to your guns and made a good job of your marriage, Sheila. I've been proud of you."

Sheila flushed at the unusual praise.

"But," her aunt continued inexorably, "I thank God you have a chance to rethink your life while you're still young. Find out who *you* are, besides Tommy's daughter and Tyler's wife."

Sheila took a deep breath to steady her voice. "Right now I'm Administrative Assistant to the President of Markham, and I'd better be getting back." She rose to fetch her coat and gloves. "But," she added, winding her scarf around her throat, "I don't want to discuss this again, Aunt Mary."

"Very well, dear, we don't need to discuss it again. But I don't want you pretending to be a grieving widow for my benefit."

Sheila bent down to plant a kiss on her aunt's butter-soft cheek. "I do grieve, Aunt Mary—for what we might have become for each other if we'd ever really tried. The fault wasn't all Tyler's, you know."

She wasn't exactly comforted, however, by Aunt Mary's brisk "Of course not, dear."

Sheila paused at the door. "I think I'll walk. They're predicting snow this afternoon, and I don't want to lose my parking space. Besides, I can use the fresh air. Just put the dishes in the sink, will you?"

"Yes, dear. But first, I think I'll have a little nap, to recover from my flight." She tottered across the room as if she had just personally piloted a small plane in from Antipodes.

On her walk through the university quadrangle, Sheila couldn't contain a chuckle. So Aunt Mary had currently elected her Family Member Least Likely to Make Demands? She remembered what her dad had always said about his elder sister: "Getting that woman to stir herself is harder than pouring molasses in January."

But when she arrived at Markham and saw the police cars pulled up to the door, she remembered something else her dad often said about Aunt Mary. As she leaned her weight against the heavy front door, she murmured to herself. "Trouble follows that woman like fleas on a dog."

SIX

THE BUILDING SWARMED with investigating officers, fingerprint men, photographers, and students arriving for Wednesday afternoon seminars. Sheila and Capeletti tried to steer students upstairs without giving information, but no one took them seriously. A growing crowd milled around in the reception hall or sat on the benches and steps, balancing books on their knees. Speculations grew wilder and louder, until the hall was filled with a low-pitched roar.

Suddenly the door to Wentworth opened. Dr. Dehaviland stepped into the hall. As he appeared, the noise dwindled to an uneasy hush. He raised frosty eyebrows. "And what," he asked in his reedy tenor, "is the meaning of this?"

The students looked at their feet, at one another, and finally—imploringly—toward Sheila. She went to meet him. "I think they are wondering what is going on, sir." She regretted the "sir" as soon as she had said it, but such was the influence of the president on even the strong-minded.

He swept them once again with his gaze, then inclined his head. "If you will meet in the third-floor conference room in ten minutes, Detective Flannagan will address you all." He crossed the lobby. "And, Sheila, Mr. Flannagan wants to speak to you at once, in Wentworth." Taking her assent for granted, he walked briskly to his office while the students trooped upstairs.

As Sheila entered the big parlor, a giant of a man stood before the fireplace, gazing up at Eusebius Wentworth. He was handsome in the florid, virile way she associated with Southern men and was unprepared to meet in Chicago. Tyler had stood like that, exuded that aura of command. So did his brother, and all their cousins. This man should be in a Faulkner novel, perhaps, but not in Wentworth.

He turned as she closed the door. "A real swinger," he said, jerking his head toward the portrait.

His shoulders were so broad and his torso so square that Sheila felt she was meeting a gigantic teddy bear, a bear with thick golden curls that incongruously topped his craggy gaze. When God gave out big noses, she thought irrelevantly, you must have been first in line.

He waved her to a chair with a huge paw. "Mrs. Travis? I'm Michael Flannagan. I'd like to ask you a few questions."

The questions were brief and to the point. At last he asked casually, "And no one tried to discourage you from visiting those rooms? Or deliberately steered you toward them?"

She shook her head.

"How did the other two react to finding the body? In your opinion, were they as surprised as you were?"

She considered. "Mr. Capeletti turned gray, and Yusuf threw up all over the floor. I think either of those would have been hard to fake."

He nodded, flipped shut a yellow notebook that looked ridiculously small in his hand. "Thanks for your help. After I've talked with the students and faculty, meet me in the president's office. About two-thirty?" The interview was over.

Sheila entered the president's office a few minutes early. Dr. Dehaviland was on the phone. He waved her to the other end of the room, where Yoshiko and Capeletti already sat side by side on a charcoal tweed love seat. Uneasy, not speaking, they stared into the low fire burning across the room. The fire was too small to give out much warmth, but provided cheery relief from the dreary skies beyond the windows. At its gentle insistence, the dull burgundy carpet glowed and the glass-topped coffee table picked up splinters of light and flung them across the room.

Sheila took one of the two black leather armchairs. "You've got your color back," Yoshiko whispered. Otherwise, nobody felt much like talking.

At last the president joined them. "Mr. Flannagan will be here in a moment." He carefully matched his fingertips and studied them. "He has a few questions to ask us. I want you to be as frank as possible. At the same time"— he raised his eyes to meet theirs—"I want to remind you that there is nothing, nothing at all, to connect this terrible crime with Markham or our people."

Nothing, Sheila thought, but a storeroom, a carpet, and a body. She watched a few flakes of snow drift down outside the window by the fireplace.

When Flannagan took his seat, the chair became the head of the room. Gone was the teddy-bear impression. Now the detective exuded a subtle air that said, "Being bigger than all of you, I am also more competent."

"I want to know anything you remember about the weekend the carpet disappeared," he told Yoshiko and Capeletti.

"I know it was there Friday," Yoshiko told him. "One of our secretaries was leaving that day, and we went in there for a special afternoon break. I'd have noticed if it had been missing."

He nodded. "And it was gone Monday morning?"

Dr. Dehaviland stepped in like a smooth lawyer. "A complete police report was filed at the time, Mr. Flannagan. I'm sure you will find it in your records."

Flannagan paused. "What can you tell me about who was around then—had the students left for their holidays?"

The business manager sat a little taller as he consulted a pad he'd brought. "I have already checked with Stan Frieze about that. We believe everyone had left by then except Dr. Williams' seminar. They met Friday afternoon."

"Jim Lucas," Yoshiko murmured, almost under her breath.

He looked at her, thought a second, then nodded. "Oh, right. He changed his mind and waited to travel with Peter Saturday." He ran one sausage finger down the pad. "Yusuf Jaffari is from overseas, and the aunt Stan Frieze lived with in Denver died last fall. I think they were both here the entire holiday."

"Stan came to us for Christmas dinner," Yoshiko confirmed. She met Sheila's surprised look with a shrug. "Nobody should be alone on Christmas."

Dehaviland leaned forward to instruct them. "Mr. Flannagan is interested in *whether* students were in town, not why."

"Yes, sir. Well, Todd and Jenny Walte left the next Tuesday."

"Todd had flu," Yoshiko enlarged, "and Jenny had to work until Tuesday afternoon."

Dehaviland tightened his lips slightly and the business manager hurried on. "Brad D'Arcy also left Tuesday."

Yoshiko was not so easy to suppress. "He had a late paper he had to complete. Then he flew to the Bahamas to meet his parents." She leaned toward Sheila and whispered behind one hand, "Scads of money."

Dehaviland's head shake was barely perceptible, but his secretary subsided at last. Capeletti's pudgy finger ran down to the last entry on his pad. "Addison Barringer left Friday afternoon."

Yoshiko's hand jerked, as if it would speak for her sealed lips. But she said nothing. Flannagan ticked a pencil against a list he held. "For the students I have Jaffari, Frieze, two Lucases, D'Arcy, and the Waltes. How about faculty members?"

Dehaviland leaned forward. "You will have to ask them, Mr. Flannagan." His voice was chillier than the weather.

Flannagan pocketed his notebook without comment. "You have viewed the body, Mr. Capeletti. Do you know who she is?"

Capeletti hesitated. When he spoke, he was addressing not the detective, but the president. "I didn't know the young woman personally, sir, but I believe Addison Barringer, Brad D'Arcy, or Todd Walte might be able to identify her."

"Yes, Nick?" The president's voice was pleasant, but his eyes were as compelling as those of an adder.

Mr. Capeletti weighed each word. "I believe, sir, from my own rather hurried look at the, uh, body, that this *may* be a young woman who... that is, perhaps they..." He trailed off, mesmerized by those ice-blue eyes.

The president spoke to Flannagan. "Addison Barringer is away at the moment, on a delicate job interview, but Todd and Brad, I am certain, will be glad to assist you in the matter of identification." He stressed the last word.

Flannagan's eyes met his, blue steel against blue ice. At last the huge detective stood. "Ask D'Arcy and Walte to meet me in the basement in ten minutes. Thank you," he added to the others.

As he left, the two women also stood. Dehaviland stopped them. "Before you go, I hope I need not tell you not to discuss this matter beyond this room. I have an important engagement and will be out of the office the rest of the day. Sheila, I leave you and Nick in charge."

Yoshiko's face went blank. She didn't know about the appointment, Sheila thought, followed by, There is no appointment! He's ducking out, leaving us with the whole mess.

The business manager gave no sign of similar suspicions. "I'll do what I can," he said, "I'll be at my desk as soon as I've lined up Todd and Brad." He walked across the room with the heavy tread of a man carrying well the weight of the world on his shoulders.

Dehaviland called him back. "Before you go, Nick, would you just shove the desk chair back?" Reduced once more to servant, Capelleti did as he was bid.

Beside Yoshiko's desk, Sheila paused and whispered impulsively, "What was it you almost said and didn't?"

Yoshiko grew very still, her face as impassive as when Dehaviland mentioned his appointment. "I think we had better do as the president asked, and not discuss it," she murmured, her lips tight. She reached for her earphones.

Rebuffed, Sheila went to her own desk. Common sense—or was it Tyler's voice?—commanded: Don't get involved. You've not been here a week, you've got a job to do, and Mr. Flannagan is perfectly capable of handling this case. Common sense, however, couldn't prevent her asking herself a few questions: Who was this young woman who had come to Markham to die? Why? And what was it Yoshiko had been about to say about Addison Barringer?

SEVEN

SHE'D BEEN AT her desk about half an hour when she started to tremble. Her hands shook, her teeth chattered, her knees beat a tattoo on the side of her desk. Managing to stand, she crossed the hall. "I'm going up for coffee," she told Yoshiko.

"Take a proper break," the secretary urged. "You've been very brave, but you look like you could use a rest."

"I think it's finally all hit me," Sheila agreed. She was glad to find the coffee room deserted. Most students had finished for the day, and gone. The coffee samovar was almost empty, but still hot. Carrying her steaming cup and two cookies back to the old leather chair, she started to nudge it with her knee to face the window more nearly. Then she stopped. Snow was flailing the panes. She nudged the chair back to its original position and gratefully snuggled into it.

Now she faced the fireplace, where several logs still burned. With the room bathed in soft light from brass sconces, her awareness of the snow lashing the world only made her more comfortable. Her eyes roamed the room, taking pleasure in the polished oak and gently worn carpet. Then she stiffened. Stan Frieze lay like a log on the couch, fast asleep.

Stan was several years older than other students, almost thirty. Perhaps that was why he'd been chosen proctor—it certainly wasn't for his looks. Even in sleep his face looked pinched, and his long, pointed nose did make him resemble a weasel. His skin was the color of kneaded dough, and his hair—if she were an artist, would she paint it a dull, lifeless brown or a muddy gray? She munched her cookie and considered the question.

As if responding to her scrutiny, he stirred and opened his eyes. Seeing her there, he swung his legs around and sat up. "Hello, Sheila." He shoved back one lank piece of hair out of his face and fumbled for his shoes without a trace of embarrassment.

Before Sheila could reply, Jenny Walte came in. She made herself a cup of chocolate, chose a cookie, and perched on the arm of the sofa beside Stan. "Welcome to 'Days of our Lives,' Markham style," she greeted them.

Jenny was everything a much younger Sheila had wanted to be: tiny—scarcely five feet—and petite. Jenny was blessed with straight gold hair that flowed almost to her waist. Deep-blue eyes usually peeped mischievously from wire-rimmed glasses, but today those eyes were sober.

Like Todd, she dressed in a style quintessentially Hyde Park: the world's ugliest clothes worn with a certain flair. Today her camel corduroy skirt was topped by a brown jacket of nubby wool and a faded plaid blouse whose muted reds and blues almost explained the purple stockings rising from her Scandinavian clogs.

Sheila smiled at her. "I see you've heard. When you didn't meet with the rest of the staff, I wondered if you'd been told."

Jenny nibbled her cookie. "They treated me like an honorary student—I guess so I'd be back to reopen the library." As she talked, her eyes kept straying toward the door.

"Where's Todd?" Stan asked.

Jenny shuddered. "He and Brad had to go look at the body. They haven't come back yet."

On cue, Todd and Brad came into the room. Jenny shot them a questioning look.

"It's Melanie, all right," Todd said with a grim nod. "What's left of her."

He drew a cup of black coffee and took a long swallow in spite of its temperature. As Brad made a cup of tea, Sheila saw that his hands were shaking.

Jenny went around to sit in the center of the couch and Todd took the other corner, beside her. Brad dropped into a chair.

Brad reminded Sheila of a young Elizabethan, just home from the sea. Short, slim and bronzed (the Bahamas, she remembered), he wore his almost-white hair below his ears, flowing into a well-trimmed beard. He not so much sat as lay in his chair, spreading the gray coat of his three-piece suit to display a thick gold watch chain across his vest. He stretched his short legs and crossed his neat ankles. His black shoes, Sheila noted with approval, gleamed with polish. Leaning his head against the back of the chair so that his beard jutted out, he closed his eyes.

Stan asked, "Melanie who?"

Brad didn't bother to open his eyes. "Something around here you don't know, Stan?" he murmured drowsily. "I wonder if we should tell you. Nick said we're to be discreet."

"I was discreet," Todd told Jenny. "I took one look and discreetly keeled over. If Brad hadn't caught me...but he's right. I'm not sure we ought to tell Stan, or even Sheila..."

"What difference does it make?" Jenny asked. "It'll be common knowledge soon enough anyway." She turned to Stan. "Melanie Forbes. Remember her? She dated Quint last spring, and in the fall she'd sometimes come by and have a cup of coffee with Evelyn. Evelyn always referred to her as 'my really good friend Melanie.'"

Stan nodded. "I remember. Didn't Brad used to date her, too?"

Jenny bit her lip and Todd checked a nod. Brad grunted gently. His profile stirred some memory in Sheila, but she couldn't remember what. Nobody said a word.

Stan considered his fellow students with disgust. "As proctor, I have a responsibility to know." Did he cultivate that high, reedy voice deliberately, to ape the president?

Brad slitted one eye in his direction. "You'll know what we damn well tell you, Frieze," he said gently.

Stan pouted in his corner. "I thought maybe she was part of your research." It was clearly an insinuation, but Brad didn't deign to respond.

Jenny turned to her husband. "Was this related to drugs?"

Todd shrugged. "Who can tell at this point?"

Brad murmured, as though reassuring Jenny, "Mellie didn't use."

Stan smiled his sly, wide smile. "You ought to know, Brad."

Jenny hurried to explain to Sheila (as to a maiden great-aunt, Sheila thought wryly), "Brad is doing special research on the international drug market and its effects on political decision-making." Her voice rambled off the long subject with practiced ease. "But"—she turned to Brad, almost pleading—"Melanie wasn't part of that, was she?"

Brad's head barely moved as he shook it. "Uh-uh. Melanie wasn't part of anything."

"It's weird to think of her dead," Jenny said, a small tremble in her voice. "She was so alive, so..." Again she turned to Sheila. "Melanie was beautiful. She always made you feel like you were wearing leftovers from your high school wardrobe. Oh, not you," she said pointedly, her eyes admiring Sheila's wool skirt and matching sweater, "but girls her own age."

As soon as the words were out, she realized how they could sound. A blush rushed to her cheeks. Todd didn't help by slapping her thigh. "Way to go, Jen. Now you've made Sheila feel ancient. What she's trying to say, Sheila, is that Melanie was a model."

Brad's voice was scarcely audible. "Melanie was also a bitch."

"Poor analogy," Jenny objected. "Melanie hated dogs."

Todd stood abruptly. "Melanie is no longer a bitch," he said with finality, "and she is no longer beautiful. Believe me, I know." He strode to the window and opened it slightly. Flakes of snow hurled themselves into the room, but he pressed his nose to the crack and inhaled deeply. They could hear the somber chimes of Rockefeller Chapel tolling four.

"Any food left?" The two Lucases glided through the door, straight toward the table. Peter's cheeks were red, as if he'd just come inside, but Jim looked pale and tired. Probably been working on that paper all day, Sheila thought with pity. He pulled the samovar toward him to drain it of coffee, then drifted over to munch cookies on the arm of the sofa beside Todd's vacated corner. Peter carried his tea to the piano and lightly touched a few chords as if greeting the instrument.

"Did we hear that you had to look at the body?" Jim asked.

"Yeah." Todd spoke without turning from the window.

"Why you, Todd?" Jim wondered. "I mean, Melanie was sweet on Brad, but you..."

It was Brad who replied. "Melanie was sweet on Melanie, Jimmy," he drawled, "but for identification purposes, anybody who knew her would do. Even you."

Simultaneously Sheila saw a dull red stain Jim's translucent cheeks and heard a rush from the piano. Peter grasped Brad by the collar, twisted it hard.

"Hey," Brad choked, "lay off it, man."

"Then you lay off Jimmy," Peter blazed. "That's twice today."

The red in Jim's cheeks grew darker. "It's okay, Pete. He really needed that book, and he's had a rough afternoon."

Peter looked from Jim to Brad. For once, Brad's eyes were fully open, and bulging slightly. Peter threw him back against the chair. Then he strode to the piano, slid onto the bench, and began a series of menacing chords.

"Sorry, Jim," Brad drawled.

"It's okay." But Jim joined Peter on the piano bench.

Stan went to stand behind them and Jenny slid to her feet and joined Todd at the window, one hand gently resting on his shoulder. Sheila was about to leave, when an unexpected question startled her. "You Tyler Travis' wife?"

Brad spoke so softly she almost missed it; looked quickly, to be sure he was addressing her. Navy-blue eyes met hers.

She nodded. "His widow."

"So what are you doing at Markham?" His voice was totally devoid of sympathy.

She stood. "I'm supposed to be working, and I'd better get back to it." His lips curved in a lazy smile that made her ask, "Why?"

He shrugged, an elaborate motion. "I thought it might be something else." His eyes drifted closed as he murmured, "Your reputation has followed you, Mrs. Travis."

Puzzled eyes stared at her from all around the room and a current flowed among them. Sheila left quickly, but not before she knew what it was. Fear had invaded the coffee room.

EIGHT

SHEILA WAS CLEARING her desk for the day when her phone rang. "Mrs. Travis, this is Michael Flannagan." Before he said his name she had already pictured him on the other end of the line. When you're five nine, you don't forget men who tower over you. "There are a few details I failed to get this afternoon. Your home address, for onc."

She raised her eyebrows, but gave it obediently.

"And your husband's name."

"My husband is deceased."

"I see." He paused, waiting. "And his name was...?"

"Tyler Travis. No middle name."

"Thanks very much." He sounded pleased about something. She hoped he wasn't planning to ask her out. Dr. Dehaviland would have kittens if he thought she was consorting with the Chicago police.

As she started for her coat, the phone rang again. "Sheila?" Aunt Mary's husky voice was deep with concern. "Are you safe to walk home? Maybe you should take a cab."

"Nonsense, Aunt Mary. I'll be fine."

"Isn't it snowing there, dear? Over here it's snowing cats and canaries." Aunt Mary spoke as if the few blocks between them were a continent.

"Yes, it's snowing here, Aunt Mary, but this is the first big snow I've seen in years. I look forward to walking in it. Make some coffee. I'll be home soon."

Her confidence, however, trembled a little as she stepped off Markham's bottom step into snow over her boots. The wind's icy fingers crept up her skirt, searched for openings in her fleecy mohair muffler, flung wet handfuls of snow into her eyes. She had to lean forward in order to make headway, and found the experience more exhausting than exhilarating. Further, the pale gold streetlights lent a Gothic air to the white-and-gray gloom—it was the kind of night favored by old movies about Jack the Ripper, Sherlock Homes, or dingy waterfronts. Unbidden, a picture rose before her; a carpet and a foot. In spite of her coat and muffler, her teeth began to chatter.

At the corner she paused to check for cars. Had someone behind her also stopped? She whirled, but saw no one. Was he lurking behind that huge cedar?

"Get hold of yourself," she muttered aloud with a vigorous shake. But she decided to take a shortcut through university buildings.

Striding down the bright, damp corridor, jostled by students intent on finding supper, at first she felt glowingly safe. But gradually she regained a sense of being watched, of footsteps that paused when she paused, hurried when she hurried.

At last she had gone as far as she could inside. Desperately she wished she'd brought her car, or heeded Aunt Mary's advice. But she had no alternative. With a deep breath she left the warmth and entered the gloom outside. Head down against the onslaught of flakes, she more ran than walked across the quadrangle.

Suddenly a hand grabbed her arm. "What's your hurry?"

She stopped, terrified.

"Sorry, I didn't mean to give you a fright, but you were about to plow me under." David MacLean's gray eyes twinkled into hers. Sheila spun to see if anyone else was near. The only other people in the quad were heading in other directions. "Are you all right?" David asked.

Sheila laughed, silly with relief. "You are always having to ask me that, aren't you? But I'll admit, you nearly scared me to death. I think I was being followed."

His eyes roamed the thick, snowy air. "If you were, he's gone. Here, let me walk you home. It's nae bother." He took her elbow and gently steered her down buried sidewalks.

"That's just what Tyler's grandmother would have said." She smiled. "But surely you were going somewhere."

He raised his bare head to meet snowflakes that also dusted his lashes. "Och, no, I was just out enjoying the snow."

"Enjoying?" Until now she'd been in too much of a hurry. She looked about them, letting the heavy silence fill and anchor her. The shadowy buildings hovered protectingly, their soft grays punctuated by the glow of scattered windows and streetlights. Tall bare trees held out their arms to welcome the storm's violent embrace, while the ground had become one soft drift of white.

They passed a streetlight. "I'm escorting royalty," he teased. "You've got diamonds in your hair."

Sheila peered up toward her bangs. "Is it frizzing?"

"Terribly." He nodded. "You shouldn't be seen in public."

Her mouth dropped.

"That's exactly what my sister asks whenever she's caught in the damp. I decided years ago that's the answer it deserves."

"You're a brute," she informed him.

"Aye. So she tells me. Her name's Margaret. What's yours?"

It seemed strange to tell him when she already felt so comfortable in his presence.

At the edge of the university she stopped. Before them spread the Midway. A wide grassy strip several blocks long, it was usually merely a pretty interlude in her walk. Tonight it was a vast, empty span of dreadful possibilities.

David took her elbow. "I'll take you the whole way, quine." His voice rose and fell in a gentle lilt. "I need the exercise."

She considered the tunnel of gloom beyond and gratefully accepted. "Will you stay for dinner?" she offered. "My aunt will have prepared more than enough for two."

He shook his head regretfully. "I'm meeting some chaps for a basketball game. Maybe another time?"

"Of course." They fell into a companionable silence. Their strides matched so well she wondered if he was deliberately copying hers, but when she glanced sideways at him, he seemed lost in contented thought.

He left her at the outside door. "Cheerio!"

She closed the foyer door behind her and started up the stairs, unexpectedly warmed and rested. But only for a moment.

Aunt Mary leaned over the top railing. "Sheila, is that you?" she called softly. Catching a glimpse of her niece as she rounded the first landing, she added urgently, "Phone."

Sheila climbed the last step quickly. Aunt Mary pushed her toward the apartment and shut the door behind them. "I didn't like to say so before the neighbors, dear, but it's the police."

"MRS. TRAVIS, this is Mike Flannagan again. There are a few details I'd like to go over once more. Could I drop by your place tonight about eight?'' Reluctantly, Sheila assented.

She entered the living room five minutes later to find Aunt Mary placing turnip greens on the table. From somewhere she had unearthed Sheila's only apron, a fluffy affair left over from bridal days, and it made her look more like a mischievous child playing house than the gourmet cook she was.

"We're ready as soon as I fetch the pork chops, dear. After dinner, you can tell me all about it."

"Pork chops?" Sheila mentally inventoried the freezer as she had left it that morning.

Aunt Mary trotted back toward the kitchen. "Oh, I added a few things to the larder. Just odds and ends."

"You went shopping?" Sheila was incredulous enough to gape. The closest she had ever seen Aunt Mary come to doing her own shopping was when she used to call the general store in Kennedy's Landing, South Carolina, to place her daily (delivered) order.

"Oh, no." Aunt Mary answered in the tone of one accused of great indiscretion. "I ran into a neighbor of yours, a very nice young woman, on the stairs. She was going shopping, and offered to pick up a few things."

Sheila suppressed a snort. From experience she could picture the scene: Aunt Mary hovering near a crack in the door, letter in hand ready for mailing, listening until she heard her prey on the stairs and then tripping down for an "accidental" encounter that would result, inevitably, in the neighbor's actually volunteering to shop for her.

She strolled casually into the kitchen toward the refrigerator, schooling her voice to innocent curiosity. "What did I need?"

Aunt Mary was suddenly very busy at the oven door. "Just a few trifles, dear. Odds and ends."

Sheila considered a box of petits fours, a leg of lamb, vintage white wine, a box of winter strawberries, and real cream. Then she looked to where Aunt Mary was arranging three thick pork chops stuffed with almonds and mushrooms. The older woman picked up the platter with a complacent smile. "Open the wine, and we're ready." As Sheila followed her to the table, she resisted a strong impulse to check to see if her hands were clean.

True to her code, not until they were ensconced on the couch, stockinged feet tucked beneath them and steaming coffee beside them, did Aunt Mary give her curiosity full rein. "Now, tell me about your afternoon," she commanded. "Every bit of it." She spooned three mounds of sugar into coffee white with cream. Then she settled back placidly. "I do like a little excitement in my life, you know."

"Well..." Sheila sipped her own coffee black to leave room for a petit four. She described the police activities, her own interview, the meeting in the president's office, and the student conversation later. "That's all I know," she concluded, "but maybe you can get more from Mr. Flannagan when he arrives."

"Arrives?" Aunt Mary permitted her voice to betray a slight degree of surprise.

Sheila drained her cup and placed it carefully in its saucer. "He's coming at eight. He said he had a few things to go over."

"Sheila?" Aunt Mary's voice was worried. "You seem to be getting very involved in this case. You don't think we need to call Wyndham, do you? I know he'd drop everything..."

Sheila shuddered. She, too, knew that Wyndham Travis would drop his lucrative Mississippi law practice in a moment to get his younger brother's widow out of a jam. But she also knew what lectures she'd have to endure in the process. "I think we can handle this between us, Aunt Mary. Now I'll get the dishes." She stood.

"Thanks, dear." Aunt Mary slid from the couch and wriggled her feet into their tiny shoes. She bent to pick up a Bible from the coffee table. "I'll be reading in my room." As an afterthought, she also picked up a murder mystery with a marker halfway through.

DETECTIVE FLANNAGAN arrived punctually. "Thanks for letting me come." As he shrugged out of his massive gray coat, his muscles rippled under his jacket. She brought him a cup of coffee, wondering how long he would take to reveal his real reason for coming. His presence was disturbing. Unlike Tyler in appearance (except for height), there was something so like Tyler in the way he moved to a large chair and took possession of it that Sheila felt her stomach give a sophomoric quiver.

As she again took her place on the couch, he settled deeper into the biggest chair and came right to the point. "Do you know a lawyer in Mississippi named Wyndham Travis?"

"Wyndham?" Astonishment mingled with apprehension. Had Aunt Mary already called him, and he the Chicago police? "He's my brother-in-law. Why?"

The detective's bass chuckle rumbled through the room. "I grew up in Tupelo with those Travis boys. Lordy, what scrapes we used to get into! When I saw your information, I wondered if you might be Tyler's..." he hesitated, sipped his coffee.

"Widow," Sheila supplied.

He rubbed one hand over his tawny curls. "Er, yeah. Well, I think we might need to have a little talk." He took a swallow of coffee that should have scalded his eyeballs, shifted his bulk to lean toward her, and looked so directly into her eyes that she saw that his were flecked with gold. "Last time I was in Tupelo I ran into old Wyndham. He said Tyler's wife had a habit of getting involved with the police." His smile was more intense than friendly.

"I never!" she gasped, caught off-guard. He raised his thick eyebrows inquiringly. "Well—once or twice, when I knew something that could help," she admitted, "but trust Wyndham to exaggerate. He probably hinted I committed all the crimes myself."

Flannagan grunted. "No, he tried to make me think you'd solved them all yourself. But I know to take old Wyndham with a grain of salt." He rubbed one huge hand over the lower half of his face. "Now what I came to say is this: You let me handle this case, all right? If I need information from you, I'll ask for it."

His voice was genial, but her eyes narrowed. "Is this a warning?"

He shook his head. "Not yet, it isn't—so long as you keep busy with your own work and let me do mine."

"What if I overhear something important?"

"You won't hear anything we don't already know."

Before she could reply, Aunt Mary's door opened and the tiny woman tripped into the living room. "Why, Sheila, do you have a guest? No, don't get up." The last remark was directed to the detective, who had lumbered to his feet at her entrance.

Sheila made the introductions, and the detective's huge hand enclosed Aunt Mary's. "And what are you doing in Chicago, Miss Mary?" The old familiar form of address startled Sheila, but she wasn't surprised. She had often noticed how, in Aunt Mary's presence, people who had long ago abandoned the South began to relax back into its language and customs. She found it an amusing balance to the hard-nosed Mike of Dehaviland's office.

Aunt Mary perched on her usual end of the couch. "Oh, a little of this and a little of that. As long as I am imposing on Sheila's hospitality, the least I can do is prepare the food and keep her place looking nice." She gazed about her with the complacent look of a woman who has scrubbed and polished all day.

"Your niece is lucky to have you, ma'am. This city can be a hard place for a woman alone."

Aunt Mary nodded. "Oh yes, indeed. Sheila was telling me about that poor girl she found in the basement this morning."

He gave Sheila a warning look. "Was she now?" he growled.

Aunt Mary inclined her head toward her niece. "I'd like some coffee, Sheila. Would you bring in the pot? And there is a cake in the larder."

Sheila hadn't had a larder in her married life, but she rose in exasperated amusement and went to search the cupboards. So Aunt Mary had heard him warning them off, had she? Poor Mr. Flannagan. As she left the room, Aunt Mary's husky voice followed her in waves. "...can't divulge official secrets, Mike—I may call you Mike...?...practically home folks." Mike's rumble of assent sounded distinctly like a purr. Five minutes later, when Sheila returned with the coffee and slices of home-made chocolate cake, she found Aunt Mary curled on the sofa, feet tucked neatly beneath her, saying confidingly, "I just hate to think how her poor mother must be feeling."

He fell for it like a crab for chicken necks. "Nobody seems to give a damn, Miss Mary, if you'll pardon my French. Her mom's dead, and her dad's been remarried about ten years. He's overseas on business, and the Philadelphia officer who went by reported the stepmother just said she'd always predicted the girl would come to a bad end. The little stepsister was worse. As soon as she heard, she asked, 'Can I have her skis?' " He shook his massive head. "Pots of money doesn't always mean a family has everything."

As Sheila passed the cake, she tried to picture this family—and failed. Aunt Mary's eyes were wide with concern. "What about her friends? Surely they miss her?"

Flannagan leaned back and let his hand dangle off the chair's fat arm, prepared to be generous to the maker of chocolate cake. "No friend we can find. She lived up near Water Tower Place, a high-rent district. People come and go all the time. She was gone eight weeks last summer, and nobody seems to have cared." Did he sound despondent because the girl had been so alone, or because that made his job harder? Sheila couldn't help wondering.

"How old was she?" Aunt Mary wanted to know. She leaned forward and asked by a tilt of her silver head whether Mike would have more coffee.

He would. "Twenty-three." He held out his cup.

"She was a model," Sheila contributed. Flannagan slewed his eyes her way as if he had momentarily forgotten her presence. "I heard that in the coffee room this afternoon," she explained. Why should she feel so defensive?

He scowled at her, but reached for his notebook nevertheless. "Did they say who she worked for?" Sheila shook her head. "Okay, we'll check it out. But remember what I said."

Aunt Mary gave him a sunny smile. "So many women have to earn their own way these days, don't they, Mike?"

He shook his head. "Melanie Forbes wasn't working for the money. Her daddy manufactures equipment for pro-football teams and he gave her a hefty allowance. Her stepmama is on the board of every charity in town," he added irrelevantly.

"If I have not charity, it profiteth me nothing."

"I beg your pardon, ma'am?"

She shook her silver curls. "Nothing, Mike. Just thinking aloud." But her brown eyes were troubled and tiny wrinkles had appeared between her delicate brows. "I am surprised no one noticed if her allowance checks weren't cashed."

Flannagan grunted. "That's how rich folks do things—they have so much money they can't keep track of it."

Aunt Mary widened her eyes. "Do tell, Mike!" Sheila nearly choked, turned it into a cough. The detective didn't notice.

"Yes ma'am. Melanie Forbes' allowance was paid directly into her bank account each month by her dad's accountant, who also paid her rent and utilities. That's why her apartment manager never missed her—the rent's been paid."

For a moment no one spoke, then Sheila rose and strode across the living room to stare out the window at the city beyond. An easy place to get lost in—but this easy? She thrust her hands deep in the big pockets of her skirt. "You're sure, Mr. Flannagan, this setup wasn't arranged just so someone *could* kill her?" Aunt Mary might be on a first-name basis, but Sheila wasn't.

He shrugged. "Could be. But personally I don't think the killer knew how easily she could disappear. If she'd been dumped somewhere in the Forest Preserve west of here, she might never have been found, or identified. Where she was, it was only a question of waiting for the first good thaw."

"So you think that rules out the family?"

He remembered he didn't want her involved. "I'll let you know when we crack the case." He shifted, ready to leave.

Sheila drew her dark eyebrows together. "Someone in the coffee room today said that Evelyn Parsons, a secretary at Markham that got fired at Christmas, called Melanie her really good friend."

Fire smoldered behind Flannagan's eyes. "Why didn't anybody tell *me* that?" he growled.

Sheila shrugged. "It just came up in the conversation."

Aunt Mary's voice was worried. "Why was Evelyn fired? You don't want to make the same mistake, dear."

"Don't worry, Aunt Mary. It's a mistake that can't be repeated—she was suspected of stealing a valuable clock."

"And did she?"

Sheila remembered her conversation the day before. "Yusuf Jaffari doesn't think so." She repeated their conversation.

Flannagan scratched one cheek reflectively, as if making up his mind whether to speak or not. "I read that file this afternoon. This Parsons woman swore she didn't take it, of course, but she was the only person with opportunity."

"Why would she want it?" Aunt Mary asked. "If, of course, you can tell us about it, Mike."

The detective accepted the second piece of cake she was placing on his plate. "I can tell you what I know—it doesn't seem to be related to this current case in any way. The motive seems to have been money. Mr. Capeletti claimed it was very valuable. However"—hc chewed and swallowed—"Dehaviland insisted it had little value. He was out of town when the theft occurred, and called us off the case when he found out about it."

"That must be why Capeletti and Yoshiko wouldn't call you immediately yesterday," Sheila concluded.

"They could have gotten in trouble for that." He glared. Sheila hoped she would never have to choose between his displeasure and Dehaviland's.

He placed his plate on the table and sighed appreciatively. "Well, I gotta run. I'll check Evelyn Parsons' story tomorrow. We kept tabs on her at her new job, but we never proved she took the clock." He stood and beamed down at Aunt Mary. "The cake was great, Miss Mary."

She dimpled up at him. "Come anytime, Mike. The coffee's always on." She put out one slim hand sparkling with diamonds, and he buried it briefly between his. "Oh, Mike, may I ask two questions before you go? Just to satisfy an old woman's curiosity? When and how was this young woman killed? You haven't said."

He hesitated, and Sheila wondered why. A Southern reluctance to bother ladies with sordid facts, or police reluctance to give out official information? His reply gave her an inkling that it might be both.

"It's not pretty, Miss Mary, and it's not out yet. But it will be in the papers tomorrow, so I can tell you, I guess. Somebody just put their hands around her neck and squeezed hard. We don't know exactly when, but we think it was during the weekend before Christmas."

Sheila rose to see him to the door. He shrugged into his coat. "If this Parsons woman gives us anything, it will be more than we've come up with so far," he admitted somewhat sourly. He stepped so near that she took an involuntary step backward, then flushed in embarrassment. He didn't seem to notice. "Now you remember what I said. Leave this case to me."

He started to leave, then turned back. "That aunt of yours is fantastic." He chuckled. "Reminds me of my own

Aunt Lucy. Take good care of her, you hear? Chicago's not Kennedy's Landing."

Sheila hesitated. Should she tell him that Aunt Mary hadn't actually lived in Kennedy's Landing for years, that she managed her own considerable fortune and spent her life shuttling between Florida, Atlanta, the mountains of North Carolina, her relatives, and outlandish parts of the world? She decided to give him a test.

"Would you believe that little lady once bagged her own lion?"

He grinned. "Sure. A dandelion. I've heard that one before."

She nodded. "I suspected you had. Well, I'll take care of her while she takes care of me."

Reassured, he turned and went heavily down the stairs. Sheila watched him go, then turned back to the living room with a smile on her lips. Why fight it? Aunt Mary's role was too firmly established by those big brown eyes and bewitching dimples ever to be shattered by mere facts.

NINE

THE NEXT MORNING Sheila accomplished very little beyond steering reporters out the door and assuring her students she knew no more than they did. To her astonishment, however, Dr. Dehaviland insisted on going ahead with the afternoon lecture. She was checking last-minute details when Jim Lucas stopped by her door.

"Do you know what the menu is for the Community Dinner?"

She looked at him blankly. "Community Dinner?"

"Sure. We have them every month. Dinner, light entertainment, and a big-name speaker. Tomorrow night Dr. Williams is the speaker and Pete and I are the light entertainment. You'll be there, won't you?" His eyes were so like a spaniel's that she nodded without thinking.

"Am I supposed to do something about it?" she wondered aloud.

He shook his head. "Not until next month. This one's all planned. I just hadn't heard what the menu was going—"

He broke off, and his face brightened. "Hi, Dr. Williams!"

A burly man with a bushy beard eyed Sheila appreciatively. "I see they've been improving the place while I was away."

"This is Mrs. Travis—Sheila," Jim told him. "She's the new Administrative Assistant to the President. Her husband was Tyler Travis."

"I knew Tyler well." He was speaking to Sheila, not Jim. Unobtrusively the young man faded down the hall. "We all feel his loss." Warmed by his smile, Sheila could see why this man was such an asset at international bargaining tables, in spite of a ruggedness that would look far more at home in a wide-brimmed leather hat and wool poncho than in the gray three-piece suit he now wore. "Are you enjoying your work here?" he asked.

"Frankly, Dr. Williams, I'm not doing much work yet," she told him. "Mainly putting names with faces."

He threw back his head and laughed, showing a mouthful of fillings. "Call me Cal, will you? And call me quick if you start to die of boredom in these fusty—I mean hallowed—halls."

She stared at him, incredulous. Had he heard nothing of yesterday's events? She was just about to ask when the front door scraped open and Dr. Dehaviland strolled in. Under his cashmere overcoat the president wore a suit of charcoal gray, a light-gray shirt, and a soft plaid tie. Immediately Sheila was aware that Cal's beard needed a trim. "Good morning, Sheila. Welcome back, Calvin. How was Washington?"

"Moving like glaciers, as usual," Cal said shortly.

Pulling back leather gloves off his well-manicured hands, Dr. Dehaviland leaned over her door in a fatherly fashion. "Are you ready for the lecture this afternoon, Sheila? Notify the secretaries that we'll want it ready for mailing by Tuesday." She looked at him in disbelief. "Tuesday? Mr. Rareby said..."

He pursed his lips and shook his head. "I spoke with Mr. Rareby last evening. We agreed that in light of, ah, recent events, we should get this first one out as soon as possible."

"I'm not certain that *is* possible, sir." Again the infuriating word slipped out. "The women are already busy, and the manuscript will have to be transcribed, edited, printed..."

He held up a hand to forestall more dreary details. "Yoshiko can help when she completes her other work. Now please call my wife and tell her I'll be bringing Dr. Henderson for dinner after his lecture."

Sheila's blood froze. "She doesn't know?" The president had said when they first discussed the lecturer's visit that Dr. Henderson would dine at his home.

He dismissed the matter with a wave of his hand. "I didn't want her to feel the pressure ahead of time."

Sheila couldn't help thinking that if it had been the president's body in the cellar, she'd have known where to look for a suspect.

He wasn't through. "Oh, and Sheila? If people cluster around your door, I trust you will send them on their way. Calvin, I'd like to see you in my office immediately, if that is convenient."

Cal nodded. "Fine, John. I'll be right in."

Dehaviland inclined his head and went down the hall toward his office. Giving Sheila a broad wink, Cal hissed over her door. "Speaking as a cluster of one, what goes on here?"

She shook her head. "I think the president wants to tell you in his own way."

"Okay." He grinned through his bristling beard. "I'll go get his version, then come back for yours."

But when the president's door opened a few moments later, Cal turned toward the unused lobby and she heard him clatter down the stairs to his basement office. "Like the wise men of old," she murmured, "he departeth to his own country by another way."

A voice at her door startled her. "Howdy, Sheila. How's it going?" Bertha propped her round elbows on the lower door.

"It's been a madhouse this morning," Sheila admitted, flexing her fingers and arching her back to relax.

Bertha nodded sympathetically. "And you've got most of it to bear. There's some around here"—she jerked a thumb down the hall—"who make themselves *conspicuously* absent when trouble comes. Not to be naming any names."

Sheila chuckled. "Let's not."

Bertha stood on tiptoe to scrunch herself farther over the top of the door. "But I tell you what. If you get swamped, you run down to the basement and eat that soup I promised you."

"Maybe tomorrow, Bertha? I'm picking up Dr. Henderson today."

"Sure thing. I've got somebody else coming, too, but that will be fine. Be seeing you." She flapped one hand in farewell.

The limousine driver was not inclined to talk, so Sheila rested her head against the seat and considered the forty-minute drive to O'Hare a mini-vacation. Dr. Henderson, a former adviser to several NATO countries, turned out to be colorless in body and personality, an elderly man who was lost for conversation that did not center on national defense. Once he'd given her a pallid handshake and placed her as Tyler's widow—"Wonderful man, I met him once out in Bangkok"—he let his head sink to his chest and dozed all the way back to Hyde Park. Sheila was left to converse with Aunt Mary in her mind: "If you think I'm ever going to be somebody besides Tyler Travis' wife, you can think again."

Thankfully she delivered Dr. Henderson to Mr. Rareby, Brad, and Todd—today carefully clad in a dark three-piece suit—for lunch at the Quadrangle Club, and decided a quick walk and a hot Reuben at a nearby deli were just what she needed.

But first, she'd put on the snow boots that vanity had kept her from wearing to meet the ambassador. As she plunged her feet into her right boot, her toes met something sharp and hard. Impatiently she wiggled her toes. She didn't have time to investigate just now. Unless she hurried, she'd be late getting back for the lecture. She grabbed her coat and started toward the door.

Whatever was in her boot continued to jab and bruise her big toe all the way to the restaurant. To make matters worse, the day was colder than she had expected. As she limped the five blocks with all deliberate speed, her cheeks began first to burn, then to ache, while tears began to slide down her cheeks. Angrily she wiped at them with her mitten. Between the cold and the pain in her toe, she arrived at the restaurant mad enough to cry or swear.

SHE COLLAPSED INTO a chair near the door and tugged at the boot. ''What the devil are you doing here?'' A familiar bulky figure loomed over the table's red Formica top.

''Having lunch,'' she said between clenched teeth. With one final tug her boot flew off. She tilted it. A pair of delicate gold lyres slid into her palm. Each ended in a sharp point like an arrow's tip.

She tested one point. ''No wonder!'' Ruefully she considered her toe, which was slowly oozing blood. She scrubbed it with a napkin, then put back on her boot.

Flannagan, meanwhile, picked up the earrings. ''Not yours?''

She shook her head. "I never saw them before. Somebody must have dropped them into my boot this morning."

He let them fall to the table with a click. "Strange way to give a present." He sounded somewhat sour, she thought.

"Unorthodox and useless." She pulled back her hair to show her unpierced ears.

He pushed the earrings to one side. "Well, when we get these other mysteries cleared up, we'll take on the case of the appearing earrings. Meanwhile, I'm about to interview the Parsons woman on her lunch hour. I'll give you the benefit of the doubt and say you didn't track me down here"—he held up one hand to forestall any reply—"since this deli is equidistant between Markham and her new office. But we're going to be sitting right over there"—he indicated a table in the far corner where a cup of coffee was cooling—"and I don't want you..."

She was taking a breath to cool her temper before speaking when someone paused beside her table and looked around the room while unbuttoning her coat.

The woman was about thirty, tall and slightly stooped. Her heavy makeup failed to disguise scars from what must have been a heartbreaking case of teenage acne. Behind glasses her eyes were a lovely gray-green, but surrounded by enough shadow to follow beauty editors' advice to accent your best feature. Her hair, light brown and falling to her shoulders, was cut in a style that just missed being smart. Only her taste in clothes was faultless. Her silky beige blouse and soft wool suit were probably inexpensive, but well chosen for her figure and coloring. And the swath of gold chains across the front was the perfect accessory.

She waited by the table, gangling and awkward, looking hesitantly at every table but Sheila's. Flannagan spoke. "Evelyn Parsons?" She jumped, nodded. "We're going to sit over there." He jerked a thick thumb. "I just came over to speak to Mrs. Travis here for a minute. But she has *nothing* to do with this case."

Evelyn tensed. "Case? You didn't mention a case when you called." Her voice was wary, a low whine. "Is this about that clock again? I've told all I know. You can't harass—"

"Of course not, Miss Parsons." Flannagan sounded about as soothing as a purring tiger. She was not reassured.

She looked at Sheila, made a sudden decision, and sat quickly in one of the vacant chairs. "I won't talk to you without a witness. Mrs. Travis, if you don't mind, can we talk here?" Sheila raised her brows at the detective. He nodded a short, glowering assent and fetched his coffee.

"Order what you want," Flannagan told Evelyn. "This is on the City of Chicago."

Listening to the size of his own order, Sheila leaned toward Evelyn and said sotto voce, "I hope the City of Chicago can afford it." Evelyn gave her a tenuous smile.

Not until they had ordered did he begin to explain the purpose of the interview. "This has to do with a friend of yours, Melanie Forbes."

She nodded. "I haven't seen her for several months, you know."

"When was the last time you did see her?"

She considered. "I guess the weekend before Christmas." She sipped her glass of milk as if gaining time to be sure. "I stopped by her place that Friday afternoon. Why?"

"Yesterday morning, Miss Parsons, Melanie Forbes was found in the basement of Markham Institute. She'd been murdered."

Evelyn's eyes widened in horror. For a long moment she didn't move, then she clasped the front of her blouse and clung to her swath of chains. "Oh, no!"

Watching, Sheila was reminded of the reaction of rock fans when one of their idols dies. Evelyn's green eyes had the same avid look: horror coupled with self-importance at being even peripherally associated with a public tragedy.

The waitress brought their orders, and Flannagan devoted himself to dousing his Polish sausage with half a jar of mustard while Evelyn recovered. She took three gulps of water and several deep breaths. "How... how did she die?"

Flannagan told her, adding, "You may have been one of the last persons to see her alive."

Evelyn's eyes widened in fear. "You don't think that I...?"

"No, but anything you can tell us may help us find her killer."

She shook her head as she spoke. "But, I mean, I don't think anything we said will help, you know. We didn't talk about dying, or anything." Was there a slight note of regret in her voice?

Flannagan took a huge bite of sausage and followed it with three fries. Then he leaned forward and said, "You may not know anything of the least importance, Miss Parsons, but often the smallest detail gives us a lead."

It had the desired effect. "Well, I did know her pretty well," Evelyn admitted, preening a little and smoothing her skirt.

"For starters, how did you two get acquainted?"

"We met at Markham, you know." She peered back and forth between them to be sure they both understood her. "Melanie was dating Quint, Quint Barringer. He's a senior this year at Markham."

"Is this Quint also called Addison?"

Evelyn looked surprised that he needed to ask. "Of course. I mean, his real name is Addison Alston Barringer the Fifth. They call him Quint because it's latin for 'fifth,' you know?" She was looking at Sheila, so Sheila nodded through a bite of corned beef, but all these linguistic crutches were beginning to get on her nerves. Couldn't the woman tell her story straight?

Apparently not, for she continued, "I mean, nobody except Dr. Dehaviland calls him Addison. And Mr. Capeletti, of course, when he's with the president, you know." She took a too-dainty bite of tuna salad and followed it with one small potato chip. The next five minutes elicited very little information: Melanie Forbes dated Quint, she often drove "the cutest little red car" down to pick him up, but Quint and Melanie had stopped dating before summer.

"Why did they break up?" Flannagan asked.

"I don't know." She stopped, plucked at her chains.

"Then why was Melanie still around Markham this fall?" Sheila wanted the conversation updated. After all, Melanie didn't get killed last spring.

"Well, she was friends with Brad. And she came by sometimes just to see me." Evelyn didn't try to conceal the pride in her voice. "We'd go up to the coffee room if I had time, for girl talk, you know." She gave a self-conscious little laugh.

"Did she and Quint ever run into one another on these visits?" Flannagan asked bluntly.

Evelyn paused to consider. "Not that I remember. The only guy I remember her being with specially was Brad. She told me once that she found Brad restful because he let her be herself. I think she felt a little strange around the institute because she wasn't...well, I mean, Melanie was kind of wild, you know? Not stuffy like the women Markham men usually marry—I guess that's because they're going to work in embassies, or something."

The former embassy wife took a bigger swallow of coffee than she'd intended. Flannagan thumped her with one ham hand and continued his questioning. "How often did she go out with D'Arcy last fall—just make a guess?"

Evelyn shrugged. "I don't really know. They came to the Christmas Community Dinner together, I remember. We chatted and made a date..." Her voice suddenly broke. "Oh, dear"—she gulped a little sob—"I can't get used to the idea that she's *dead*."

Flannagan nodded and Sheila reached out to touch her arm gently. Then they waited while she carved a pallid tomato wedge into bite-sized pieces. When Evelyn had barely recovered, he asked, "How did she seem at the Community Dinner?" Tears would never keep him from a goal, Sheila thought, then rebuked herself. The man had a job to do, after all.

"At the dinner?" Evelyn shrugged. "The same as usual. I mean, she laughed a lot, teased people she knew."

Brad D'Arcy's description of Melanie Forbes sprang into Sheila's mind. "Teased them how?"

"Oh, like she asked Dr. Williams if he was getting inspiration for his book—he's writing something on Latin American revolutions. And she told Yoshiko she looked like a plum blossom. She called one of the students Red Rover, and she offered to teach Mr. Rareby to cha-cha-cha. Oh, and she called Peter Lucas 'Schroeder,' like in the comics—you know? Because he played carols after dinner.''

"Did she offend anyone—make them angry?" Flannagan asked.

Evelyn hesitated. "Nooo, I don't think so. I mean, that's just how Melanie is—was. She had pet names for everyone. She always called me Evangeline." A slow flush rose in her scarred cheeks. "That's a girl in a poem or something." She tossed the fact off as if it didn't matter, but Sheila suspected she had looked it up and cherished the image of Longfellow's lovely heroine who had sacrificed her whole life for the one she loved. Sheila herself, more pragmatic, couldn't help remembering that Evangeline had died an ugly old maid. Melanie Forbes' humor had carried a sting in its tail.

She brought her thoughts back to the conversation.

"... she tease him too?" Flannagan was asking.

Again Evelyn shook her head. "I don't think they spoke all evening. He was at another table, you see."

"Did he have another date?"

"Quint?" She seemed surprised by the question. "No, he didn't date all fall that I knew. He was gone a lot, of course, helping with the Massachusetts senatorial race, and that took a lot of time. And he's been interviewing for two jobs out near Boston. His family is very prominent there. The Barringers came over before the American Revolution." Clearly Quint's prestige had been added to the other glories of Markham in some minds. Evelyn was still talking. "... and pots of money. So these two multinational corporations want him for their overseas offices, and he's trying to make up his mind. Or," she amended bleakly, realizing what a gap of time separated her from Markham, "he was. He may have decided by now."

"How long did you work at Markham?" Sheila asked on impulse.

Evelyn bit her lip. "Nine years. I went there when I left secretarial school, to work for Mr. Southard, you know. Then when Dr. Dehaviland's secretary left, he asked me to work for him. I was with him for six years." The bleakness in her voice had deepened to despair. Had she been in love with the man? Sheila wondered.

"A long time," she said gently.

Evelyn peered sadly over her glasses. "That's what made it so hard when . . ." Her voice broke. "He didn't even tell me good-bye."

Flannagan gave Sheila a warning look. "This is not what we are here to discuss," it seemed to say. She meekly subsided to nibble one last potato chip and a limp dill pickle while he got on with his case.

He spoke crisply, to stem Evelyn's tears. "How serious would you say Barringer and Melanie Forbes were last spring?"

Her eyes widened behind their thick lenses. "They were almost engaged. I mean, his parents came out to meet her, and he went home with her at Easter break. We all thought they would be engaged by the end of the year, or even married. But"—her thin shoulders rose under the silky blouse—"I guess it just didn't work out."

"And you got the impression that Barringer called it off?"

She nodded. "Maybe it had something to do with the way she lived, you know?"

"No, we don't know," said Sheila with a trace of acerbity.

Evelyn didn't pick it up. "Oh, she liked to party and drink, like I said. And Quint doesn't. He doesn't smoke, or drink much, or even swear."

Obviously a man of whom Eusebius Wentworth could be proud. Sheila caught Flannagan's eye and they both looked quickly away.

He switched the conversation. "Let's go back to the last time you saw Melanie. When was that again?"

The waitress came with dessert. Sheila eyed with distaste the soggy chocolate pie with spongy meringue set before her, but Flannagan attacked his apple pie à la mode with zest.

Evelyn stirred her ice cream with her spoon. "The Friday before Christmas. We had made plans, like I told you, at the Community Dinner, to meet for dinner and a movie. But then I...I..." She paused, then said defiantly, "I got fired." She sighed. "I won't go into all that, but it was horribly unfair. I was really upset. I called and said I wanted to come by her place to talk first."

Tears filled her eyes. "I didn't know it would be the last time I ever saw her." She sniffed, found a tissue and blew her nose hard. "I got to her place about, oh, maybe five-thirty. We had drinks, and I told her about what had happened, you know? While we were talking, the phone rang."

"Who was it?" Flannagan asked.

She took a small bite of ice cream and let it completely melt on her tongue. "Melanie didn't say."

"Did you overhear the conversation?"

She had her mouth full of ice cream again, and spoke through it. "No. She took it in the bedroom after she'd answered it."

Flannagan concealed his annoyance well, but Sheila saw a powerful muscle in his jaw begin to throb. "And then what?"

"Well, then she came out and said something had come up. That there was someone she had to see. She asked if we could postpone the movie to another night, you know? So of course I did. I mean, you know, when a guy calls, of course you go." She tossed it off like one with much experience, but Sheila doubted she'd ever gotten to live up to this dubious code. Flannagan, however, was interested in other things.

"How did you know it was a man who called?"

Evelyn looked at him as if his intelligence were suddenly in question. "Melanie wouldn't have broken our date for another *girl*," she protested. "I mean, she said this was somebody she had to see. Of course it was a man."

"But she didn't say who?"

Sheila was watching her closely, or she might have missed the flicker in the green eyes before they met Flannagan's. "No."

Flannagan halted his questions long enough to tackle another huge bite of pie, spoke thickly around it. "What did you do then?"

"I had another drink and lay on her bed watching her dress. Melanie had such marvelous clothes. I mean, really."

"What did she put on?"

In these matters dear to her heart, Evelyn didn't hesitate. "A navy wool skirt, a green sweater, and a scarf that tied the whole ensemble together. Oh, and navy boots." She sighed. "Melanie had a pair of boots to match anything."

Sheila raised her eyebrows at Flannagan, and he nodded. "Then you must have been one of the last people to see Melanie Forbes alive, Miss Parsons. You have just described what she was wearing when she died."

Evelyn dropped her fork with a clang, and her eyes grew very wide. "Oh, no!" she breathed for what seemed to Sheila like the hundredth time at least. To conceal her own irritation she reached for an extra paper napkin lying on the table and crumpled it. Underneath lay the little gold earrings.

Evelyn saw them, and grew very still. "Why did you bring those here?" she asked in a flat voice. "Why didn't you just leave them in her ears?"

Flannagan and Sheila both gaped. Sheila found her voice first. "These belonged to Melanie Forbes?" She needn't have asked. Evelyn's face had already told them.

Flannagan leaned across the table. "Was she wearing them that night you watched her dress?"

"Of course. She always wore them. They were her lucky harps." The earrings seemed to convince her it was really true. Tears coursed down her plain cheeks. "I'm sorry," she muttered, pulling off her glasses and swabbing at the tears first with her napkin and then with a wad of tissues Sheila found in her purse. At last, red-eyed and crumpled, she lifted her eyes to theirs, swamped in misery. But she did not speak.

"And you still say you do not know who called her?" Flannagan asked like a volley of shots. "It could have been the murderer, you know."

Evelyn pressed the last tissue against her lips tightly and regarded him nearsightedly. Slowly her eyes dropped to the table and lit, as if by accident, on her watch. She pushed back her chair hurriedly. "Oh my goodness! I didn't realize it was so late. I really must go. My boss will be furious." She struggled into her coat and rushed out.

"How not to answer a question," Sheila mused appreciatively.

Flannagan rubbed the side of his nose. "You noticed, huh?" She nodded. He leaned back in his chair and contemplated her with an expression she did not understand. Finally he shook his head. "I hate to admit it, but you were a help. Not," he added, raising one finger, "that that gives you license to butt in any further."

She pushed back her chair. "Believe me, Mr. Flannagan..."

He gave her his teddy-bear smile. "Call me Mike, won't you? After all, as Miss Mary said, I'm practically home folks."

She shook her head. "Not in my home. Not yet." But his grin was contagious, and he was definitely attractive. She smiled back. "But you and Aunt Mary have such a thing going, I assume we'll be seeing more of you."

He nodded. "I'll keep you informed, at least."

She stood. "Well, the lady was right, Mike. Lunch hour is definitely over. I'll have to hurry if I'm to be on time for the first lecture. Keep the earrings."

"I intended to." As she started to leave, he called her back. "Oh, Sheila? At the risk of sounding like a bad television show, at this point all roads lead to Markham. Whoever did this may not still be around, of course. But somebody who has killed once may not hesitate to kill again."

TEN

As SHE REMOVED her coat and boots in the unused lobby, Sheila found herself remembering Mike's words, but was annoyed at herself for feeling any apprehension. The lobby was empty, as usual. Except for staff depositing and fetching coats and the five Pres-Res students who got all their mail at the institute, no one visited the lobby regularly. Most students checked their boxes once or twice a week for an occasional letter or routine university notice.

She cast a nervous, exploratory look toward the staircase—then froze. Someone stood on the dimly lit landing, watching her.

"Hello, Sheila." It was Stan Frieze. He seemed to float up through the dimness toward her, wearing his weasel smile. In the poor light his pasty face was paler than ever.

"Stan, don't materialize out of nowhere." Relief made her voice shrill. "Give people warning that you are coming."

"Did I frighten you? Sorry." He sidled over to her, bent very close. She took a quick, instinctive step backward. "Who did you think I was?" he asked softly. "The murderer?"

When she didn't immediately reply, he continued in his soft insinuating voice. "Really, Sheila, do you think someone would do away with you here in the middle of the hall during school hours?" He laughed, scornful and superior. "People are getting rather silly over this, aren't they? After all, it happened so very long ago." He brushed past her and padded toward Wentworth.

In one sense he's right, Sheila admitted to herself as she slipped on her shoes and followed him down the hall. If we start suspecting everybody, we'll all be living on the fringes of hell.

Capeletti stopped her as she passed his door. "Sheila, Dr. Dehaviland has instructed me to give you a key to the building, in case you have to come in early or on Saturdays." Luckily he missed her expression as he went to his drawer, pulled out a single key, and thrust two forms before her. What, no fingerprints? She didn't ask.

The topic of murder, however, was submerged by the lecture—at least for the rest of the workday. The lecture was worse than Sheila had expected. Dr. Henderson scarcely seemed to wake up to deliver it, which he did in a dull, low monotone. When he finally finished and asked for questions, not a hand was raised.

Sheila left as Dr. Dehaviland approached to accompany the lecturer back to his office, and hurried there herself to make sure Bertha had stocked the bar and brought down coffee. She need not have worried. Bertha had even made a plateful of hors d'oeuvres.

She hovered by the door, anticipating another hour of boredom, but the president surprised her. After accompanying his guest to a comfortable seat by the fire, he motioned her to the door and said in a low voice, "Why don't you run upstairs and have coffee with the students, Sheila—get their initial impressions?" She ascended the stairs with a grateful sense of escape.

The coffee room, as usual, radiated warm lamplight, cheerful fire, soft leathers, and faded colors—but not peace. Not today. At the piano, Peter was engrossed in Debussy's *La cathédrale engloutie*, tolling somber buried bells across the room. Students sprawled across chairs and sofas, munching cookies and balancing mugs, but conversation stopped as she entered. Wary eyes followed her as she crossed to the samovar and drew a steaming cup of coffee. She felt like waving a white flag, saying, "Hey, guys, I was as bored as you were. Don't blame me."

Only Todd retained a semblance of humor. Standing, he struck a pose and declaimed, "Our little world goes on its curved and unswerving path..." He beckoned. "Come on over, Sheila. Join the party." She palmed a couple of cookies and climbed over several pairs of legs to a vacant seat.

"Conrad?" she asked Todd in passing.

He nodded appreciatively. "Remember the rest?"

Her memory supplied it: "...carrying a discontented and aspiring population." "Apt," she said briefly.

For a moment, nobody spoke. Yusuf finally dared. "Not, certainly, an impassioned delivery."

"To say the least," she agreed with a small smile.

Todd cast discretion aside. "One more lecture like that, and I will probably puke. All over the Wentworth Oriental."

"Oh, no," Brad admonished through his perpetual doze. "Not on the only one left."

She expected the conversation to turn, then, to murder. But the students were single-minded about their injustices.

"What's the point?" demanded an underclassman. "I could have read that lecture in an encyclopedia."

"He probably did," chimed in another. Several laughed.

"Lucre, man." Todd rubbed his fingertips with his thumbs. "Alums around the world have been conned into subscribing to this wonderful series for mucho moola."

The son of an African leader protested in his soft, musical English, "But if they want to teach European politics, why not let Mr. Southard do it? Why bring in men who know less? All this man seems to know is war, war, war.''

''You forget our conservative alumni,'' Todd replied. ''And Mr. Southard's recent sharp remarks concerning European foreign policy.''

Sheila wondered what exactly had been John Dehaviland's purpose in sending her into this hotbed. Did he merely want a report? If so, she could tell him the students seemed, to a man, to resent spending valuable study time on these lectures. But if he expected her to stem their fury, he'd chosen the wrong emissary. She heartily agreed with them. Her mind wandered, returned as a thin young man spread his arms and teetered in his chair. ''Balance, men, balance is the key to good diplomacy.'' Sheila wasn't certain whom he was quoting, but the others laughed.

''Me, I think it unfair to require attendance,'' Yusuf said. ''I need to work on my paper for Cal. Perhaps, Sheila, you could speak to him about that?''

She wasn't ready for that role, either. But she was saved by Stan Frieze, lounging behind Peter at the piano, where Jim shared the bench. ''The president considers it unfair to ask men of this caliber to address a mere handful of students.''

''Ve're adults,'' protested a young man with an accent as thick as Kissinger's. ''Required lectures are for college freshmen.''

Stan regarded him coolly. ''You all know that were the lectures not required, few of you would bother to attend, no matter how excellent they might be. Our attendance makes it worth the lecturers' while to come.''

A student in the corner spat out one short expletive, then added, ''Has-beens? They come for the glory and the honorarium.''

Jim earnestly disagreed. "But it would look terrible for them to come all this way to speak to just—"

He was cut short by Peter, who crashed down on a major chord and leapt to his feet. "What's your beef?" he demanded, eyes burning beneath his red hair. "Markham needs money, we need an education. Why knock lectures that provide both?"

"Attack Markham, attack me," Todd muttered to Sheila out of the corner of his mouth. "The Lucas family motto. A dynasty of tempers like cayenne pepper and absolute loyalty to this school. Blind loyalty," he amended. He twisted in his seat to address Peter. "*My* beef, Peter, is that today's lecture wasn't education. It was a rehash of the past. Markham's resting on its laurels. We need new blood, dynamic leadership."

"My own beef," said the African, obviously trying out the word, "Is that the topics are of little interest for my own studies, and I badly need a course that's only offered Thursday afternoon at university."

"Not to mention," Brad murmured, "that Dehaviland's Quadrangle Club bills alone could consume the entire profits of the series." Sheila eyed him suspiciously. She could have sworn he was asleep.

Again Peter came down on the keyboard with a crash. "If you feel that way about Markham, why stay?" he blazed. "Nobody is keeping you. Go!" He swept one arm toward the door. "Go, all of you!" He slumped to the bench and began a furious rendition of Chopin's "Minute Waltz." It sounded more like a minute scourge.

When he was done, Todd spoke gently. "Yes, they are keeping us here, Peter. I may loathe these lectures, but I appreciate the education. And I have invested years in Markham—pledged my whole future on what I can learn here. I think somebody needs to talk to the president."

"Wait for Quint," Brad advised in a grunt.

"Oh, yes," Yusuf agreed. "He carries a lot of—how do you say?—cloud."

Todd pulled himself to his feet. "Okay. We'll give this second guy a chance. If he's awful, we'll take Quint and go to Dehaviland. Agreed?"

There was a general nod. Todd climbed over feet and left the room. With that herd instinct that announces when the party is over, everyone else left too—except Brad, dozing, and Peter, who had abruptly begun to hit the same note over and over again. It was, Sheila realized as he continued to play, the opening chime from Saint-Saëns' "Danse Macabre."

As she rose to go, Brad spoke softly. "Learn anything of interest?" His eyes were only half open, but they mocked her.

Outside the door she paused, and shivered. Guilt, she admitted. *I feel like a spy among these guys.*

SHE WAS clearing her desk for the day when Jim Lucas stopped at her door dangling a set of keys. He thumped a large envelope on the top of her door. "I've got to deliver this for Dr. Dehaviland. If you don't have your car, do you want me to run you home?"

She gave the near-zero temperature a quick thought and gladly accepted.

As they stepped from the building, the cold met them like a wall. Sheila clutched her coat as the wind gnawed her with persistent ferocity. "Brrr. I really appreciate this, Jim. I didn't know you had a car."

"...Stan's" was all she heard of his reply. Strong gusts snatched the rest away.

Jim must have been feeling the cold through his slacks and overcoat, for Sheila was having a hard time keeping up with him despite her long-legged stride. At a fast lope she followed him across the street and into an alley behind Pres-Res, where a solitary Volvo sat under a street lamp. How like Stan, she thought, to choose such a colorless beige.

The wind was less strong here, and conversation possible. As Jim unlocked her door she asked, "Is this car as new as it looks?"

"Sure is." Jim held her door with unexpected gallantry. "An uncle sent money for Christmas and Stan decided to get one while he could. He'll need it when he graduates. For now he just uses it for school errands that pay mileage."

"And to lend to friends?" She lowered herself into the bucket seat and dropped her purse on the floor.

He shook his head. "Stan's not much on lending. I'm helping him out just now." He shut her door and went around the car.

Sheila took an appreciative sniff. The car still smelled new. Consistent with Stan, it was also the most impersonal car she had ever seen. Not one sticker, not one scrap of paper, not even a map indicated who owned it.

Ahead of her, the bleak back of Pres-Res loomed gray and formal in the gloomy twilight. The only spot of color in her whole range of vision was a bright-blue dumpster stenciled ACE #63. As Jim got into the car she looked up at the windows of Pres-Res and asked, "Where were you the Friday night they think Melanie Forbes was killed?"

Jim started the car before he replied. "Peter was playing in a club, and I went along to listen. Why?"

She gave a small shrug. "Oh, I thought maybe somebody who lived here might have seen something. Lights, for instance."

He looked at her with obvious admiration. "You know, I thought of the very same thing. I even asked around. But it was a dead end. Nobody was here that night. Even Mr. Southard had gone to his sister's for dinner."

"Too bad. Supersleuths strike out." She smiled at him, and his bony face lit with a grin. "What do you mean, Peter was playing at a club?" she asked. "Does he play professionally?"

He answered absently, concentrating more on backing and turning in the small alley than on the conversation. "Not anymore, he doesn't. Until Christmas he played Friday and Saturday nights at a club up near the Loop."

"That seems an unlikely way to prepare oneself for a life of diplomacy," she mused. She pulled her collar closer and huddled into her seat. Would that heater never get warm?

Jim was absorbed in watching the steady stream of traffic for an opening, so he only threw her a quick nod. "That's what the folks back home said over Christmas holidays—our family, and the senator. They're pretty conservative where we come from, and wouldn't tolerate him playing in what one aunt called 'a sleazy joint.' It wasn't fair!" His face flushed at the injustice. "They'd never seen the place, and Pete was changing it. They only wanted jazz when he first went there, but he persuaded the management to let him do some classical stuff, and he was bringing in really high-class customers. That's why he plays so much at Markham these days," he concluded, finally maneuvering them into the crawling procession. "He doesn't have any other piano to play. Peter without a piano is like the rest of us without hands."

They drove the next block without speaking, each occupied in private thoughts. Sheila, sneaking a look at his clear pale profile, wondered how long Jim could continue as buffer between Peter and the world.

"Jim, this may sound like prying, but is it possible that Peter is, well, heading for a nervous breakdown? He seems strung pretty taut."

Jim chewed his lower lip. "Pete's okay," he finally said. "He's just under a lot of pressure just now. His last term, you know, and all that, that . . ." He clenched his fist and hit the steering wheel once, hard. "Why don't they just go to the lectures and learn what they can?"

"You think Peter's worried about the other students?" she asked, feeling like a Rogerian therapist.

He nodded shortly. "Among other things."

"The murder?" she hazarded. "It's certainly not doing Markham any good. Dehaviland's muzzled the press this far, but the reporters I talked to this morning were growling for a story."

"Damn it all to hell!" Sheila turned, surprised less by his language than by the fierceness of his tone. His jaw was clenched and his hands gripped the wheel so tightly that his knuckles stood out white. She waited for him to go on, but he took so long to speak again that she thought he might not. Finally he said with a ragged sigh, "Melanie wasn't *always* unkind."

Sheila was all at sea. Was Jim upset because of the effects of the murder on Markham, or genuinely mourning the dead girl? "Did you know her well?" she asked in a puzzled voice.

"Not very well." His voice was taut, and tears were gathering in his eyes. He blinked hard to control them, but his voice was unsteady when he spoke again. "I used to talk to her some last year, when Quint had to get dressed to go out. Then, when they stopped going out, she used to call me sometimes, just to talk." He sounded forlorn, like a little boy.

Sheila spoke on impulse. "You liked her, didn't you?"

Her guess was on target. Even in the limited light she could see a flush stain his cheeks as he looked at her, then quickly away. "Yeah," he muttered, "but she never knew it." He shook his head. "She wouldn't have cared."

Sheila remembered Brad's unkind remark in the coffee room and agreed. There was little in the pallid too-young man beside her to attract a woman like Melanie Forbes.

She couldn't think of anything to help him in his misery, so decided to leave him alone with it. He swung the car in against the curb and shot her a look of shy pride. "This supersleuth did one right thing. I was doing some work for Nick one day and I looked up your address."

"With these talents, I'm certain you'll solve Markham's murder in no time," she assured him lightly, reaching for her purse. It had caught on something under the seat, and when she tugged at it, it flew open—distributing its contents. "Oh, no!" She scooped up keys, a Visa receipt, a blue scrap of paper, cosmetics, wallet, tissues, and a comb, then fumbled under the seat to be sure she wasn't leaving anything behind.

Jim gave her a wry smile. "It's not your fault. Volvos eat purses."

She found one last stray pen, stuffed everything into the purse in a jumble, and slid out of her seat. "Well, I hope I've got everything. Thanks for the ride, Jim."

"Glad to do it." He shifted into gear. As she closed the door she heard his predictable farewell, "Be seeing you."

But Sheila went to her door with a troubled frown. It looked as if Mike might be right. Who but a Markham man would know that Pres-Res would be empty of witnesses on that fatal night?

ELEVEN

WHILE THEY RELAXED with after-dinner coffee, Sheila told Aunt Mary about the day's events. The little woman settled herself more comfortably against the sofa cushions with a contented sigh. "Thank you, Sheila. You bring a little excitement into my life."

"That's not much of a compliment. I've known you to get equally excited about surviving a hurricane and finding your favorite brand of pancake syrup in a new grocer's stock."

Aunt Mary raised her brows in what the family called her grand-duchess manner. "Each part of life provides its own kind of stimulation, dear."

The doorbell rang.

Sheila unfolded herself from the other end of the sofa to buzz the caller up, and was surprised to see Mike Flannagan appear in the peephole of her door. "I wouldn't have barged in without calling, but I was in the neighborhood and thought I would drop off some pralines for Miss Mary." He proffered a yellow paper bag.

Aunt Mary had already set out a third cup. "Mike, how lovely to see you again." Her husky voice was warm with delight. She indicated a chair with a small hand sparkling with topazes to match her brown-and-gray tweed skirt. "Sit down and remind me again how you like your coffee."

"Black and sweet." He lowered himself to fill the armchair.

"Mike brought you some pralines, Aunt Mary." Sheila handed her the bag.

The older woman's face wrinkled into a childlike smile. "Oh, Mike, aren't you sweet to think of me." She passed them around and nibbled one herself. "Are you getting along with your mystery?"

He bit off a hunk of praline and shook his head. "Oh, I don't think there's going to be much mystery about this case, Miss Mary."

Her brown eyes grew very wide. "You have a suspect?"

He gave her a golden teddy-bear smile. "Let's just say we have suspicions." He took an appreciative gulp of coffee.

"Quint Barringer?" Sheila wasn't really guessing—who else was there?

He shot her a look of reproach. "I'll be telling you as soon as we have enough evidence for an arrest, Sheila."

"You poor man, I hope you get it." Aunt Mary leaned forward to pass him the pralines again. "Are you having to work awfully hard?"

He took two and spoke around a mouthful of nuts and brown sugar. "Pretty hard," he admitted. "We went through the victim's apartment this afternoon."

Aunt Mary's eyes shone with admiration. "Did you find any clues?"

He shook his head. "Just the usual female folderol— bathroom full of cosmetics, several pieces of gold jewelry, fancy French perfume I couldn't pronounce, much less afford. She liked to stock up—had several pairs of unopened stockings, three unopened boxes of bath powder, even a lacy nightie with its tags on. Pretty fancy for someone living alone. But no clues."

"Poor Mike." Sheila was just repeating what Aunt Mary had said, but it came out different. Aunt Mary threw her a look of reproof before explaining, "We ladies don't like to run out. Some French brands of bath powder are hard to get when you need them."

Mike shook his head. "The powder was just Avon, ma'am."

Aunt Mary nodded sagely. "Probably got it on sale. What about a diary, Mike? Wouldn't that be of use?"

He smiled indulgently. "I wish it were that easy, Miss Mary. But real life isn't much like detective stories. We don't mess much with diaries. She did have," he said to Sheila, who would appreciate it, "three phones in a three-room apartment. Didn't want to overexert herself."

"How about an address book?" Sheila wondered.

He shook his head warningly. "I told you, Sheila, if we get the evidence, I'll let you know." He leaned forward and prepared to lecture. "In America these days we need hard evidence to take to court—hairs, fingerprints, witnesses." He reached into his breast pocket and pulled out a written report. "Normally I wouldn't show this, but there's not much in it. It will give you an idea of what we look for."

Aunt Mary donned the tortoiseshell half-glasses she wore for reading. "Hair from pillowcase," she read aloud. "Hair from foyer carpet. Thumbprint from kitchen cabinet." She raised her head and looked at him curiously over her glasses. "But won't these all turn out to be Melanie's own?"

He shrugged. "Probably. I told you there wasn't anything there. I don't think anyone had been in that place since she died. The glasses from her drinks with the Parsons woman were still on the coffee table with a film in the bottom."

"We are looking for a murderer, not a maid," Sheila pointed out. "If someone had gone into the apartment, he wouldn't have necessarily washed glasses."

Mike took another bite of praline. "*We* aren't looking for anything," he said with emphasis, "but *I* had the Parsons woman up there after work, and in between mild hysterics she confirmed that the place was the same as when she was last there."

"So you are pretty sure she died that Friday night?"

He nodded. "We don't have to prove time of death, but I think so, yes. Our biggest problem is that our suspect has an alibi for the whole weekend. We are concentrating just now on breaking it."

Aunt Mary fluttered her lashes at him over the rim of her cup. How on earth did she get away with it? "Could there be other suspects, Mike? Someone you haven't thought of yet?"

"Mr. X?" He grinned, then shook his tight gold curls. "I think I'll stick with this suspect, Miss Mary. There's too much to connect him with the deceased. One hair, a disproven alibi, and his relationship with the girl will give me as good a case as many I've taken to court and won."

"But what if it's the wrong man?" Sheila asked, appalled. "He could have left a hair there months ago."

He shook his head indulgently. "There's not so much mystery in most cases as novels would have you ladies think. Usually the most likely suspect is also the killer. For us, the biggest mystery is how to get the evidence we need."

It was clearly a bid for sympathy, but Sheila wanted to shake him. Aunt Mary intervened. "Did Melanie decorate with plants, Mike? Keep scrapbooks or souvenirs?" As if reading his mind, she added, "Just to help me know what the young woman was like."

Flannagan reached for the next-to-last praline. "Her plants were dead, of course. She had an album of snapshots from childhood—nothing more recent. And I don't recall any souvenirs except a brandy snifter full of match-books on her coffee table.''

"Matchbooks!'' Aunt Mary positively crowed. "Any from interesting places?'' Sheila shot her a suspicious look. "Don't look at me like that, dear,'' Aunt Mary told her. "I have a matchbook collection myself. They are such a marvelous record of places you have been, don't you think? And so inexpensive, too.''

She beamed at Mike over her cup. He was looking thoughtful, then his face broke into a wide grin. Aunt Mary fluttered her lashes at him and refilled his cup.

Sheila dragged them ruthlessly from their flirtation. "What else did you find, Mike? Any sign of drugs?''

"Not yet. But we sent some stuff to the lab for a check. I think D'Arcy is right about that angle. This case has all the hallmarks of a lover's quarrel.''

"Lovers quarrel all the time without committing mur-der,'' Sheila said dryly.

"Yeah,'' he grunted, and a bass chuckle rumbled through the apartment. "Thank the good Lord for that.''

Aunt Mary leaned back and asked, "What about her checkbook, Mike? Any suspicious entries there?''

He shook his head. He was getting the look, Sheila thought, of a man weary of discussing on an elementary level what he had to deal with on a much higher plane. He was still polite, but he was sitting low in his chair and she caught him sneaking a glance at his watch. "Her check-book was probably in her purse, Miss Mary. It's long gone by now.''

Aunt Mary cocked her head to one side and fluttered like a little bird. "Oh, do you think so, Mike? A checkbook is so hard to throw away, don't you think?''

He shook his massive head. "Not at all. The city is full of dumpsters.''

Aunt Mary pursed her lips thoughtfully. "Poor little girl, I hope she wasn't killed for her money."

Mike yielded to an impulse to shock them. "She could have been. She had two thousand dollars in her checking account on her last statement.

"Surely not!" Aunt Mary was scandalized.

"Yes, indeedy, ma'am. That little girl had money. She had it in one of those savings accounts you can write checks on."

Aunt Mary sighed faintly. "I see."

Listening to them, Sheila hid a smile behind her cup. Mike was obviously amazed that Melanie Forbes possessed two thousand dollars extra. Aunt Mary—to whom two thousand dollars was a trifle—was horrified to think for even a moment that any money wasn't invested and thus making more. Should she point out the comedy? No, she was sure no one else would find it funny.

"Did she bank at home, or in Chicago?" Aunt Mary asked.

Sheila swiveled to stare at her in astonishment. In Aunt Mary's code, it was the height of rudeness—right up there with staring, or scratching in public—to ask such a personal financial question, even about the dead.

Mike, however, didn't seem to know that and named a bank in downtown Chicago. "But she hasn't been banking anywhere lately," he pointed out. With that, he rose. "I hate to run, ladies, but I really must go."

Aunt Mary smiled roguishly. "Your wife will want you home sometime tonight, won't she?"

He grinned down at her. "I married young, Miss Mary, and it didn't last. Since then I've never found the right woman."

She dimpled. "If I were a few years younger..."

"Only a *very* few, ma'am." Her deep chuckle and his bass rumble met across the coffee table.

She offered her hand. "Mike, you do me a world of good."

Sheila went to see him out. In the hall he stood awkwardly, as if he still had something to say. Finally he bent his head so close to hers that his after-shave started unwelcome prickles up her spine. She moved away, but he followed and spoke in a voice too low to be heard in the next room. "I wondered . . . well, I know you are still missing Tyler, Sheila, but I'm off tomorrow night, and I really came by to see if you'd like to take in a movie. What do you say?"

She was so astonished that it took her a minute to realize she was standing there shaking her head. "I'm sorry, Mike, but I've promised to attend the Markham Community Dinner tomorrow night."

He put one big hand out and gave her shoulder a squeeze that nearly crippled her. "Well, you can't fault a fellow for trying. I'll call you when I get another day off." He was already in the hall when he turned. "Oh, and Sheila? For now, you forget this case. It's my job, and I'm going to solve it, one way or another."

He clumped down the stairs without waiting for a reply. But Sheila whispered one anyway. "That's what I'm afraid of, Mike."

TWELVE

BACK IN THE living room, her eyes met Aunt Mary's placid, almost complacent gaze. "Well, dear?"

"Well what?"

"Are you going out with Mr. Flannagan?"

Sheila shook her head in reluctant admiration. "You really do see it all, don't you? I thought Mike came only to visit you."

Aunt Mary laughed. "These old charms can't bring a man like Mike Flannagan around more than once or twice. But you haven't answered my question. Are you going out with him?"

"No."

The laughter died in the brown eyes. Sheila left her in suspense a moment longer before explaining. "He asked me for tomorrow night, and I'm already committed to Markham's Community Dinner." She began to gather cups. "Besides, Aunt Mary, I told you I am not interested in men just now."

"But you do like Mike?"

"Sometimes. But he exasperates me almost to tears with his determination to focus on only one suspect. And there are times when he's terribly Knight of the Forest in his treatment of women."

"A knight is handy to have around if you need rescuing, dear."

"And a bore when you don't. So don't start any matchmaking, Aunt Mary, or it's back to Alabama and the garden for you!"

Aunt Mary's eyes widened. "Are you becoming a feminist, dear? It suits you. When you first got out of college you were such a clinging vine I could have shaken you, except you can't shake vines—they wither and die. And as for saying anything about your getting interested in Mr. Flannagan, *I* certainly did not. If you got attached to him just now, it could be a real problem for us."

At first Sheila wondered if Aunt Mary was referring to their current living arrangement. Was she contemplating making it permanent? But the older woman continued, "It would make our job much more complicated."

Sheila, in the process of picking up Mike's cup from beside his chair, halted halfway up so that her eyes were level with Aunt Mary's. "What job?"

Aunt Mary answered with the tiny shrug of one who explains the obvious. "Solving this murder. You do see, don't you, dear, that it's up to us?"

"No!"

Sheila plunked the cup and saucer onto the coffee table and perched on the edge of the chair Mike had vacated so recently it was still warm. She leaned forward and gave her aunt a stern stare. "We are *not* going to solve this murder, as you so casually put it. We are not even going to try."

"But, dear..."

"No. Mike just explicitly warned me off any amateur sleuthing and reminded me it's his turf. If you think I want to make that gorilla mad, you can think again. Besides..."

Aunt Mary waited what she considered a decent length of time, then inquired in a voice that conveyed only a proper amount of curiosity, "Besides what, dear?"

Sheila sighed and slumped back in the chair. "Besides, I don't like it. Digging into people's sordid pasts and suspecting everyone. Turning lives inside out for motives."

Aunt Mary cocked her head to one side and regarded her with a puzzled frown. "But we've done it before, Sheila. In Japan..."

Sheila grinned. "Every time you came to visit, in fact. But," she sobered, "those times were different. In those cases we knew something the police didn't. And even then we got involved against my will. Frankly, Aunt Mary, I find your taste for solving mysteries hard to justify."

She let her eyes rove to the mystery novel on the table beside Aunt Mary's Bible. But Aunt Mary merely gave her niece a shrewd glance. "Fighting evil is always justified, dear."

Sheila shook her head fondly. "You always have the right answer, don't you? And deep inside me I must know that, or I wouldn't have worked on the other cases. I guess my real reluctance this time is that I've been at Markham such a short time—what do we have that Mike doesn't?"

Aunt Mary held up pearl-tipped fingers to enumerate. "We've got your mule-headed insistence on truth, for one. We've got both our knacks for seeing straight, as your daddy so inelegantly puts it. And we've got a lump of a policeman, Lord love him, who's wearing blinders so he can only see in one direction. Look at all he missed just in that apartment."

"The matchbooks?"

"Of course, dear. You pick up one here and one there, until you do it so automatically that even the people you're with don't notice. If there *is* a Mr. X in Melanie's life, Mike could find a trail to him in that brandy snifter."

Sheila nodded. "I thought you might be working along those lines. Why didn't you just tell him?"

Aunt Mary sighed. "Sheila, this kind of man you can't go at like a roasted oyster, with heavy gloves and a knife."

"Someday I might like to try. Meanwhile, I hope he got the hint. What about the checkbook?"

Aunt Mary shook her head with a laugh of despair. "Would you have believed he'd be so dense? He must have thought me a country bumpkin—if not an old fool—for not knowing how easily anything can disappear in a dumpster. What *I* meant was..."

"...a checkbook is so hard to let go of," Sheila finished.

"Exactly. Especially the checkbook of a wealthy woman whose body is not going to be found for a while, and whose date of death may be uncertain. How tempting to write yourself a check or two before you toss it into one of Mike's convenient dumpsters."

"Of course, if Quint actually turns out to have done it, he's not likely to have written checks. He's wealthy himself."

"But since Mike's concentrating on Quint, don't you think we ought to look for other suspects, dear? Her bank statements might prove extremely interesting."

Sheila shook her head. "I'm not sure I'm on this case, after those lies you told about your matchbook collection. Really, Aunt Mary, if we work together, I must have truth from you, too!"

Aunt Mary patted her curls. "But I *do* have a matchbook collection, dear. My apartment in St. Petersburg has an ancient gas stove and the pilots are constantly blowing out. You don't expect me to *buy* matches, do you?"

"Not you," Sheila agreed. "I can't think of any way to get her bank statements, though, without Mike. Will you just march into the bank president's office and charm him into revealing all?"

Aunt Mary looked pained at the thought. "Goodness, dear, how exhausting that sounds! At my age one has to conserve one's strength. I thought I'd just call Charlie."

Aunt Mary's broker in Atlanta was such a formal man that even his wife called him "Charles." But not Aunt Mary. "I can't call someone Charles," she said within the family, "whom I knew before he was in pants." Sheila always assumed she referred to the Edwardian custom of dresses for infant boys, but with Aunt Mary one never knew—and it was usually safer not to ask.

Still, she felt sympathy for Charles Davidson. He put up with a lot from this old friend and wealthy client. "Poor Charlie, what makes you think he can get bank records for you?"

"Oh, just an idea I have. He's on a lot of boards and things." She waved her hands vaguely, and her topazes flashed.

"So you are going to check on the bank statements, and I"—Sheila pulled her long body to its feet—"am going to wash the dishes. I don't think there's anything I can do about the case tonight. And tomorrow—well, I'm still not sure Mike can't handle it alone. He seems perfectly capable..."

"...of missing the obvious," Aunt Mary finished tartly.

Sheila turned at the kitchen door. "Something else?"

Aunt Mary nodded. "The bath powder, dear. Don't you think it strange that a young woman who wore French perfume and all those lovely nighties should have three boxes of common bath powder in her bureau drawer?"

Sheila regarded her blankly. "Maybe she just hadn't needed them yet—bought them at a sale, or got them as presents. I've got a box around here somewhere that I got for Christmas."

Aunt Mary shook her head with a sigh of sheer pity. "But you don't understand men, dear. Melanie Forbes did."

Sheila put one hand on her hip. "And what does that mean?"

"French perfume and lacy nighties belong to a woman who dresses for men. A woman who wears a special scent is not going to muddy it with different brands of bath powder. She wants the scent to always remind men of her, whoever is wearing it."

"Like honeysuckle makes us all think of you," Sheila said, not very kindly. That remark about not understanding men still stung.

Aunt Mary was unruffled. "Exactly. Except when I first started using it, only the French could produce it. Now a stronger version is available in a much cheaper brand. So unfair, I always thought." She paused for personal reflection. Sheila drew her firmly back to the topic at hand.

"So what's your theory about the powder?"

"Well, dear, if you wanted to give friends something they shouldn't have, don't you think it would be wise to conceal it in something they *should* have?"

Sheila's eyes narrowed. "Drugs? You may be right. But honestly, Aunt Mary, some of the things you know about are—well—almost indecent for one of your upbringing."

"I know, dear." Aunt Mary smoothed her skirt. "But about this bath powder..."

"We can't just ask Mike for it," Sheila pointed out. "He'll think we're a couple of freeloaders."

"No, it needs to be analyzed, and he'll have the lab to do it. If Mike didn't think of it himself, we'll just suggest it to him gently."

Sheila crossed the room and stood by the window, peering down at the grimy street below. "I still don't like it, Aunt Mary. I feel like a spy and a counterspy. In the past I've worked with the police, not around them. Don't you think we can just trust Mike with this case?"

"With blinders on?"

Sheila leaned her cheek against the icy pane. Aunt Mary came to stand beside her, her silver head barely reaching Sheila's shoulder.

On the sidewalk three young women, probably students, hurried down the street together, hugging their coats against the cold. Under a street lamp they paused, and one threw back her head to laugh.

"Melanie Forbes should be alive tonight to laugh with her friends," Aunt Mary said softly. Sheila followed the girls down the block with her gaze before she replied.

"Okay, Aunt Mary, you've convinced me. We'll give it a try. But we're going to have to be awfully careful about Mike. We don't want him thinking we're stepping on those big toes of his."

Aunt Marry nodded in emphatic agreement. "Of course not!"

"And I confess I don't know where we go from here."

The doorbell rang.

Aunt Mary brightened. "Why don't we go to the door?"

SHEILA HAD A sense of déjà vu, except this time the man at the doorway proffering a bag was David MacLean. "Dessert, if you've not had it."

She peered into the bag. "Shortbread? David, how marvelous. Come in and meet my aunt. Coffee? Or tea?"

"Coffee would be fine."

"I just put some on, dear." Aunt Mary tripped across the room and offered David her hand. "You must be David MacLean. Welcome. I'm Sheila's aunt, Mary Beaufort." She led him to the chair Mike had filled earlier.

David was so slender he seemed almost frail in comparison with the chair's previous occupant. He settled back, crossed one calf over the other knee, and immediately seemed perfectly at home. Fumbling in the pocket of his tweed coat he directed a look at Aunt Mary. "May I smoke a pipe?"

"Of course. Sheila, get the man an ashtray."

Sheila brought a saucer—the best she could do—and curled up on the other end of the couch from Aunt Mary. David lit his pipe.

"Sheila and I were just discussing the death of that dear girl at Markham," Aunt Mary told him.

Sheila shook her head in protest. "I don't think Melanie Forbes was ever a dear girl, Aunt Mary. Not even Evelyn Parsons made her sound very likable. And Jim Lucas said Melanie wasn't *always* unkind—which I took to mean that she usually was."

David blew a cloud of pungent smoke. "I'll admit I formed the same impression myself."

Two pairs of eyes swiveled to stare in astonishment. "You *knew* her?" Sheila asked.

He shook his head. "Not to say 'knew.' I saw her once, at Markham's Christmas Dinner. She had come with Brad, I think, but she spent most of her time talking and laughing with Evelyn or trying to attract Cal Williams across the room."

"Cal?" Sheila asked, puzzled. "Not Quint Barringer?"

David considered. "Aye, it could have been Quint, right enough. He was at the same table. But she did call out something to Cal at one point. Something about a book, I think it was."

"But why was Melanie interested in Cal's book? She doesn't sound the type to care about Latin American politics."

Aunt Mary lightly buffed her nails against her skirt and held them up to examine the polish for chips. "Who is Cal, dear?"

"Calvin Williams, the presidential adviser on Latin America."

"Oh, of course," Aunt Mary murmured. "I was at school with his mother. Is he married, dear?"

Sheila shrugged, but David nodded. "She is an archaeologist, currently digging in Montana, I believe. She's here in Hyde Park with him for the winter."

"Ummm." Aunt Mary could almost have been humming. Sheila waited, and the older woman raised her eyes. "Oh, I was just thinking how things that seem simple at the beginning have a way of getting complicated." Without further explanation she cocked her head. "Wasn't that the coffee bell?"

Sheila rose and padded to the kitchen in stocking feet. But when she returned a few minutes later, Aunt Mary waved her back. "Not yet, dear. Plans have changed."

"Plans?" Sheila looked from one to the other, bewildered.

David hoisted his thin body from the chair. "Your aunt thinks you and I should call on Evelyn Parsons this evening. I know her fairly well, you see. Her mother is a Scot, and an invalid. I visit them occasionally." He took her elbow to steer her toward the foyer. "Miss Beaufort thinks Evelyn may share what she knows or suspects more readily with us than with the police." As he put on his coat he added in a low voice, "We needn't stay long."

"But it's late—past eight-thirty."

"Och, no bother. No Scot would go to bed without a bite at nine. And it's not far. We'll be back for our own coffee not long after that."

EVELYN HERSELF answered their ring. When she saw David, her sallow cheeks flushed under their bright spots of rouge. "Come in," she gushed, smoothing the long velour robe she wore. "It's David MacLean," she called over her shoulder as she stepped back to let them enter. Again Sheila was impressed by Evelyn's clothes sense. The dark gold showed to advantage her tall spare frame.

A stately woman with iron-gray hair wheeled herself in from a back room and greeted David with restrained but obvious pleasure. "And how've ye been keeping yoursel'?"

He bent to squeeze her shoulder gently. "Och, nae bad." He spoke far more broadly than Sheila had heard him do before.

As the three of them exchanged greetings, she glanced around the small living room. Its large worn furniture was spaced so that a wheel chair could maneuver comfortably about it. A yellow-and-orange afghan over the back of the couch and a vase of orange silk flowers on the television showed brave attempts to brighten what must be essentially dull lives. David was obviously another bright spot for the two women. Evelyn's plain face was pink, and her mother's eyes glowed.

David reached back to draw her into their circle. "This is Sheila Travis, who's taking Eleanor Quincy's place at Markham. Evelyn, she's told me you might know something about the murder. If so, I don't want you keeping it to yourself—that's dangerous."

Evelyn's eyes were wary as she considered Sheila. "I thought you were a friend of Mr. Flannagan—you know, the detective."

"Mr. Flannagan and my husband were boys together. I ran into him at the deli just before you arrived."

Evelyn relaxed, but Sheila suspected it was not really her explanation that had done it. The first change in Evelyn's expression had come when Sheila said the word "husband."

After initial chitchat David again steered the conversation around to Melanie Forbes' murder. "I don't want to sound like a third-rate telly film," he told Evelyn, "but if you know or even just suspect something—anything at all—it is important not to keep it to yourself."

"Do you, Evie?" her mother asked.

Evelyn didn't reply immediately, and when she did, her voice was sullen. "I've told Mr. Flannagan everything I can think of."

There was a long silence.

David turned to Sheila. "Mrs. Parsons has some pictures in the next room I want to see. We'll be right back." He rose and followed the older woman as she wheeled herself from the room. Sheila noted with approval that he made no attempt to offer unwanted assistance.

When they were alone, Sheila spoke urgently. "Evelyn, this is very important. Did you think it was Quint who called Melanie?"

Evelyn's face assumed what Sheila's mother would have called a balky look. "It couldn't have been. I mean, Quint was out of town, you know? He left Friday morning." With one large hand she smoothed and roughed the nap of her robe. "But then that call came, and . . ." She paused, then wailed, "Oh, why can't everybody leave me alone?"

Sheila resisted an urge to shake her by shoving her fingers through her own thick hair instead. "Is there anyone else it could have been?" she prodded. Evelyn didn't reply. "Evelyn, the police need all the help they can get!"

Evelyn was unimpressed. "I don't owe the police anything. Or Markham. Not after..." She paused, spoke defiantly. "I guess you haven't heard about me. They think I'm a thief."

"No, they don't," Sheila assured her. "The only person who has even mentioned the clock incident was Yusuf, and he thinks you were framed—or, as he puts it, bordered."

Evelyn permitted herself a flicker of a smile. "Well, it's true. I never touched that clock. I noticed it was gone in the morning when I took in the mail. I mean, the president had left a cup on the mantelpiece, and when I went to get it I saw the clock was missing. But I didn't tell anybody, you know? I mean, I thought maybe he'd sent it to be fixed or something." Sheila nodded, but inwardly fumed. Evelyn's string of extra phrases was getting harder to endure. But Evelyn hadn't even waited for her nod. Her colorless voice droned on.

"Then that afternoon, when Bertha went in to dust, she ran out calling for Mr. Capeletti. The police came and everything, but then the next day, when the president was back, Mr. Capeletti called me in and asked why I hadn't, you know, reported it missing. Then... then he said Dr. Dehaviland said I had to go." Her thin voice broke. "Six years I worked for that man," she cried, "and he couldn't even tell me himself!" She yanked off her glasses, covered her face, and wept.

When she had wiped away her tears, she sat in damp silence. Sheila waited.

Finally Evelyn spoke again, in a voice so low Sheila had to strain to hear her. "I've been thinking about her all afternoon. Melanie, I mean. I began to remember things—how she really was, you know? She could be really cruel to people she didn't like. Stan—she always said he gave her the willies, you know? So she called him Willy. And Peter—you know Peter Lucas?"

Sheila was so accustomed to "you know" as a filler that she failed to nod at once. Evelyn jogged her memory. "He plays the piano."

It was rather like saying Phil Niekro played baseball. "Of course," she said quickly. "What about him?"

"Well, Melanie was always after him to play rock music. If she went into the coffee room and he was playing something classical, she'd say, 'Bor-r-ring' in this really disgusted way, you know? He got so mad at her one day I really thought he was going to..." She stopped, pressed her hands against her sallow cheeks with a stricken look. "Oh, I didn't mean... It wasn't only Peter, it was everybody. Even people she liked. She used us. Me, Brad, poor Jim. When Quint broke up with her last year she'd called Jim, hoping Quint would answer." Evelyn sniffed, fumbled for another tissue and blew her nose. "Sometimes...sometimes she could be *so cruel*." Her weak eyes met Sheila's. "I told you at lunch that when she made jokes at the Christmas Dinner, nobody minded, you know?" Sheila nodded. "That wasn't true. When she told Mr. Rareby she'd teach him to cha-cha-cha, Cal got really mad. I know, because she told me later he took her into a corner and let her have it. I mean, Mr. Rareby was shot in the leg, and it hurts him almost all the time. She shouldn't have been so...so callous about it."

"How did Melanie take Cal's criticism?"

Evelyn shrugged. "Oh, she sort of laughed and said she'd have to mend her ways. But she didn't sound like she really cared."

"Could anything she said that night have made somebody mad enough to kill her?"

Evelyn thought it over, then shook her head. "I don't think so. Not that night. But do you know what I do think?" She paused, then spoke in a rush. "I think whoever killed her . . . I mean, I think she deserved it!"

Sheila would probably sound like a prig, but she had to say it. "Nobody deserves it, Evelyn—or maybe we all deserve it sometimes, but nobody has the right to eliminate another."

Rebuked, Evelyn was silent and sullen once more. Sheila was glad to see David coming through the door. "Ready?" he asked.

They made their farewells as brief as possible. At the door, Evelyn said with a weak smile, "Tell Yoshiko and the others I said hello. I miss them awfully . . ." Her voice trailed off.

Sheila nodded. "I will." She started to follow David down the steps, on impulse turned back. "There's the Community Dinner tomorrow night. Why don't you come? Dehaviland won't be there."

Evelyn considered, started to shake her head. Then she asked wistfully, "Do you think anybody would mind?"

"I think they'd be glad to see you," Sheila told her. "And Jim Lucas assures me the program will be wonderful."

Evelyn's face lit up. "Oh, is it the Lucas program? I heard them practicing, and . . ." She broke off, as if catching herself about to betray a secret.

Sheila clutched her coat closely around her and tried not to shiver visibly while she waited for Evelyn to finish. With the air of one coming back after a brief absence, Evelyn finally said vaguely, ''I'll need to think about that.'' With no other word of farewell, she stepped back into the room and closed the door.

THIRTEEN

"WAS THAT IMPORTANT?" David asked as Sheila started the car.

She shook her head. "I don't think so. Evelyn's trying to decide whether to come to the Community Dinner."

He lit his pipe and a lovely aroma filled the car. "That's wonderful; what is it?" she asked.

"Cherry tobacco." He took a couple of puffs. "Will you be coming to the dinner, then?"

She was too busy trying to edge the car into ruts in the crusted snow to do more than nod. "That's fine," he said in obvious satisfaction. "Sit with Yoshiko—you'll like her husband, I think. He's a philosophy prof at the university."

"Is he Japanese-American, too?"

"Aye. They met in an internment camp during the war—World War Two, that was. Yoshiko's story is that they were both trying to run the youth program, and finally decided to stop fighting and work together." He chuckled. "They make a fine team."

Sheila shook her head in amazement. "How on earth do you learn so much about people in such a short time?"

"My sister says I have an overdeveloped bump of curiosity."

If so, it was on holiday where she was concerned. For several blocks they rode without speaking while Chopin preludes rolled over them from the radio. "Home, sweet home," Sheila murmured as Markham loomed ahead. David reached out and touched her arm. "Look!"

She looked, then struggled with the wheel as her car swerved on ice. "What was it?" She had seen nothing but Markham's blank gray face and the faint glow of the stairwell security light shining through her own office window.

"A light," David said urgently, "on the top floor. Stop!"

She braked so suddenly that a car behind them blared. She pulled hard toward a vacant space, fought the ridge of snow between the lanes, and finally turned off the engine. "I hope you're right. My reputation as a driver is ruined."

"It wasn't much to speak of anyway," David assured her. "Riding with you makes me want to burst into 'Nearer My God to Thee.'"

She opened her mouth to make an indignant retort, but he was already peering back down the block. "Now there's a flicker in the stacks. Or could it have been a reflection of car lights?"

"I didn't see any car." She leaned across him. "But you're right about that light on the third floor. It's the big conference room." She almost lay on him to peer over his shoulder. "I don't see anything in the stacks, though."

He shoved her firmly upright. "This is no time for embraces, quine. You stay here. I'll just ring the bell. If this is on the up and up, they'll answer. If not, you phone the police."

Sheila opened the door. "After that last crack, you think I take orders from you? Besides, I've got a key. We can call from my office. Nobody will hear us from the third floor or the stacks."

David joined her on the sidewalk. "We may both look like fools, but I suppose two fools are better than . . ."

This time they both saw it—a faint light flickering in the first-floor windows of the stacks. "I think it's moving up from the basement," Sheila whispered.

"Aye." David spoke in a normal tone, and she jumped. He grinned. "There's no need to whisper yet, Sheila. Save it."

They watched as the light, faint but unmistakable once they had seen it, made its wavering way up the stairs.

"Look!" Sheila pointed. "The third-floor light just went out."

"So did the one in the stacks," David said grimly, "on the top floor." He mounted the wide, shallow stone steps. "This may be perfectly legitimate, of course." He leaned hard on the bell.

They heard it shrill through the empty halls, then die. Sheila shivered, dug her hands deep in her coat pockets and wished she'd thought to put on slacks. The lecherous wind was creeping steadily up her skirt.

She pressed her ear against the door. So far no sound answered their ring—but how much could they hear through that thick weathered oak?

She had her answer immediately. They could hear a hoarse cry, then a thud.

Black eyes met gray ones. "We've got to go in," Sheila whispered. "Someone is hurt."

"I will," David insisted. "You stay here, and go for help if we need it."

"I'd freeze." Sheila was already fingering her keys like a rosary, trying to find the right one in the dim light. It turned the lock smoothly and the big door scraped open with a screech.

"No secret now that we're here." David knocked out his pipe and dropped it into his pocket. "We might as well have some lights.'' He felt along the wall and the vestibule sprang into sudden brightness.

Sheila stood, blinking. Beyond this pool of radiance the stairwell loomed dimly above them, filled with malevolent shadows. She edged closer to David.

''Who's there?'' David's voice echoed from the unused lobby.

''What's going . . . ?'' Brad D'Arcy's voice halted midsentence. ''Good Lord.'' His face appeared on the landing. ''Get an ambulance. Nick's hurt.''

They stood, sharing one thought: it could be a trap. ''I'll have a look.'' David took the steps two at a time, with Sheila right behind him. ''Don't move him,'' he called up.

Nick Capeletti sprawled face down on the second floor, just at the foot of the steps. It didn't take a crime specialist to see that he must have fallen—or been pushed. His face was so pale Sheila feared he was dead, but as they arrived, Brad murmured, ''He's breathing. Is somebody calling an ambulance?''

David dropped to his knees and felt for Nick's pulse. ''I'm on a mountain rescue team,'' he explained, bending to listen to Nick's chest. ''If someone else will call the ambulance, I'll stay here.''

''I'll do it.'' Brad was already on his way.

He disappeared down the stairs and Sheila stood over David, feeling futile and useless. She strained to listen, but could not hear Nick breathe. She bent down to listen, and, as if she had triggered it, all the lights went out.

''Sheila?'' She felt David grope for her, grab her knee. With relief she clutched him, straining now to hear any sound at all.

''What's going on?'' Brad's voice rang loud and clear from below. Had he had time to flip the switch and get up the basement stairs? Sheila couldn't decide.

"Must be the main switch," David called back. "Do you know where it is?"

"I do," Sheila was forced to admit. "Nick showed me my first day here." How could she explain to him, that her greatest weakness was a foolish but nevertheless terrifying fear of the dark?

Thankfully, it didn't occur to David that a grown woman was able to take care of herself. "Come up with Nick and we'll go," David called to Brad. "Sheila knows where it is."

"Right." Brad's voice was already approaching them up the stairs.

Even David's nearness didn't make the trip into nothingness one Sheila would willingly make. As they groped down two flights of stairs and felt their way along the basement hall, she listened with every pore of her body. The building seemed as dead as a tomb.

At last her fingers felt cold metal and the handle responded to her tug. When David reached past her and flipped a switch, dim stairwell lights glowed at each end of the hall.

Her courage returned with the light. "There's a blanket in the staff coat closet we could use to cover Nick. You go back to him, and I'll bring it." He turned toward the far stairs as she hurried up toward the unused lobby, and the sound of his footsteps followed her reassuringly. It was only as she reached the dim vacant space that she felt uneasy. Quickly she fumbled for the switch and flooded the big lobby with light, then bent to reach into the closet for the blanket she remembered on the floor in the back.

The push came suddenly, without a sound. She fell into the closet on top of the blanket and heard the door shut behind her with a faint click. Then a sliding sound—a bolt being shot home.

The closet was dark, cold, and musty with years of coats and wet boots. But what Sheila noticed first was how angry she was. "Let me out of here!" She pounded on the door. "Somebody, help me!" Her fists pummeled wood for what seemed several minutes before she heard the bolt slide back and her eyes saw light again.

"A strange place for praying," Cal Williams remarked as she climbed up from her knees.

She glared at him. "Somebody locked me in!"

"Somebody's playing with the lights, too. What's going on?"

"Nick's hurt." She stiffly rotated her shoulders and stretched her long legs. "On the second floor." Cal was already hurrying in that direction.

She followed him, but Brad motioned her into her office. "Try to make this operator understand what we need," he hissed, handing her the receiver.

Sheila's knees were trembling and her voice unsteady. Her eyes followed Brad and Cal up the stairs. Had one of them pushed her into the closet? And why?

In talking on the phone, Sheila turned away from her door. She jumped when a voice behind her demanded, "What's going on?" Peter Lucas' red hair flamed at the door.

Sheila waved him to silence until she was certain the ambulance and police were on their way, then turned to accost him. "Nick's been hurt, up on the staircase." The murmur of voices drifted down to them. Peter turned, but she spoke before he could leave. "What are you doing here?"

"I'd been over at the library, and saw lights on my way home. I figured if somebody was here, I'd come get a mike I want to test for tomorrow night."

Sheila regarded him through narrowed eyes. "Do you always wear velvet pants to the library? And shirts that look like silk?"

He flushed to the hairline. "What's it to you?"

"Nothing, as long as you weren't prowling around in the basement earlier."

His brows met fiercely. "Of course not. Why?"

"Somebody was. They just locked me in the closet."

If she'd hoped to surprise him into a guilty reaction, she was disappointed. He merely stared at her as if she belonged in a loony bin. "A closet?"

She sighed, and suddenly her desk chair looked wonderful. She collapsed into it. "I'll be all right in a minute. Go check on Nick." As he turned, she called him back. "Wait, take him this blanket." She'd forgotten she still held it.

"Okay." He glided across the reception hall, and Sheila sat—her eyes open just enough to make sure she wasn't surprised again—and willed herself not to scream.

With relief she heard a siren wail to silence just outside and heavy fists pound on Markham's front door.

The men moved quickly and efficiently, and in almost no time Sheila stood at the front door with David, Cal, Brad, and Peter and watched Nick being lifted gently into the waiting vehicle.

"Should one of us ride with him in the ambulance?" she asked.

The ambulance driver shook his head. "I think the police will want to talk with all of you. You could call his family to meet us, though, if you would."

Sheila was just hanging up when the police arrived.

These young officers were not as large as Mike Flannagan, but just as thorough. "Please tell me what you were doing in the building when the gentleman fell." One of them flipped through a notebook looking for a blank sheet.

Sheila and David exchanged a wordless agreement. Convinced as they were that Nick had been pushed, they would wait to say so.

Brad looked quickly at Cal, then away. "I had a paper to do, so I was in the library."

"But the library is closed on Thursday nights," Cal objected.

"We didn't see a light in the library," Sheila felt compelled to add.

Brad shrugged, an elaborate affair that involved his whole frame. "Come and see," he offered. They all followed him back up the stairs. Sheila couldn't control a shudder as they passed the place where Nick had lain. Brad, beside her, nodded soberly. "I nearly stepped on him coming out the door."

He walked surely through the dark and clicked a switch. They saw a study nook created out of what must be desperation. A small table sat between two shelves, a table covered with books and carefully lit by a lamp shaded by a sweater. "See?" Brad said with pride in his voice. "Just me and the ghosties."

The policeman wrote something down and turned to Cal. "And you, sir, what were you doing here?"

"I've been out of town, and had some work to catch up on. I've been in my office down in the basement all evening, but I didn't know Brad was here. Or Nick, either, for that matter."

Sheila was making a calculation. A light from Cal's office would have to penetrate the furnace room at the front to show on the sidewalk, making his alibi impossible to prove.

Meanwhile, Cal was turning to Brad. "Is that paper you're working on the one you told me you'd have ready before I got back?"

Brad nodded ruefully. "An over-optimistic estimation."

The policeman raised one arm in its leather sleeve. "If I could just get a statement from the others, please."

Sheila, David, and Peter each told their stories, and he laboriously wrote them down. "So none of you knew anybody else was in the building?" his partner finally asked. Cal and Brad shook their heads in unison. "But you"—he turned to Sheila and David—"think you saw a light at the other end of the building?" They nodded. "Has anybody left?"

They looked at one another blankly. "I don't think so," Sheila said, "unless somebody got past Brad after he shoved me in the closet."

Now it was everyone else's turn to stare—at her. "What?" David demanded.

She told the story. "And that's where I found her," Cal confirmed, "down on her knees like a good penitent."

"Okay," said the officer. "Let's have a look around."

Like a gaggle of realtors inspecting a new listing, they all tagged in the wake of his flashlight's powerful beam. Cal switched on lights as they came to them, and Peter turned them off.

"To the outside world," David whispered, "we must look like a series of bright ideas."

In the conference room they discovered papers spread across the table, mute witness to Capeletti's late-night work, but they found no one else there—nor in the parlors, classrooms, offices, or basement.

When they'd checked the furnace room, Cal asked, "Do you want to enter the stacks from the top, the bottom, or the middle?" Sheila suspected he was being facetious, but his face was perfectly straight.

"The top?" she asked, curious.

He nodded. "There's an exit up in the conference room—hidden by that huge tapestry. I found it when I was a student here. The closest way," he added to the policemen, "is through a door down here in the storeroom."

The stacks, of course, were dim even when Cal switched on the four lights that dangled far above them. Peter obligingly began to flick switches above various shelves. But the vast room was empty.

They arrived back in the lobby to find Stan and Jim, peering up and down the long hall.

"What *is* going on?" Stan sounded so much like Dr. Dehaviland that Sheila had to turn her head to hide a smile.

"Sheila thought she saw a light in the stacks," Cal explained, draping one arm over her shoulders. "So we all came to help her check it out."

"Why wasn't I called?" Stan demanded of her. "If Jim here hadn't noticed the lights . . ."

Sheila moved away from Cal and started to answer, but Brad beat her to it.

"Nobody was called," he drawled. "Invitations were sent by ESP. Too bad you missed yours, Stanley."

The policeman pulled out his notebook again. Stan gave his name and address in the peevish tone of a child being left out of grown-up affairs.

Finally they all stood in a circle, feeling anticlimactic. "Well," one officer said, stowing his notebook in one leather pocket. "It's a good thing somebody was here when the old man fell. He might not have made it through the night."

"What old man?" Jim demanded.

"Nick," Peter told him. "He fell down the stairs."

"Is he hurt bad?" Jim asked.

"We don't know," David replied. A somber silence descended on the group. Awkwardly the officers bid the others good night and clumped down the steps.

Cal turned off the last switch, and the hall softened to the dim glow of security lights. The crowd made the darkness friendly, but Sheila did not want to be the last to leave.

"Does everybody have a key?" she asked.

Nobody spoke for an instant, then Cal said, "I do, of course. But how did you get in, Brad?"

Brad moved uneasily. "I, uh, pinched one from Nick last year and had it copied. I run behind so often, you see." He fished in the pocket of his sweat suit and handed it to Cal. "I'd better turn it in, huh?"

Cal clapped him on the shoulders. "We're going to make an honest man of you yet, D'Arcy. Come on, I'll drive you home."

Peter, Jim, and Stan crossed the street as Brad and Cal climbed into a silver BMW.

David followed Sheila to her car and lit his pipe before he turned sober eyes to hers. "Do you think Nick fell?"

She shook her head. "That's not what I heard."

"The shout?"

"No." She shook her head again. "After that. The sound of running feet."

FOURTEEN

SHEILA'S MIND the next morning was so preoccupied that she scarcely noticed the students as they trudged up to class, feet sliding on the stairs to wear the mark of their generation in the gently cupping stone. An occasional remark or sudden burst of laughter, however, suggested that the students, at least, maintained that special brand of self-absorption higher education demands, in which all outside events are measured primarily by how they impinge on one's own studies.

Yoshiko bustled in half an hour late and out of breath. "I called the hospital about Nick. He's too ill to see visitors yet, and Annette, his wife, says he seems to be in a sort of shock." Her face was pale and drawn.

Sheila herself had called Dr. Dehaviland last night. But she hadn't thought to call Yoshiko, and doubted that John Dehaviland would have bothered to dial a number himself. "How did you hear?"

Yoshiko's eyes lost their worried look and twinkled behind her glasses. "Stan called. He was quite put out with you for calling Dehaviland before he did."

Sheila grunted. "Tough. But I'm glad you called to ask about Nick. Did he . . ." She hesitated. "Is he talking yet, I wonder?"

Yoshiko's eyes narrowed. "Talking about what?"

"Oh, I don't know. How he fell, or anything?"

"I didn't hear anything about him falling. All Stan said was that he'd had a heart attack." Before Yoshiko's mouth was fully open with the next question, Sheila decided on an abrupt change of subject.

"Could we send him some flowers? Would he like that?"

"He can't have flowers—he's using oxygen."

"Well, you've known him longer than I have. What do you think he'd like to have?"

"Who you talking 'bout needing flowers?" Bertha demanded, stopping to join them and balancing a tray of cookies and clean cups on one ample hip.

"Nick," Yoshiko informed her. "He had a heart attack last night, and is in the hospital."

"He can't have flowers," Sheila explained further, "and we were wondering what else he'd like."

"A pack of cigarettes," Bertha said promptly. "Even when they's killing him. But if it was me, I'd send fruit. If he don't eat it, his wife and the nurses can."

"The very thing," Yoshiko agreed. "I'll call the grocer down the street and have them pack him a basket, and I can take it after work tonight."

Having solved yet another problem for Markham, Bertha continued on her way upstairs. Yoshiko also turned to go, but Sheila called her back. "I guess they are still going to want the first-anniversary lecture to go out next week. We're about ready to print the introduction and cover pages as soon as I proof them. How do I go about getting that done?"

"Check with Jim Lucas. He should be in soon, and he's on a work scholarship and gets credit for that kind of thing."

Sheila settled into the large green chair in her office to proofread and wait for Jim.

About half past ten he draped himself over her door. He wore a thin gray jacket and no gloves, his only concession to the bitter cold a knitted scarf so old and grimy that it was impossible to tell if it was dirty white or faded beige.

"Are you trying to catch your death of pneumonia?" she demanded.

His bony face softened into a smile. "We all have to go sometime. How's Nick?" He blew on his fingers to warm them.

She shook her head. "Not so good."

Before he could speak again, Todd came in, stamping snow off his boots. Sheila greeted him, then said to Jim, "Yoshiko said you run the press downstairs. Could you possibly work for me this morning? We need to get the introduction to the lectures printed."

Jim nodded. "Sure. Now that my paper's done, I'm a free man until next week."

Todd unzipped his parka. "I'll help, too. I used to run a press in the Peace Corps, and have just been waiting for a chance to show off my skills."

Sheila gathered up the work and they trooped downstairs.

Markham's mystique did not extend to its lower regions, and the workroom's two bare bulbs did little to relieve the gloom. Sheila set Jim to gluing red labels on each binder cover while Todd introduced himself to the press and got it clacking. Under the pretext of checking supplies, Sheila hung around—feeling like an inept spy. She couldn't even think what questions to ask.

Jim finally pointed a direction. "When's Quint due back?" he called to Todd.

Todd spoke without taking his eyes off the press. "I think he's coming in today. Wonder if he's going to take that job?"

Sheila seized this opportunity to discuss the elusive Mr. Barringer. "I haven't even met Quint. What's he like?"

"A real nice guy," Jim told her.

"A rebel," Todd grinned, thumping paper on the table to even it. "His family has gone to Harvard for generations, but Quint came to the University of Chicago and stayed on at Markham."

"They're better schools," Jim said matter-of-factly.

Todd's grin widened. "Spoken like a Lucas. Did you know, Sheila, there were Lucases at Markham when my folks were slaves?"

"There you go again, picking at Markham and the Lucases!" Jim clenched his fists, flushed to the roots of his copper hair. "Looks like you'd show a little gratitude that Markham accepted you!"

Sheila held up a warning hand. "No wars down here, fellows."

He flushed. "Sorry, Sheila. I didn't mean to lose my temper."

"You do a far better job of controlling it than your cousin," she assured him. "I didn't even know you had one."

As she set him to work punching holes in paper, she tried to make amends by getting to know this thin, gentle boy.

"Do you have brothers and sisters?"

He shook his head. "It's just Mom and me. My dad and sister were killed in a car crash when I was seven. Mom was so smashed up she's been in a wheelchair since."

"I didn't know that, Jim." Todd's sympathy was sincere. "Who takes care of her when you're away?"

Jim's bony face softened with pride. "She takes care of herself. She trained as a computer programmer, and the house is fixed so she can live alone."

"She sounds terrific," Sheila told him, "but I'll bet she'll be glad when you graduate. Will she live with you then?"

"Not likely. I'll be going overseas, probably. But she won't mind. She thinks I was, well…" He flushed. "…sort of saved for something important. I was supposed to be in the car the day they had the accident, and at the last minute they decided to leave me at Peter's. Mom's always said it was because . . ."

Whatever he was about to say they would have to wait to know, for just then Yoshiko's voice floated down the hall. "Peter? Peter Lucas. Telephone."

Jim turned and raised his voice. "Pete's in class, Yoshiko. I'll get it." His voice returned to normal. "It's probably the shop saying our slide projector is ready for tonight. I'll come back this afternoon." He glided from the room.

Sheila turned to Todd. "Did Brad tell you about last night?"

"You mean about Nick falling downstairs? Yeah, he told me. Is Nick going to be all right?"

Sheila shook her head. "We don't know yet. Tell me, who besides Brad and Quint around here knew Melanie Forbes?"

Todd chewed his lip. "You think Nick's falling had something to do with that?"

Sheila turned her back and pretended to check boxes of pencils. "I don't know. Do you?" She turned back to face him.

He considered the question. "No, I don't. Melanie was, as Brad said, a real bitch. Sweet as sugar, then went for the jugular. But Nick scarcely knew her. He certainly wouldn't be having heart attacks over her, unless he thought finding her body here was going to tarnish Markham's silver image forever."

She decided on a frontal attack. "What if he'd found out that the murderer was a Markham student?"

He shook his head vehemently, and immediately jumped to the conclusion she'd hoped to avoid. "Who? Quint's been done with her for months, and killing former girl-friends is just not the done thing in Boston. Nobody else cared enough to kill her."

"What about Brad—or Stan, or Peter?"

"No way. She and Brad hung around sometimes, but it wasn't serious. She never looked twice at poor old Stanley, and Pete only notices women built like grand pianos."

It seemed a dead end. Sheila glanced at her watch. "It's lunchtime. Let's call it quits for now and work later."

"I've got a seminar. Sorry. But Jim can finish for you."

"Maybe Mike's right," she said to herself as she checked her lipstick in the restroom mirror. "I certainly can't find a suspect to replace Quint Barringer." Frustrated and hungry, she went to join Bertha in the kitchen for lunch.

MARKHAM'S BASEMENT KITCHEN, which occupied the space directly under Wentworth, was used to serve tea and occasional meals. An oak dumbwaiter ran between the two floors. But in the past decade, Markham had seldom served full meals, and Bertha and Jack had claimed the kitchen for their own. Here it was that she prepared the coffee for upstairs, and here it was that she and Jack—and those they invited—had lunch.

The kitchen had much in common with the rest of the basement: exposed water pipes, institutional gray walls, and a floor of dark-brown ceramic tiles. But Bertha and Jack had decorated it with the kind of love that incorporates rather than conceals defects. Jack had installed a table, three straight chairs, and two rockers. Bertha had covered their worn cushions with red towels. Jack had polished the floor until the tiles glowed, Bertha had splashed them with red and blue rugs. From the pipes overhead, Jack had suspended several mobiles of shiny fish that lazed in the warm air currents against their sea-gray background. And above the stove, Bertha had hung a calender for 1981 that showed two chubby boys, one black and one white, caressing a smug duck.

Usually the kitchen was a cheerful place. But this morning Sheila found Bertha sitting dejectedly at her table. Chin on one plump palm, she stared out the window at an empty courtyard that separated Markham from houses at the rear. Wednesday's snow had frozen into a solid crust that shot sunlight in all directions, but the view was nothing to command such total absorption.

"You look lower than a snake's belly," Sheila told her. "Am I still invited to lunch?"

Bertha heaved herself to her feet and started toward the stove. "You sure are. I was just thinking about all the awful things happening around here. Have some homemade vegetable soup."

"It smells scrumptious." Sheila accepted.

They heard feet clumping down the stairs and, to Sheila's surprise, David MacLean joined them. "The snow's lovely today," he greeted them.

Bertha rolled her eyes at Sheila. "This man. He's crazy about snow. I guess where he comes from, there's nothing *but* snow—is that right, Davy?"

"Well..." He considered the question, and his accent broadened. "We do have summer, ye ken. I mind last year it was on a Thursday afternoon..."

His mood was infectious. They had as merry a lunch as if murder had never come into their lives, finishing with cups of steaming coffee.

The tingly aroma made Sheila sneeze. As she rummaged in her purse for a tissue, she dislodged a tumble of tissues, pencils, paper scraps, and receipts.

"A regular rat's nest," Bertha grunted.

"Afraid there'll be a paper shortage?" David asked.

"It's just that I'm a tidy soul," she said in mock defense. "I can't stand to see a scrap of paper lying about, so I pick them up to toss."

"Well, get to tossing," Bertha suggested. "It might put off your heart attack for a while." She helped herself liberally to sugar.

Sheila pulled a wastebasket beside her chair and began sorting through the debris. But almost immediately the horror of the past few days returned. When or where had she picked up this scrap of blue paper? With puckered forehead, she swept it back into her purse—a small rectangle on which someone had practiced in an unfamiliar hand a most familiar name:

Melanie J. Forbes

Melanie J. Forbes

Melanie J. Forbes

The paper seemed to smolder in her purse, and as soon as she could decently do so, she left the kitchen. In spite of his warnings, Mike needed to see this. At the top of the stairs she paused. Yoshiko was flying across the lobby with a glad cry.

"Quint! Welcome home!" The little secretary was enveloped in a bear hug by someone standing by Sheila's door.

So this was Quint Barringer.

Sheila wasn't certain what she had expected. Because Brad, Todd, and Yusuf had relied on Quint to tackle Dehaviland, she had been prepared for a forceful young radical, bearded and dressed in the "ready for the barricades" garb of the sixties. Evelyn's description had made him sound like a stuffy young New Englander Eusebius Wentworth would have loved.

The young man across the lobby was neither. Several inches taller than Sheila, he was loosely constructed of such large bones he could be called rawboned except for the grace with which he moved in his three-piece navy suit. His straight dark hair, worn just below his ears, shaped his head as only very well-cut hair will do. His smile was wide and lopsided, slightly foolish. It could easily deceive you into dismissing Quint as a clown—before you met his gaze. There was nothing foolish about the light-blue eyes behind steel-rimmed spectacles. Those eyes were warm, friendly, and highly intelligent.

Sheila realized with a shock that she knew about his eyes because she had been looking directly into them for several moments. Yoshiko had dragged him across the lobby to where Sheila stood, staring. She blushed. Instead of pretending he didn't notice, Quint gave her a comrade's grin, as if he didn't mind in the least being stared at like a slide specimen.

"This is Sheila Travis, the newest member of our family," Yoshiko informed him, beaming up like a pygmy between them. "She's taken Eleanor Quincy's place. Her husband was Tyler Travis. Sheila, this is Addison Barringer. The Fifth."

He shot out one hand. "Hi, Sheila. My friends call me Quint."

"I hope I'll be one of them." She smiled.

"I hope so, too." He dropped her hand, but fixed her with such an intent gaze that she felt they were still in physical contact. "How do you like Markham?"

Before she could answer, Yoshiko tugged at his arm. "I want to talk to you for a minute."

His brows lifted in surprise, but his smile was still warm. "Sure. See you later, Sheila?" He followed the tiny secretary, who pulled him into her office and firmly shut the door.

Sheila returned to her office with a strange sense of peace. Quint carried himself in a way she'd formerly associated with men like Mahatma Gandhi or Abraham Lincoln. What was it, humility? Yes, and gentleness. But a gentleness born of confidence and strength, not of weakness. It was, she decided fancifully, the gentleness of steel cables holding aloft the Golden Gate Bridge, the gentleness of a warm, weathered boulder that welcomes a climber to the mountain's crest. He was not, she was certain, someone who would strangle a woman.

Two noises brought her out of her reverie—the front door scraping open, and the buzzer on her desk. She answered the buzzer.

"Sheila, would you step into my office for a moment?" The voice on her phone did not bother to identify itself. The light tenor was unmistakable.

"Right away." She checked the "sir," and rose from her desk to confront Peter Lucas in his gold leonine parka. With one mittened paw he shoved back his hood. "Jim's sick," he said without preliminaries. "I just found him throwing up in the john. He asked me to tell you that he can't work this afternoon."

She checked a sigh. "What seems to be the matter? He was fine this morning."

Peter shrugged. "I don't know, but he's positively green. He thinks it may be bacon he ate for breakfast. It's been around awhile. But I think it's just nerves about tonight. Jimmy gets nerve attacks when something is important to him."

He spoke gruffly, but underneath his use of their childhood name Sheila sensed a deep concern. "Should I check on him later?"

He shook his head. "I gave him a couple of pills that will knock him out. He's got no more tolerance for medicine than a baby. On my way back, I ran into Stan, looking almost as green as Jim. They'll listen out for each other."

He left, and she went to the president's office.

He was standing beside the fireplace, resting one elbow against the mantel. The pose was calculated, she suspected, to suggest Thomas Jefferson. It more nearly resembled a scene from Masterpiece Theatre.

"Yes?" she asked from the open doorway.

"Please come in and close the door behind you." He took a chair and waved her to the love seat. When they were seated, he continued. "Mr. Flannagan is coming out today to interview two students and..." he paused, examined his nails for an infinitesimal moment, and continued, "...and one member of our faculty. He feels that each of them might have information which could, ah, assist his investigation."

"I see." Actually she saw nothing—especially why the president was telling *her* all this.

At last the blue eyes met hers directly. It was like gazing into a frozen pond. The color was identical with Quint's, but the effect was not.

"I want you to be present for those interviews, Sheila. I cannot and will not permit the police to harass our people."

"But..."

He held up a hand to forestall her. "Nick would be the logical person, of course, if he were not...incapacitated."

The effect of that small pause was to imply that Nick Capeletti was malingering. It almost, but not quite, distracted her from the truth.

"It would seem to me that you, Dr. Dehaviland, would..."

He shook his head. "Unfortunately, I am occupied this afternoon getting out some important correspondence. I realize that you are new to Markham, Sheila, but I feel that your years in diplomatic circles have equipped you to sit in on those interviews. Your newness to Markham may even prove an advantage. It makes you a little more, shall we say, impersonal?"

"Expendable" was the word that had sprung to her own mind. But what she said was "What did Mr. Flannagan say to my being there?"

He inclined his head and gave her a frosty smile. "Let us just say that he bowed to necessity. You are to meet him in Wentworth at two." He consulted his watch. "That's about ten minutes from now. And, Sheila, I want you to take extensive notes. Mr. Flannagan may object—he plans to tape the interviews—but I feel that tapes are..." he paused, a post-Watergate Republican facing an unpleasant truth, "...well, unreliable. If Mr. Flannagan gives you trouble, refer him to me."

She nodded. So he and the big detective had crossed swords, had they? And this time the honors went to Dehaviland. Strangely enough, she found herself siding with the president. She was as reluctant as he to see anyone from Markham accused of murder.

FIFTEEN

FLANNAGAN TOOK HER presence with better grace than she'd expected. She was piqued by their last conversation, and disconcerted that her body chemistry welcomed him when she would have preferred to feel cool and distant. He didn't help matters, as she led him and a young black officer into Wentworth, by leaning close to murmur, "I'm glad you're here. You look terrific in that color." She moved briskly to open the draperies, beyond the smell of his after-shave.

His warning of the evening before seemed days, not hours earlier, and Sheila wondered if he'd even heard about the later excitement at Markham.

He had. As he flicked on the lights he said casually, "I read a report that people were running all over this place last night. Said you got locked in a closet. How did that happen?"

She explained. He regarded her sternly. "Were you sleuthing after I specifically warned you against it?"

"Not very successfully. We saw a light and came in to check on it, but Nick fell—or was pushed—before we got inside."

"We?" He was busy shoving a couch nearer a chair. Only Mike would do it that way instead of the other way around.

"David MacLean, from the university." Why did she make him sound twenty-two and harmless? she wondered, furious with herself.

Mike's reply was lost in the reaction of Jerry, the young officer, who'd just caught sight of Eusebius. "Now there's a dude I'd hate to meet on a dark and stormy night!" He was still chuckling as he went to set up recording equipment at a side table.

Mike sprawled on the chair he'd chosen and motioned her to one end of the sofa that now adjoined it. She took her seat primly, willing herself to Della Street poise. He helped, by turning on his obnoxious teddy-bear act in an attempt to charm her.

"Well, looks like last night was more sound than fury. Let's talk about this afternoon. I meant it when I said I'm glad you're here, Sheila. You can really be a help. You know these people. Watch for signs they are lying—body movements, hands, that sort of thing. If you see something, cough and I'll know to pursue it."

She bit her lower lip. "I already have orders, Mike. I'm to be taking notes."

He waved one hand impatiently. "No notes. If the president wants to, he can listen to the tapes when we're done. I said—"

She interrupted. "...and *he* said I am to take notes. Sorry, Mike, but I am here to represent Markham."

He made an unpleasant noise of disgust. Then he seemed to reconsider. "Okay, play it your way. But you aren't going to want notes on some of this, I guarantee you." He turned. "Ready, Jerry?" The young officer nodded, and Mike said to Sheila, "Would you tell Brad D'Arcy we're ready for him?"

BRAD WAS IN the coffee room, lying in a chair with his head back and his eyes closed. When Sheila spoke his name, he slowly raised his lids. "Come with the tumbril?" he drawled.

"Maybe it won't be that bad," she suggested.

He gave an elaborate shrug. "When the police send for a man with my name, we automatically expect the guillotine." He led the way downstairs. When she started to follow him into Wentworth, however, he looked at her quizzically. "I think she fancies herself Saint Catherine," he murmured to Flannagan, dropping to a sofa, "and plans to hold my head in her lap while you cut it off."

"Mrs. Travis is here at Dr. Dehaviland's request," Mike told him. "For your protection."

Brad gave her a lazy smile. "Protect away." Then he leaned his head back on the sofa and waited for Mike to begin.

Flannagan got quickly through the preliminaries and went to the heart of what he wanted to know. "Did you know the deceased was dealing drugs?"

Brad shook his head. "She passed out joints to friends, but she didn't use the stuff and she didn't deal."

Mike flicked a finger toward Jerry, who came forward with a small black case. "We found these in her bureau drawer," Mike told Brad, opening the case and taking out three boxes of bath powder.

Score one for Aunt Mary, Sheila thought, repressing a smile.

Mike opened the boxes to reveal, tucked in the center of each mound of powder, a small plastic bag also filled with powder. Brad leaned forward to reach for one of them, then paused.

"It's okay," Flannagan assured him. "You can touch them."

Brad opened one packet and sniffed, wet a finger and tasted an infinitesimal bit of the powder. Then he shook his head, not quite convinced. "You found these at Melanie's?"

Flannagan nodded. "And since you are the only person at Markham who is known to be interested in drugs, *and* since you dated the deceased, I thought you might know something about them."

Brad hesitated. "No, I didn't. But I wish I had." He fished in his hip pocket, dug out his wallet, and handed Mike a card.

Mike scanned it, handed it back. "I suspected as much. What can you tell us?"

Brad leaned back, but kept his head erect and his eyes open. "Not much, except that in spite of looks and money, that was one needy lady. This was probably a set of kinky Christmas presents."

Flannagan closed the black case with a click and set it beside his chair. "Let the record show Brad D'Arcy carries identification of an undercover agent for the Chicago narcotics squad."

Sheila's eyes flew to Brad in surprise. "We all have our covers," he murmured.

"Do Jenny and Todd know?" she asked.

He shook his head. "Too risky. Jenny's transparent as a window, and Todd doesn't keep secrets from her." Remembering Jenny's fear in the coffee room, Sheila hoped they found out soon.

"Is Markham just a good cover, or for real?" Mike was no longer using his interrogation voice.

Brad turned his head toward him. "Oh, it's for real. The undercover bit pays for Markham, actually."

Sheila was puzzled. "But I thought your parents..."

He completed the sentence for her. "Were loaded? They are. And fine people. But my old man swings to the right, the far right. He thinks most people in Latin America are Communists, which makes my wanting to work there highly unpopular." His lips curled in a gentle, mocking grin. "So here I am, cut down to barely enough for socks, shorts, and Wheaties."

"And vacations in the Bahamas," she added.

For the first time she saw Brad at a loss for words. "Yeah, well, right. They provide for everything, actually, except tuition. The City of Chicago supplies that."

Flannagan gave Sheila a look that she interpreted to mean he wanted to take over again. "What else can you tell us about the deceased? Especially last fall?"

"She wasn't happy, but then I never knew her to be happy—except maybe when she was dating Quint."

"They weren't dating last fall?"

His head shifted slowly from side to side. "Uh-uh. Quint got smart last May. What else can I tell you about the charming Melanie?" he continued drowsily. "She had a most unlovely habit of finding a person's weakness and bringing it up in public. Made her feel a bit powerful, I think, to know things about people. Anything else you want to know you ought to ask Evelyn Parsons. She knew Melanie probably better than anybody. Yoshiko could give you her number."

"Fine." Flannagan shifted as if the interview were over, then shot out one last question. "Where were you on the Friday night before Christmas?"

The suddenness didn't shake Brad's poise. "Holding Todd's head while he puked. Jenny had shopping to do."

"Can they verify that?"

Brad shrugged again. "Depends on their memories."

"Strange kid," Flannagan said as he left.

"I keep feeling I ought to know him," Sheila mused. "He looks very familiar. But I'm certain that I don't. Wonder what he's like under all that pose?"

Flannagan grinned, blue eyes twinkling. "To quote Mr. D'Arcy..." He gave an elaborate shrug.

Sheila chuckled. "You'll need to practice it before a mirror. You get too much shoulder into it."

He sighed and considered his bulk. "I have so much shoulder to *put* into it."

Her mind was already back to the interview. "Does his work with the police eliminate him as a suspect?" She knew her own answer, but wanted his. It was the same.

"No. If this crime were connected with drugs, maybe. But since it doesn't seem to be, he's a good second-stringer."

"He has no motive."

"And Barringer wasn't here. Which do you prefer to believe?"

She sighed. "I prefer a tramp off the street. Both of them are such nice guys."

"Lots of murderers are nice guys, Sheila."

She chewed her lower lip. "I know. But if you find what you're looking for here, Mike, it could give the whole place a bad name. You know that, don't you?"

He nodded. "It's not fair, of course. You get a plumber who kills somebody, nobody says all plumbers are bad. But you get somebody in government, or a preacher, or a cop"—he smiled ruefully—"and some folks will blame the lot of them."

She didn't return his smile, so he leaned close and whispered, "Tell you what I'll do. You figure out why Melanie Forbes came in here with that tramp off the street, how they got in, why he killed her, and how he got a key to that basement storeroom, and I'll tie a bow around it for the prosecution."

She finally rewarded him with a very small smile. After all, it wasn't Mike's fault someone had stored a body in Markham's basement. "And in the meantime?"

"In the meantime, ask Calvin Williams down. I got a call from your aunt this morning that gives us a few things to discuss."

CAL WAS IN the coffee room too. Polished boots propped on a table, he was rehashing last week's basketball scores with a couple of first-year students.

When she came in, he pulled his long frame out of his chair. "Ah, 'how beautiful on the mountains are the feet of them that bring good tidings,'" he quoted. "You really should try the mountains, Sheila. They might do wonders for your feet." He picked up his briefcase and strode to the door. "That," he explained to the bewildered students, "is by way of saying that this lady bringeth not good tidings, but ill. My presence is required below. Stick around and we shall continue our discussion anon."

"Very cool," Sheila admired as the door closed behind them.

"I try, Sheila, I try. What do the police want, do you know?"

"To talk about murder, I should think."

He paused, one foot poised mid-air. "Are you serious?" She nodded. "Why me?"

She shook her head. "I'm just a messenger. Ask the police."

Mike was standing to greet them, and Cal wasted no time. "What's this about?"

"Have a seat." Mike resumed his chair, Sheila settled herself on one end of the couch, and Cal perched on the front of the other cushion like a man who has no intention of staying long.

"Dr. Williams, let me first inform you that this interview is being taped. Have you any objections?" Cal shook his head. "Would you answer aloud, please?"

"No, as long as I can leave at any time."

"Of course. This is merely a preliminary questioning. It concerns the death of a young woman, Melanie Forbes..."

Cal sat quietly through Mike's introduction until he reached the sentence, "We are talking with those at the institute who knew her well." Then he sat bolt upright.

"Hey, man," he interrupted, "I don't know her at all! I saw her a couple of times in the coffee room. If you are looking for her friends, you'd better look elsewhere."

Flannagan's voice was very mild. "We are interviewing students, Dr. Williams, but we want you to help us fill in a few gaps. Such as the period between June second and July fifteenth."

Cal narrowed his eyes and gave every appearance of a man thinking furiously. "What about those weeks?"

Flannagan dug into his pocket and pulled out something that for the moment was still concealed. "We have information that during those weeks Melanie was out of town with a friend, possibly male. We also have information that during those weeks you were on an island in Wisconsin writing a book, and that your wife was in Montana doing archaeological research."

Cal made an impatient motion with one hand. "It was summer, Mr. Flannagan. *Everyone* was somewhere. So what?"

"So we also have these." Mike leaned forward and opened his hand. "Let the record show I am holding five matchbooks from restaurants near where Dr. Williams spent the summer."

Cal looked at them and shook his head. "I don't understand."

"They were in a brandy snifter at Melanie Forbes' apartment."

"So maybe she has a summer place up there." Cal's tone was casual, but Sheila noticed his large hands trembled.

"Maybe," Flannagan agreed pleasantly, "but I have a man up there right now looking for witnesses who saw the two of you together. If those witnesses exist, we'll find them. Now suppose we have a little straight talk."

Before he could continue, Cal threw an angry look at Sheila. "What's she doing here?"

Sheila dropped her own gaze to her lap. She wasn't a prude, but she was beginning to feel distinctly nauseous.

"Mrs. Travis is here on Dr. Dehaviland's orders," Mike growled. "For your protection," he added. "Do you object?"

"I certainly do. Some of this may get very personal. I don't want to spill my guts in front of her." Flannagan didn't reply, so Cal tried again. "Look, man, I don't know what you know, and none of it relates to murder. But if some of it becomes public knowledge, it could get very sticky for me professionally."

Flannagan had been pocketing the matchbooks. Now his eyes met Cal's and Sheila was surprised at how hard and cold Mike's eyes could be. "You should have thought about that earlier, Williams. The lady is here at Dr. Dehaviland's request, the lady is discreet, and she stays. Now. Let's begin at the beginning. You met Melanie Forbes when?"

"I met her one day last spring when I came to Chicago to discuss this year at Markham. Quint and I were having coffee upstairs, and she joined us. I know his father, you see."

Mike shifted abruptly. "You and your wife having trouble?"

"Not then. Not now. But last May..." He sighed, slewed his eyes to Sheila and back to Mike. "I hoped Lena would give up Montana for one summer and go to Wisconsin with me. She wanted me to be with her in Montana, as I have a few times in the past. She was right, of course. I can write anywhere, she has to dig where the fossils are. But the day she left, we were both very angry. I got in the car and drove nonstop from D.C. to Chicago, showed up at Pres-Res and asked Ralph Southard to put me up for a night or two. Markham would have lodged me at a hotel, of course, but I didn't want anybody—especially the press—to know I was in town."

"So why'd you call the Forbes woman?"

Cal shook his head. "I didn't. I planned to rest, final-ize some details here about the seminar, and drive on up to Wisconsin. The night I arrived, Melanie Forbes called."

"Called you?"

Cal shook his head. "No, Quint. He lived there last year, but he'd already moved out and gone home."

"Did Miss Forbes know your wife was not here with you?"

Cal expelled a deep breath of exasperation. "Who knows what she knew or didn't know? She certainly didn't mention it. She said she'd like to talk to me about Quint, and asked if she could come over. I'm not that dumb. I suggested we meet at Orly's for a glass of beer."

"And on the strength of one glass of beer you invited her to Wisconsin?" Mike spoke dryly. "That must have been potent beer."

Cal had the grace to grin. "It must have been, because I don't remember asking her at all. If it weren't saying things about the dead, I'd say she invited herself. She started out by talking about Quint, and how he was hurting her. Then she started talking about me. How lucky my wife was to have me. That was balm for my wounds, the way I was feeling that night.'' He paused, darted a quick look at Sheila, and again sighed deeply. ''I won't whitewash it, but I hope you won't put it in your notes, Sheila. One thing led to another, and we wound up at her place. The next morning we seem to have agreed that she'd be a definite inspiration for the book I'm writing.'' He ran both hands through his hair and gave it a hard tug. ''It was insane. I knew it all the time, and certainly know it now. By the end of two days we were both bored silly. She found the island deadly, and I couldn't write with her prowling around. She wouldn't even cook—insisted I take her to those restaurants. But I didn't see her pick up the matchbooks. You think she planned blackmail?''

''Probably just a habit. How long did she stay?''

''Five days. Then I put her on a plane for Acapulco, assuring me she'd never tell if I didn't. As if I would.''

''You see her this fall?''

Cal shook his head. ''I ran into her in the coffee room once or twice, always with a crowd, and she was as cool as if we were strangers. Which, of course, we were.''

''I see.'' Mike's voice was noncommittal. ''That's all for now. If we have further questions, we'll be in touch.''

At his tone, a vein throbbed in Cal's forehead. ''Look, man, what are you going to do with this? If this hits the papers... Adultery is bad enough, but that girl had drug connections that would ruin my work in Latin America if my name were linked with them.''

Mike stood. ''As I said, you should have thought about that sooner. But we won't leak it—unless we have to. For the record, where were you the weekend before Christmas?''

Cal unfolded himself from the couch. "Home with my wife." He turned, as if he wanted to make an appeal to Sheila. She was glad he did not. Instead, he squared his shoulders and walked to the door like a man going to the firing squad of his own volition.

Mike signaled Jerry to turn off the tape. "Well?"

Sheila shook her head. "I don't like this, Mike. The muck that's getting raked up..."

He snorted. "I noticed you didn't take many notes. But we have to rake up muck, as you call it, if muck's the truth."

Her sigh was as deep as Cal's earlier. "What's truth, Mike? Don't those years and years of good marriage and excellent leadership also count as truth?"

"Sure. But put them on a scale with this affair and see which side weighs heaviest with Dehaviland and the press. Meanwhile, call Addison Barringer, so we can finish here."

BEFORE SHEILA reached the door, there was a tap on the other side. Yoshiko entered with a tray of steaming cups and a plate of cookies. "I hope I'm not intruding." She carried the tray to a table beside Mike. "I saw Cal come out, and thought you might want something to drink before you talked with Quint."

Quint himself followed her in, bearing cream and sugar. "Hello," he said. "Ready for me?"

Flannagan nodded. "Go ahead and have a seat. I'll be with you as soon as I get sugar in my coffee. Coffee, Jerry?" Jerry came from his corner and carried a cup back with him. "Thanks," Mike told Yoshiko with his teddy-bear smile.

Quint seated himself on the couch and stretched his long legs. He gave Sheila a warm smile, then focused his whole attention on the detective. "How may I help you?"

Sheila studied him while she flipped to a clean page in her notebook. Seen from the side, Quint's long nose turned up just a bit, giving him a piquant look. He sat with no sign of nervousness, hands clasped on his lap, head bent almost deferentially.

Yoshiko, it seemed to Sheila, was taking an unnecessarily long time to be sure they had everything they needed. Finally she backed to the door. "Call me if you need anything," she said, darting one quick, furtive look at Quint as she left.

Flannagan sipped his coffee and munched a cookie. "Now, Mr. Barringer, we are interested—"

"Call me Quint," the young man suggested. "It's easier."

"Quint, then. Interesting name."

The lopsided smile widened. "It's what happens when you are the fifth to have a name. They've run out of things to call you."

Mike munched another cookie. "Will you call a kid the sixth?"

Quint's eyes twinkled. "I plan to have only daughters."

Sheila could feel her shoulder muscles relaxing. Maybe it was the coffee, or maybe it was Quint himself, but Mike seemed far less aggressive in this interview.

Swiftly he outlined for Quint the basic facts concerning Melanie's death. "How would you define your relationship with the deceased last spring? Just friends? Or more than that?"

Quint stroked one cheekbone from ear to nose and back again. "Pre-engaged, I suppose."

"And who called that off?"

"I did. We'd have made each other miserable."

"Did she agree?"

Quint shook his head. "Not at first. But we were apart all summer, and by fall she seemed to have accepted it."

"I see. What contact did you have this fall?"

"None, except at a distance. I don't think I ever spoke to her after May."

Flannagan sprawled sideways in his chair and rested one arm along its plump back as if this were a conversation between pals. "What can you tell me about her? Things like who her friends were, and her enemies."

Quint drew his brows together. "Mel rubbed people the wrong way sometimes—she had a way of pinpointing what would most deeply annoy someone, and using it to gain attention. But I don't think she had any real enemies."

Flannagan rubbed his big nose. "Somebody killed her, Quint."

Quint flushed. "Touché. I wish I could help you find out who. But I can't honestly think of anyone—"

"Any friends who might know her better?"

He shook his head. "Melanie didn't have real friends, either, and she changed acquaintances with the season. She was afraid of getting close to people, you see. The only person she seemed to hang on to was Evelyn Parsons, who—"

"We have her name, thanks." Mike stood. "Well, if that's all you know, that's all you know." As Quint stood, too, Mike asked casually, "You went home Friday before Christmas?"

Quint turned back. "I left Markham Friday morning, yes."

Mike put out one massive hand. "Thanks for your co-operation."

Quint shook his hand, then gave Sheila a smile and the man in the corner a respectful nod.

"Already running for President," Jerry chuckled from his corner, "and I'd give him my vote, too!"

"Don't vote yet, Jerry." Mike stretched and gave a huge yawn. "He may be running for another election first."

Sheila went to close the draperies, noting that it was almost dark even though it was only half past four. Another storm was nearly upon them. "So you're still not satisfied about Quint?" she asked Mike over her shoulder. "To eliminate him, I mean."

He shook his tawny head. "Barringer's still far and away the best suspect wc have."

"But what about Brad, or Cal?"

"We'll check out Williams' alibi, and D'Arcy's, too. But neither of them had the involvement with her Barringer did."

She couldn't believe he could be so pigheaded. "But Quint wasn't even here!"

Mike lived up to her worst expectations. "We have to look at all the possibilities, Sheila. It was possible, with his money, to fly home Friday morning, return that same afternoon, murder Melanie, and still get back to Boston in time to sleep most of the night in his own bed. Before Quint Barringer leaves the top of my list, I want his every hour accounted for on that Friday. Sorry, but I can't base my case on squeamishness about suspecting your friends."

She glared at him. "I have no squeamishness about suspecting friends, Mike"—she fought to keep her voice level—"but I have a good bit of squeamishness about suspecting someone with little motive, less opportunity, and no evidence against him. Sometimes I get the distinct impression you're far more interested in winding up this case than in finding out the truth."

"I assume," he said in a voice like steel, "that they will be one and the same." She turned away to flick off a lamp.

"I'm leaving, Sheila," he growled. "Do you have anything else to say?"

She did not turn back until she heard the door close behind him.

Alone at last, she permitted herself a deep, audible sigh. She was keeping two facts to herself, facts that Mike did not know. Three, if you counted the paper she'd forgotten to give him. Was she wrong? Mike, she was certain, would feel she was suppressing evidence. But Mike would have to wait a day or two.

She'd been manhandled herself in the last couple of days (and, she told herself fiercely, had enough of men to satisfy her for a long time). She didn't want Mike manhandling anyone else until she could find out what it was that Yoshiko knew about Quint, and until she could talk to Cal again. He might have a perfectly good reason for saying he hadn't spoken to Melanie Forbes since July—but Evelyn Parsons had said they quarreled at the Community Christmas Dinner.

SIXTEEN

SHE EXPECTED TO FIND a moment to speak to Cal at the Community Dinner that night. But she had never thought the place would be so crowded. Although snow was pelting down outside, making transportation difficult, and although Markham's Community Dinners were held in a Loop hotel several miles from Hyde Park, neither distance nor snow deterred Markham students, wives, and dates from flocking to a good meal and (Sheila hoped, remembering Jim's earlier illness) good program.

The noise level escalated with each wave of new arrivals, and because conversations were conducted as much by hand as by mouth, the scene eddied with constant, frenetic motion. Will she come? Sheila wondered, eyes scanning the crowd both for Evelyn and for a seat. She didn't see the former secretary, but gradually faces stood out of the mill.

In one corner Quint stood next to a thin young man whose bristling black beard concealed most of his face and much of his personality. Up at the stage, two redheads bent over equipment, plugging in cords and stringing wires. Stan sat at a round table near the stage, sweeping the room with his usual supercilious glower, but he looked paler than usual. His gaze passed over Sheila with no trace of recognition, leaving the impression that she had been rendered invisible. Todd and Jenny restored her confidence by giving her a cheery wave, but all the chairs at their table were tilted to indicate imminent returns.

"So there you are!"

Sheila turned in relief as Yoshiko took her arm. "Come meet Furutani. We've saved you a place." She towed Sheila through the crowd to a thin man not much taller than Yoshiko herself. He stood with quiet dignity, perfectly at ease in the midst of noise and youth. He looked, Sheila thought, more like a diplomat than a philosopher—but then, she didn't know any philosophers.

"Takashi Furutani," he said with a small bow.

Without thinking she returned the bow and murmured, *"Hajime mashite yoroshiku onega-ishimasu."*

Her embarrassment was relieved by the twinkle in his eyes. "I assume that means hello. My wife has told me much about you. If you agree to speak only English, we will go into a corner and I will promise not to tell what my wife has said about you if you promise not to tell what she has said about me."

"It's a bargain." They shook hands gravely.

"And how do you like Markham?" he asked.

All of a sudden, Sheila realized how tired she was. She felt so weary she wanted to lay her head on his immaculate gray shoulder and bawl. He seemed to sense how she felt, for he reached out and touched her arm gently. "First weeks at work are always hard, but this has certainly not been typical. Markham is generally a very placid place, I assure you." His gaze roamed around the large room, seeking something or someone.

As if conjured by his wish, Yoshiko—who had left them briefly—reappeared with David MacLean. "Now we are all here," she said with satisfaction. "Let's get our seats before someone else does." They obediently followed her, and had barely taken their places when the meal began.

Sheila was surprised that most people seemed to have so much to talk about besides Melanie's murder and Nick's fall. Yoshiko, Takashi, and David flitted from politics to weather to Chicago Bears and Cubs, but Sheila found it hard to concentrate on their conversation. Her eyes searched for Evelyn, while her mind kept returning to the afternoon interviews. At one point her gaze met that of Cal. His eyes bored into hers as if demanding, "What will you do with what you know?" She hoped the smile she gave him was reassuring, not smug.

He turned to the woman on his right and spoke. Her eyes, too, met Sheila's, and Sheila liked what she saw. Lena Williams sat tall—probably as tall as Sheila herself—and was not afraid to increase her height by braiding her thick brown hair into a crown. Her face was clear of makeup, so olive it appeared tanned even in midwinter, with a strong jaw, long straight nose, and wide, humorous mouth. As Sheila watched, she turned to Cal and calmly continued a conversation. She looked like a wife who could handle repentance, and Sheila was so relieved she wanted to shout.

The Williamses sat at the same table with Stan, who was now flanked by Peter and Jim. Peter, Sheila saw, ate with devotion to the task, but Jim and Stan merely shifted food around on their plates. Sheila vowed to invite all three to dinner soon.

As everyone finished eating, Peter stood on a dais beside a grand piano while Jim took a seat beside the slide projector. For the first time since she'd met him, Peter looked relaxed and happy.

"People of Markham," his amplified voice filled the room, "imagine, if you will, the tenth reunion of our senior class. As we walk the hallowed halls and sit in the hollow chairs"—he paused for a titter of appreciation—"what might we hear?" He took a seat at the piano. "First slide, Jim, please."

Peter touched the keys in the opening chords of "Pomp and Circumstance" and on the screen, Nicholas Capeletti beamed at the audience. "Tonight's program," Peter continued, "is dedicated to our own Nick Capeletti, who, I understand, has regained consciousness but cannot have visitors yet."

"Police orders," Yoshiko hissed to Sheila behind one hand. So Mike wasn't as casual about Nick's fall as he had pretended to be!

Meanwhile, up on the stage, the slide had changed to Capeletti and the president, deep in conversation. The business manager's husky voice confided, "None of them are rich yet, sir, but most of them have finally found a job." A ripple of laughter went around the tables. It broke off abruptly as the next picture appeared.

To the opening bars of a malaguena, Mr. Rareby confronted Peter himself beside the library counter. "Lucas," the little professor hissed through his beard, "did you ever return that library book on Latin American counterrevolutions?"

"No," Peter replied, "but I wrote one on counter-*point.*"

With surprise and delight Sheila realized that Peter himself was doing all the voices as well as the accompaniment. Cal asked Quint about doing a summer seminar off the family yacht. Brad, dozing in the coffee room, called for someone to wake him when the reunion was over. Mr. Southard inquired plaintively when someone was going to fix the Pres-Res kitchen faucet broken by Stan ten years before, and Stan himself held aloft a manila envelope and announced, "I have a few forms here to be filled out." The audience groaned.

Next on the screen Yusuf shivered in the cold. "I shall attend no more reunions until Markham moves to a warmer climate," he declared. "Please tell someone with—how do you say, cloud?'' Yusuf himself led the laughter that filled the room.

Finally Peter's own voice came back on the air. ''Well, that's about it, guys. I won't even attempt a Boston accent, Quint, for there are heights one can nevah reach, and I can go no fahthah.'' The room roared. ''But,'' he concluded, ''before we say good night, let us bid welcome to two foreigners among us.''

The music was a clever combination of ''Highland Fling'' and ''Tara's Theme'' from *Gone with the Wind,* and the slide had to have been taken that week. It showed Sheila and David MacLean meeting in the hall.

''When...?'' Sheila began as David's lilt filled the room.

''Och, Yank, I'm telling you, there's no comparison between good porridge and yon grits.''

''Mistah MacLean,'' a feminine drawl exclaimed, ''don't you da-ah call me a Yank!''

The room burst into wild applause while Sheila herself pounded the table in mock fury. ''I don't sound like that!''

David grinned at her. ''Just.''

Cal's speech was excellent, and as Sheila gathered up her coat afterward she marveled at what a little humor and stimulation could do to alleviate horror. Since Peter was surrounded, she went to congratulate Jim instead.

''Good job, Jim! Where did Peter learn impersonations?''

''We worked for a radio station during college.'' His voice was muffled, for he was bent to put away his equipment. ''One of the guys there was a mimic.''

''I guess his musical ear must help,'' she mused, then continued in mock anger, ''but you tell him if he makes fun of my accent again, he'll find out people besides redheads have tempers, too!''

He grinned. "I'll tell him. He'll probably shiver in his boots." She left him with a sense of well-being. In spite of the dreadful things that had happened there, Markham was still a good place to belong.

David waited at the top of the stairs. "It's still lashing snow. Would you like to stay here for a drink?"

She shook her head. "Come back to my place. I left Aunt Mary without a report on the day's events. We can all catch up together. But first I need to see Cal for a minute."

She elbowed her way through the crowd with years of embassy practice, but when she reached Cal he turned abruptly. "Wait," she said, "I need to ask you a question."

"No comment," he said, holding up one hand to shield his face from imaginary photographers.

"But it's important," she insisted. "Evelyn Parsons said—"

"I don't give a damn what Evelyn Parsons said," he snapped. "I've answered all the questions I plan to." Turning to Brad, who had just come up, he muttered audibly, "I hate nosy women."

"You'd better watch out for that one..." was all she heard of Brad's reply before he drew Cal out of earshot.

Frustrated and angry, she pushed her way back to David near the door. "You look as mad as Mary Stuart after talking with John Knox," he greeted her.

"There's a couple of people I'd like to behead," she retorted. "Let's go. But you drive—loving snow the way you do."

"Och, no, quine. I'm not used to your side of the road. Although"—he paused meditatively—"it might be safer at that."

She did not deign to reply, and on the ride home didn't speak until they were almost at her door. Then she asked, "Does it seem to you that Markham is taking this murder awfully lightly?"

"Och, it's nothing to do with most of them, and they are busy with the beginning of term. Besides, they don't know all you do."

She maneuvered into a parking place near her door and sighed. "They may before long, which could be disastrous."

David hurried her through the blizzard and into her lobby before he replied, surprising her by saying, "It may be to the good, you know, all this shifting of mossy stones."

She turned, aghast. "What on earth do you mean?"

He stamped his feet and brushed off his coat. Then he began to light his pipe, and waited until the pungent odor of cherry tobacco filled the lobby before he spoke. "Markham's been hiding a lot of things under rocks lately, which isn't healthy. Things under rocks mold, and send tendrils into other parts of life. But when the rocks are shifted, wait and see. Once the gossip dies, things will assume a proper perspective—some will be forgotten and the rest will be punished and done with. Too many people have a double fantasy—believing on the one hand that no one will ever find them out, and on the other hand persuaded that discovery will end their world. Their imaginings are generally much worse than actual results."

Sheila was still not convinced. "The coward dies a thousand times, the brave man only once?"

He laughed. "And this brave man will die of thirst if you keep him down here sermonizing all night. Where's the famous Southern hospitality I've heard about?" He reached for her hand and pulled her up the stairs after him.

Aunt Mary heard them coming, and held the door open. "Hi!" Sheila called up. "Look what I'm dragging in."

"And who's doing the dragging?" David demanded. Then they both stopped.

Aunt Mary's eyes were dark with worry, her forehead a pucker of concern. Silently she motioned them inside, then as she carefully shut the door behind them, she gave them the news. "Mike called, and Evelyn Parsons is missing. She left home at eight-fifteen this morning and hasn't returned. She didn't go to her office, and no one has seen her all day. Mike fears the worst."

SEVENTEEN

"How is Mrs. Parsons? Should we run up and see her?"

It was typical, Sheila thought, that David's first concern was for a person while her own mind was busy with theories about what might have happened to Evelyn—and why.

Aunt Mary spoke over her shoulder. "Mike said a neighbor is with her, but you might give her a call. I'll put coffee on." She went into the kitchen. David hung up his coat and followed.

Sheila flung her own coat over a chair and prowled the living room, picking up and putting down small objects. Aunt Mary would object to both the coat and the prowling, but for now she didn't care. "Evelyn knew something," she muttered, setting a small china woman back on its shelf. "Why didn't I make her tell me?"

She leaned her head against the windowpane, welcoming its icy press against her forehead, and tried to remember everything she could about her two conversations with Evelyn Parsons. What had Evelyn been holding back? And why—to protect Quint? Or for some devious purpose of her own? "You could have asked her," Sheila's inner voice accused. She winced, and felt tears sting her eyes. David was right. Truth might have freed Evelyn from whatever she faced on this freezing night.

As if her thinking about him had called him, David appeared beside her and lightly touched her shoulder. She turned, hoping he would not see how close she was to tears. But when her eyes met his, the gray ones were so full of concern and understanding that she put her head on his shoulder and wept. "If only I had made her tell me everything!" she sobbed.

He didn't reply, just held her gently. He was so close to her own size that his embrace could have been that of a dear sister except for the hardness of the shoulder beneath her cheek. When she was done, he led her without a word to the couch and handed her his handkerchief, smelling of tweed and sunshine. She sniffed, blew her nose, and gave him a weepy smile. "Thanks."

He sat down across from her and spent some moments filling and lighting his pipe until the pungence of cherry tobacco filled the space between them.

"Did you get Mrs. Parsons?" she asked with one final sniff.

He nodded. "She's pretty fair cut up. I think I'll run up and see her later if you don't mind."

"There's still no word at all?"

He shook his head. "But, Sheila, you are not to blame yourself. Having secrets was Evelyn's way of getting attention."

"But if I had only insisted!"

"She'd have told you if she wanted to," he said firmly.

She smiled across the coffee table at him. "Thanks, David. I don't know if it's true, but it helps."

Aunt Mary entered as if on cue, bearing a tray. "I decided on hot chocolate," she announced, "with some of David's shortbread." Her gaze strayed to Sheila's coat over the chair.

Sheila stood. "I think I'd better hang up my coat," she murmured to David, "before *somebody* mentions it."

When they had finished their chocolate, David rose. Sheila saw him to the door and handed him her extra keys.

"Keep the car until tomorrow—I won't need it," she assured him.

Aunt Mary had already settled more deeply into the cushions and tucked her feet daintily beneath her. "Now you tell me about your day," she commanded, "and I'll tell you about mine."

Sheila described the afternoon's interviews with Brad, Cal, and Quint. "I thought those matchbooks would turn up something," Aunt Mary said with satisfaction. "As I said before, things are seldom as simple as they seem."

"Meaning?"

"His affair with the young woman. It seemed so private at first. Now he finds it has sent out ripples that are splashing a good marriage and a promising career. Not to mention the good opinion of his students."

"Oh, I don't think his students will be shocked," Sheila told her. "Surprised, maybe, and disappointed. But they are a compassionate lot. I don't think they'll condemn him."

"No, dear," Aunt Mary said shrewdly, "but they'll never trust him again. That could be even worse."

A silence fell between them. The fragrance of David's pipe lingered, which both comforted Sheila and reminded her of his errand. She sighed. "Evelyn must have known something. Could she have gone into hiding on her own?"

Aunt Mary set her cup and saucer onto the coffee table with a firm click. "We can do nothing about Evelyn Parsons tonight, dear, except pray. I suggest we look at what I have. Charlie sent a man around this afternoon." From between the sofa cushion and its plump arm she drew forth a brown manila envelope.

Sheila drew out several sheets of paper. "Melanie Forbes' bank statement for December!"

Aunt Mary nodded. "Dear Charlie," she said softly with a faraway look in her eyes.

"I hope dear Charlie gets a cell next to your own," Sheila retorted, turning her attention to the pages she held.

They were photostats of bank statements dated December and January, and of all checks written during those months. Her eyes sought the bottom line of the statement. "Over two thousand dollars left at the end of the month, as Mike said."

Aunt Mary was not impressed. "Look where she started December, dear."

Sheila's eyes slid up the page. "Over twenty thousand! She was doing some heavy spending that month."

She thumbed through the copies of checks. They were arranged according to the date they had been received at the bank, and until number 718 had been received in jumbled order, according to when various charge companies and merchants turned them in. Numbers 719 to 725, however, were in exact order. Each had been made out to Melanie herself and endorsed with the words "For Deposit Only." Each had been deposited by mail to a local savings and loan.

"Why?" Sheila wondered aloud. "Why transfer thousands of dollars to another bank paying the same rate of interest? And why do it in seven checks over three weeks instead of all at once?" She examined the checks again. "The first one was written on December twentieth, and the last one on January—" She broke off and her eyes met her aunt's. "All of these were written after Melanie Forbes was dead."

Aunt Mary nodded, her wrinkled face expressionless.

Sheila examined the photostats carefully. "Excellent forgeries." A memory stirred. She rose to get her purse. Then she handed her aunt the scrap of paper she had found at noon. "Just touch the edges, and tell me what you make of this."

Aunt Mary looked at the paper, then picked up one of the check photostats and compared the signatures. "Someone was practicing. Where did you get this?"

Sheila sighed. "I wish I knew. You know how I am—a scrap of paper here, a scrap there."

"Which you always plan to toss and seldom do," her aunt agreed wryly. "I remember, dear. Well, hang on to this and show it to Mike. Maybe his labs can make something of it." She turned back to the papers she held.

"I meant to do it today, and forgot." Sheila picked up the statement again. "This was a strangely cautious forger. Look—the first check is only for twenty-five dollars."

"Testing the waters," Aunt Mary nodded.

"But after that first check, there's none for eight days. Wonder why?"

Aunt Mary coughed delicately. Sheila glanced her way and saw she was tracing the plaid of her skirt with one finger. "I think it was to let that check clear. I called the bank this afternoon, and they don't clear a local check for seven days."

Sheila gave her a look of approval. "Good work. So not until after the first one cleared did he—or she—milk the account for two more weeks. But why stop then, with two thousand dollars left?"

She waited. Aunt Mary would have all the answers, she was sure. But they would have to be extracted like wisdom teeth. Aunt Mary tapped pearly nails in her lap. "Well, number 725 would have been the last check in that book."

"Sure, but why not write the last one for all that was in the account? Melanie must have had stubs or a ledger."

Aunt Mary nodded. "I can see the wisdom in not closing out the account and raising curiosity too soon. But such restraint . . ." She shook her head, baffled.

"That brings up another question," Sheila said. "How could anyone get at money deposited at a second bank in her name?"

"A joint account." Aunt Mary replied so promptly that Sheila knew she had been waiting for this question. "I did a bit of sleuthing myself this afternoon, dear. I called the bank a second time, gave my name as Melanie Forbes, and told a distressing story of losing my passbook and needing to know how much I had in my account. I had to tell a few untruths, unfortunately, but eventually I got what I was looking for."

Sheila was duly impressed. Chicago bank personnel were direct descendants of the clan, so Aunt Mary's charm was greater than she had supposed. But she schooled her voice to rebuke. "Shocking!"

Aunt Mary's eyes were demurely on her lap. "Was I indiscreet?"

Sheila leaned over and gave her a hug. "I think you were magnificent, if you want the truth. But you may be hauled into court for impersonating a dead woman—or murdering her."

Aunt Mary was unperturbed. "Oh, I don't think Mike would let it go that far. And if he did, I'm sure Wyndham—"

"Tell me what you discovered," Sheila hastily interposed.

"Well, the nice lady at the bank told me that the account was closed on January thirteenth. That would have been the day after the last check cleared."

"Closed out by whom?"

Aunt Mary paused. "Rex Stendhal."

"Rex Stendhal?" Sheila asked, bewildered. "Who's he?"

Aunt Mary gave a very genteel shrug. "I don't know, dear. And as Melanie Forbes, I couldn't very well ask. The lady was most concerned, but said that it was a joint account, he had the privilege of closing it without my signature. They assumed I had been notified by the closing party."

"What did you say then?" Sheila asked.

"I gave a gasp of distress and said quickly, 'Oh, that nephew of mine!' Then I hung up."

"Leaving her to think the worst?"

Aunt Mary's brown eyes twinkled with mischief. "I probably made her day. And I don't think they will investigate further unless Melanie herself presses charges—which is highly unlikely, don't you think?"

Sheila shook her head. "How you have eluded the law thus far is the biggest mystery of all. But you got what we needed."

"Except how this Stendhal managed to open an account for Melanie when she was dead."

"That's one I can answer from my experience as an old married lady. Tyler twice opened joint accounts for us without my ever entering the bank. He established his identification, then brought the card home for me to sign and mail back.

"So Stendhal, whoever he is, could have opened an account, taken a card home, signed Melanie's name to it, and mailed it back without anyone at the bank knowing whether Melanie was alive or not?" Aunt Mary was clearly impressed. "Then the signatures wouldn't really be forgeries, would they? At least not at that bank."

"Don't sound so admiring," Sheila retorted. "We are, after all, dealing with a murderer. And we finally have a motive."

"But such restraint," Aunt Mary mused. "I still don't understand that."

They sat in silence for a while, each lost in her thoughts. Finally Aunt Mary spoke again. "But who *is* Rex Stendhal?"

Sheila shook her head. "I have no idea. Maybe Melanie's dad's accountant—he already had fingers in her financial pie."

Aunt Mary didn't reply. Carefully she replaced the photostats in their envelope and laid it on the coffee table. Sheila stood up to take the dishes to the sink. "Well, at least this widens the field beyond Cal, Quint, and Brad."

She could hear Aunt Mary's sigh from the kitchen. "I was afraid you'd think like that, dear. But any of them could be Stendhal. If he forged one name, why not two?"

"But he'd have had to present identification at the bank," Sheila objected.

"True. You don't recognize the name as another student?"

Sheila came to the door and shook her head. "He's not in the directory and he doesn't have a mailbox. But I won't sleep until I know if this is a Markham name." She glanced at her watch. "It's just past ten-thirty. I'm going to call Yoshiko."

When she returned five minutes later, her aunt's look of sympathy told her her face reflected the frustration she felt. "Good news and bad news. The good news is that Yoshiko just talked with Annette Capeletti, and Nick's on the mend. Still no visitors, though—Mike's taking no chances until Nick can be interviewed. The bad news—I guess—is that Rex Stendhal graduated from Markham last year. He was a shy young man who roomed in Pres-Res last year with—are you ready for this?—Quint Barringer. Why would someone with Quint's money live in such a desolate place?'' she wailed, as if his changing that fact would have altered all subsequent events.

"One reason people have money is that they don't spend it on things they don't need,'' Aunt Mary replied primly. "Where is this young man now?''

Sheila sighed. "In Africa, working for CARE. He's been there,'' she added, "since September.''

"Oh.'' Aunt Mary seemed at a dead end.

Sheila added her last bit of information. "Yoshiko said one thing more. Last spring Stendhal lost his wallet. It later turned up in the coffee room, but all his identification was gone.''

Aunt Mary shot her a shrewd look from beneath silver brows. "That's important, dear. Now we know for certain that whoever we are seeking is at Markham.''

EIGHTEEN

THE STORM BLEW OUT during the night, and Sheila decided to walk over to Markham to check Rex Stendhal's records and complete some work she'd left unfinished to sit in on the interviews. "I don't like the idea of your being there alone," Aunt Mary worried over her second cup of creamy coffee.

"I won't be alone. Jenny will be there to open the library, and Yoshiko often works on Saturdays, too."

But as she trudged through unshoveled paths, bent low against the constant wind off Lake Michigan, she almost changed her mind. Because it was Saturday and very cold, the entire university was deserted. Faculty members were stretching in their suburban beds and thanking the good Lord they didn't have to travel to Hyde Park. Secretaries were starting the laundry and housecleaning they had piled up all week. Students were burrowing deeper into their covers after a late Friday night. The only people abroad were a few librarians, stifling yawns and calling down curses on the heads of those who insist that academic libraries open early on Saturdays—then never show up until noon to use them.

Markham loomed gray and empty above the blanket of fresh snow. It turned back the morning sun at its small leaded panes, maintaining a strict privacy that excluded even light. Once, when this empty, it had admitted a murderer, and as Sheila put her key in the lock and shoved against the heavy front door, Aunt Mary's words flowed out to greet her: "Now we know for certain that whoever we are seeking is at Markham."

She could not repress a shudder. Then she gave herself a mental shake. "The library will open at nine," she reminded herself, opening her own office and adjusting the blinds to permit the sun to stream across the powder-blue carpet. Once again she blessed Eleanor Quincy's excellent taste. Lovely surroundings made danger seem so remote. She opened the thermos she had brought and poured a steaming cup of coffee, breathing deeply of its pungent, beloved aroma. But she didn't feel quite brave enough, she decided, to walk the length of the hall to hang up her coat. It would do fine folded on top of the filing cabinet.

Nick's records gave her no information on Rex Stendhal she didn't already know. With a sigh, she turned to unfinished tasks and worked steadily all morning. Todd and Jenny hurried in at quarter past nine, breathless, to open the library. Students began to trickle in about half past ten. At noon, with a huge stretch, she declared the day's work done, and reached to clear her desk.

A voice asked at her door, "Have you moved in? Or did they forget to tell you Saturday is a day off?"

She looked up to meet the lopsided smile of Quint Barringer. His eyes twinkled gently behind their glasses.

"Hi, Quint. Another five minutes and I'd have been half-way across the quadrangle."

"And I'd have missed my chance to offer you a ride. Helga's outside. Can we give you a lift?"

"Helga?"

He gestured to her window and she saw a red Volvo parked at the curb. "Otherwise known as my flaming chariot."

"I see." She shot him a suspicious look. "Does that refer to the way you drive?"

"You'll have to ride to see. Feeling brave?"

She nodded. "Let me close up here." He draped his lanky form over her door to wait. In down parka and jeans, he looked more like a student today.

Her filing cabinet was near the window, and as she got her coat her angle of vision permitted her to see the alley across the street. Three police cars now blocked the alley entrance, and a crowd was beginning to gather. "What's going on?" she wondered aloud. Quint came in to stand behind her.

"I don't know," he said, "but I'll find out while you're getting ready." Soon his form was added to the crowd at the mouth of the alley. Sheila was not surprised to see Mike's tawny head towering above the rest. But, glancing up, she *was* surprised to see, in a second-story window of Pres-Res, the face of Stan Frieze. He was as white as the snow in the small yard below.

Quint met her on the sidewalk, looking grave. "Nobody knows what's going on. Rumor is that a purse was snatched, but the police have the area sealed off tight."

Sheila felt cold all over. Had murder come to Markham again? If so, she was horribly afraid she knew whom it had visited.

Quint seemed to sense her unease. "I'm afraid this happens more in Chicago than places like Tokyo, Sheila. You don't exactly get used to it, but you learn to live with it." He ushered her to the car and opened the door. "Where to?"

She directed him, then—mostly to take her mind off the Pres-Res dumpster—she said, "Volvos seem popular at Markham. I rode in Stan's earlier this week."

He patted his dashboard with one slim hand. "Helga's the elder. Stan drove her a few times, and fell in love."

"I would have guessed," Sheila nodded. "His still smells newborn."

"While poor Helga smells of Polish sausage and sweaty gym shoes." He sighed in mock sorrow.

After a brief silence, she turned to him. "Quint, I don't know you well, and this will seem impertinent, but I really need to know. Why did you get involved so deeply with Melanie Forbes? She sounds like a girl you'd never date more than once or twice."

He hesitated, then answered frankly, choosing each word with care. "Mel was funny. Unlike most people, she displayed her least attractive side most of the time—she'd be cruel, even ruthless to people she genuinely liked. Yet she could also be gentle, and very, very vulnerable. When I saw that side, I guess I thought I could help her show it to the world." He shook his head. "It didn't work that way. Melanie liked who she was, the friends she had. She didn't get much pleasure out of them, but she didn't want to give them up, either. It just took me a while to realize that, and that we wanted very different things out of life."

"Did she see it your way?"

"Eventually. Whenever we met this fall, she was very cool."

Sheila remembered herself at nineteen, deliberately cool in order to make herself more appealing to Tyler Travis, who was then twenty-four, and said nothing. She felt no responsibility at this point to enlighten Quint Barringer concerning the ways of women in love. Instead she pointed. "That's my building." Her car was parked near the curb.

He pulled up at the curb with a flourish. "You are home, modom," he intoned.

"Many thanks, Jeeves." She reached for her purse. It caught under the seat as it had in Stan's car. "Volvos definitely have a taste for purses!'' She fumbled to retrieve its contents.

"Oh, Helga, how could you do that to another lady?" Quint smacked the dashboard. "Did you get everything?" he asked Sheila.

"Everything but my lipstick. It's too far under the seat." Climbing out, she crouched in the gutter to reach far under the seat. "Here it is. And what's this?" Her fingers had encountered something hard and cold. "Yours?" she asked wryly.

Quint looked at her palm and shook his head. "No," he replied in a tone of mystification.

It was an earring made of turquoise and silver. Although reminiscent of Indian design, it was large and gaudy. Sheila started to hand it to Quint, but he held up one hand in refusal. "Keep it. If I find its mate, I'll let you have them."

She shook her head. "I don't want them. Not only is it for pierced ears, which I don't have, but it's..." She paused, reluctant to express her opinion aloud.

"...big enough for a Volvo." Quint grinned. "Maybe a gift from one of Helga's admirers. Will you take it in and toss it to spare her reputation, not to mention mine?" He waved farewell.

She carried the earring upstairs, dropped it on the hall table with her gloves, and promptly forgot it.

After lunch the doorbell rang. Mike stood there, looking grim. He spoke as soon as the door had closed behind them. "We found Evelyn Parsons. Got a tip from an anonymous caller this morning. She was in the dumpster behind Markham's old president's house."

Sheila's stomach cramped with horror. "Oh, no, Mike! How was she killed?"

"Strangled—probably with a scarf, although we didn't find it. I think it's the same guy, but there's no way to prove it."

"Come on in. You look like you could use a cup of coffee, and I don't feel so good myself."

His face was reddened by the cold and his blue eyes were bleak. He nodded. "One cup. Then I'm off to headquarters."

"Has Mrs. Parsons been notified?"

"A squad car is on its way to her now."

Sheila took his coat and went to the closet.

Behind her back, Mike spoke casually, but with an undercurrent of something she couldn't define. "Where'd you get the earring?"

She replied over her shoulder. "Oh, it was under the seat of Quint's Volvo this morning. We were making dumb jokes about it . . ."

Her voice trailed off. She had turned, and now she saw Mike's face. He was staring at the earring as a man stranded on a desert island might gaze at an approaching boat. "Sheila," he said in a tone of jubilation, "I think you have just solved us a case."

He picked up the earring and examined the back of the loop. One huge finger pointed. "See that dark stain there? Blood, from where it was pulled from Melanie Forbes' ear. She was wearing its mate." He reached over and pulled her to him in a bear hug. "You're terrific. This is the final evidence we need to arrest Quint Barringer for the murder of Melanie Forbes!"

Sheila pulled away and stumbled several steps across the hall. Her ears were pounding, and she felt hot and furious all over. "But he was in Boston!"

He shook his head. "I called Boston. Quint didn't go home until Monday morning. His folks think he was in

Chicago until then.'' He pocketed the earring and headed for the kitchen. ''If you don't mind, I'll just use your phone.''

BY THE TIME Mike had finished his call, Aunt Mary had produced a pot of coffee and Sheila had prowled the living room twice. As he appeared, she whirled to face him. ''You look so smug!''

He bent to pick up the cup Aunt Mary had poured him. ''I've done my job. That feels good in a case like this.'' He flopped into his chair and breathed out a deep sigh.

Sheila came from the window to the coffee table, but waved away a cup of coffee. The very aroma was making her sick. ''What now?'' she asked.

''We take Quint in for questioning, then wrap it up for the state's attorney. If he thinks it's enough, we take it to trial.''

''Do you continue to investigate other suspects at the same time?''

He gave her an expression of disbelief mixed with frustration. ''What other suspects, Sheila? Face it. It's looked bad for Barringer since the beginning. The only reason for looking elsewhere was his alibi. Now that that has been shaken, and you've found the earring actually in his car...'' He stopped and spread his hands wide.

''What if I refuse to say I found it there?''

''You'll be subpoenaed.''

Sheila decided she needed a cup of coffee after all. Suddenly she felt very, very cold. ''So your investigation is closed until Quint is proven innocent?''

Mike snorted. ''Unless, not until.''

''How long will that take?''

He sighed. "With his money," he said bitterly, "it could take years just to *get* to trial. One thing that makes lawyers expensive is their ability to delay."

"And in the meantime?" She flopped onto the couch.

"His daddy will have come up with some hefty bail money and he'll be free to walk the streets—even commit another murder. Not until after the trial will he be beyond reach of Daddy's money." Again his voice was bitter, and his eyes were hard as they stared into the cup he held.

Aunt Mary's husky voice was barely curious. "Do you dislike him for his money, Mike, or for some other reason?"

He gave her a rueful grin. "Actually I don't dislike Quint at all, Miss Mary. He's a very pleasant guy. What I dislike is the system. In my business you see guys with bucks walk out the door while those without money—or friends with money—sweat behind bars awaiting trial. I think it should be the same for everybody."

Sheila's mind was still elsewhere. "But what if Quint *didn't* murder Melanie, Mike? He'll miss out on his last year of Markham and some very good job opportunities, maybe carry a stigma for the rest of his life. And your trail will be cold."

Mike set his saucer on the coffee table with a clunk. "Take it from me, Sheila"—he wiped his mouth with the back of his hand—"he did it. He killed both of them, Melanie first, then Evelyn because she could identify him. Everything points to it."

She made one last attempt to change his mind. "Not quite everything, Mike. Quint brought me home from Markham this morning. Before we left I asked him to see what was going on across the street. He didn't flinch. Don't you think if he'd killed Evelyn, I'd have noticed something odd in his behavior?"

He hauled himself to his feet with a sigh of exasperation. "I don't know what you might or might not notice, Sheila, especially where this Barringer is concerned. But most criminals like to return to the scene of their crimes. You probably gave him the reason to do what he wanted to anyway." He leaned over to take Aunt Mary's hand. "Good-bye, Miss Mary. Thanks for the coffee. Excellent as always."

She gave his huge hand a squeeze. "Come back, Mike. Hear?"

He cast a meaningful glance toward Sheila. "I'm not sure your niece will let me." He started for the door. "So long, Sheila."

She pulled herself to her feet and padded in stockinged feet to let him out. "Mike?" she pleaded for the last time.

He shook his head. "He did it."

She looked at him gravely, then opened the door. "Be seeing you, Mike." She didn't realize until he'd gone that she had used the Markham farewell. She was glad. Never had she felt such a part of Markham.

WHEN HIS HEAVY TREAD reached the ground floor she returned to the living room, her fingers clenched into fists. Aunt Mary looked at her in rebuke. "Put your face in order, Sheila. You look mad enough to swing a bobcat by the tail."

Sheila laughed shortly. "Your description fits your friend."

She swept through the living room and into the kitchen. Perhaps she could warn Quint. Quickly she dialed the number she found in Markham's directory.

On the second ring a girl's voice answered. "Hello."

"Quint Barringer, please."

"I'm sorry, but Quint's gone out for a few minutes. Could he call you back?" Her voice was low and musical.

Sheila thought furiously. "Who is this, please?"

The girl hesitated. "Carla. I'm a friend. If you will leave your number, I'll have Quint call you." As she spoke, Sheila could hear Quint's doorbell ring. Mike already? It was only two blocks, and he had called someone to meet him with a warrant.

"The doorbell . . ." The girl was about to leave.

"Wait. If that's Quint, tell him to come immediately to Sheila's. Don't call, just come! But if it's the police—" She'd intended to tell the girl to come. But as soon as she had said "police," the girl on the other end gave a faint cry and hung up.

Sick with worry, Sheila returned to the living room. "Do you think that call was wise, dear?" Aunt Mary chided with a slight frown. "Mike would be furious."

"Good." Sheila poured herself another cup of coffee and took a deep gulp of the burning liquid. "That would make two of us."

"Don't be too hard on Mike," her aunt said gently. "He's just doing his job the way he thinks it should be done. Besides, whoever killed Evelyn Parsons would not hesitate to frame and kill Quint, too. Having Quint in jail will both keep Mike busy, and Quint out of danger while we work on the other possibilities."

Sheila's slight knowledge of the Cook County Jail made her think "out of danger" might be a euphemism, but it was her aunt's last statement that she answered. "What other possibilities?" She flopped onto the couch.

Aunt Mary held out a pad. "I jotted down a few names while you were on the phone."

"Cal Williams," Sheila read. "He's a possibility for Melanie, yes. But I can't imagine him stuffing Evelyn into a dumpster." Her memory prodded her: Cal turning away, saying angrily, "I don't give a damn what Evelyn Parsons said." Had he cared too much?

"He's certainly a front runner," she admitted. "And with his Latin American background, Melanie's drug connections would feed newspaper stories for days, if not weeks."

"Yes, and I think you should see this, dear."

Sheila took the piece of paper her aunt held out, read it, and looked up with a question in her eyes. Aunt Mary spoke with dignity. "I cannot tell you where I got that, Sheila, but I assure you it comes from a highly reliable source. Calvin Williams is being considered as a candidate for Vice President in the next election."

"And this could ruin him."

Aunt Mary nodded. "Easily. If Melanie threatened to expose him . . ."

Their eyes met gravely. "Why, then," Sheila asked, "didn't you tell this to Mike?"

Aunt Mary's eyes twinkled. "Because, Lord love him, Mike's got a bee in his bonnet. It's buzzing too loud for him to listen."

Sheila nodded. "This certainly gives someone besides Quint a motive. Do you have one for Brad?"

"Of course, dear. Melanie might have discovered he was doing police work, and threatened to expose *him*."

Sheila sighed. "But I can't imagine Brad getting het up enough to do murder. He's as unlikely to stir himself as someone else I know and love."

Either Aunt Mary had not heard the remark or she was ignoring it. "Peter Lucas, you say, seems unbalanced. Has he a motive?"

"He was playing in a club that night," Sheila reminded her.

Aunt Mary shook her head. "We haven't established a time of death. He could have come home with Jim, waited until everything was dark, and met the girl in Markham."

"But she was planning to go out as soon as Evelyn left," Sheila objected. Before Aunt Mary could reply, she answered her own objection. "He could have met her at Markham earlier, killed her, and gone with Jim. Then he could have moved her body when the playing gig was done."

Aunt Mary nodded. "He could have. But do you think he would have killed her at the institute?"

"Not likely," Sheila agreed.

"And the same goes for Jim?"

Sheila nodded. "Plus he's the only person I've met so far who has a kind word to say for Melanie Forbes."

"I have also listed Stan Frieze."

Sheila leaned forward and refilled her cup. "Now there's a student I would like to put on the top of the list—simply because he's so awful. This morning when the police were in the alley behind his house, I saw him at an upstairs window watching their every move. Too good to mingle with the crowd below, but not about to be left out of knowing what's going on."

Aunt Mary bit the tip of one finger. "You don't suppose he already knew what was going on, do you?"

Sheila drew her brows together. "Do you suppose?" She considered for a moment. "If Melanie was killed yesterday, that could explain his sudden illness, and lack of appetite last night. But Stan seems to have known Melanie less than any of the others, and he has almost as much respect for Markham as the Lucases. No, if any of them did murder, they'd do it somewhere else." She reached for the list and scanned it. "The only people you haven't listed who were in town that weekend are Todd Walte, who had flu, and Yusuf Jaffari. And I don't think he did it.''

"No," her aunt surprised her again, "they were at a party."

"How do *you* know?" Sheila nearly choked on her coffee.

"I spent an hour yesterday afternoon with his wife," Aunt Mary said placidly. "You said they had a new baby and her husband was working on a paper, so I thought she might be lonely. I called and asked her over for tea."

"How'd you get her number?" Sheila asked, as much astonished by Aunt Mary's burst of energy as by anything else.

"It was in the Markham directory." Aunt Mary smoothed her skirt complacently. "I asked her to bring the baby to see me, and she was delighted. When I happened to bring the conversation around to the weekend before Christmas" (Sheila hid her smile in her coffee) "I believe Fatima said they attended a party that evening. Of course," Aunt Mary added somewhat apologetically, "I might have misunderstood. We were speaking Arabic at the time."

Sheila snorted. "*We* were speaking Arabic, Aunt Mary?"

"Yes, dear." Aunt Mary's voice was totally matter-of-fact. "When I was a girl I spent two years in Saudi Arabia with Cousin Louise. Her husband was in oil, you remember. She insisted I study the language. It's just as well that I did, for today I have—well, let's just say that from time to time I need it in the way of business. My Arabic is far from excellent, but I did understand Fatima to say that she and Yusuf were at a party on the Friday night in question."

Sheila scarcely heard her. She was still trying to picture her dainty aunt bartering with sheikhs in flowing robes. "Is there anything you haven't done?" she asked fondly.

Aunt Mary's brown eyes got a faraway look. "I never learned to fly," she murmured, "but I've often thought I'd like to try."

Sheila reached over and gave her thin shoulders a hug. "If you did, you'd probably wind up owning the airline."

Aunt Mary, engrossed again in her list, only murmured, "How exhausting that sounds." She didn't wait for a response. "I did not include Mr. Capeletti or Dr. Dehaviland on my list. Do you think they should be there?"

Sheila nodded. "Dehaviland, of course. The more the merrier."

As Aunt Mary reached for her pencil, the phone rang. Sheila unfolded herself from the couch to answer it. Mike's voice was gruff. "We just arrested Barringer, Sheila, and charged him with the murder of Melanie Forbes. We aren't adding Evelyn Parsons just yet." He paused, as if hoping she'd commend his restraint. Doomed to be disappointed, he continued in a somewhat truculent tone, "I shouldn't be calling, but I thought you'd want to know."

"What does Quint say?"

She could almost see him shaking his tawny curls as he growled, "Denies it, of course. But he refuses to account for where he was that weekend. Admits he didn't go home, but won't say where he did go. We've got something else, too. In January Barringer deposited several thousand dollars into a bank account—almost as much as was taken from Melanie Forbes' account and deposited into an account under the name of—are you ready for this?—Barringer's old Markham roommate."

Sheila thought she'd better play dumb. "Maybe the roommate did the murder."

"Not unless he flew in from Africa to do it. He's in an area that takes three days to get in and three days to get out. And he was there on Sunday the weekend she died."

"What does Quint say about the money?"

His scorn was heavy on the wire. "Claims it was a dividend. Some dividend, huh?"

She strove to keep her voice patient. "He's rich, Mike."

"Yeah, and he's also guilty as hell. Look, Sheila, you want to help your friend? You get him to tell us where he was that weekend—and he'd better have a witness or two. Barringer can have visitors every Monday. Division Two, Cook County Jail. He'll be there awhile—bail's been denied. You get down there Monday anytime before two forty-five. See if *you* can get him to talk. Otherwise he's as good as shut away for years."

She was about to hang up, when he added, "Oh, there's something else you could do well. Mr. Capeletti is out of the woods, but the docs say don't excite him. I think he'd talk with you better than me. Can you get over to University Hospital tomorrow afternoon? Today he's still a little dopey."

Sheila sighed. "Sure, Mike. Just anything you say. Looks like somebody's got to solve this case before you blow it." She hung up before he could reply.

NINETEEN

SUNDAY WAS a very long day.

Sheila had been planning to attend a small community church, but Aunt Mary insisted she accompany her to Fourth Presbyterian downtown. "Of course we can worship anywhere, dear," she explained as she adjusted her furs, "but I worship so much more *thoroughly* among Presbyterians." Sheila spent the service in fervent petitions for Quint Barringer.

After lunch, she read the paper while Aunt Mary napped. Passing over clashes between Chicago's mayor and city council, and skirting the current debates over military buildup, she scanned page after page for a report of a young woman's body found in a dumpster and the story of a wealthy young student arrested for another murder. She found nothing about the latter. Yet surely the arrest of a Markham student was of national interest to the press. Who had muzzled reporters—Mike? Quint's dad? Dehaviland?

(When the police had told him Saturday afternoon about Evelyn's death and Quint's arrest, he had called Sheila with a long list of instructions for Monday, adding that he would need to be out of the office all day.)

Far into the second section she found a paragraph about Evelyn Parsons. Her name was misspelled, and it said she had been found in an alley in Hyde Park. It mentioned her mother and a brother serving in Germany. That was all. Evelyn died as she had lived, Sheila thought sadly, making scarcely a ripple in the stream of life.

Her thoughts kept returning to Quint. Was he comfortable? Was he even safe? Was he having to share a cell with one of the gang toughs who made up such a large segment of Chicago's jail population? What were his thoughts on this long, long day?

She also wondered about the girl, Carla. She'd tried to call Quint's apartment all Saturday afternoon, hoping to reach Carla, but no one answered. Now she wondered if perhaps someone else might have her number. On a hunch she dialed Pres-Res.

Peter was at the Laundromat, Jim informed her, and he himself didn't know anything about Quint's current women friends.

"Have Peter call me," she told him. "I'm going to see Nick, but my aunt will be here and can take a message."

"Stan said Nick can't have visitors," Jim informed her.

"I know, but the police are making an exception for me this afternoon," she told him.

"Police?"

Sheila could have kicked herself. "I meant doctors, Jim. I must have police on the brain. Just have Peter call if he knows anything about Carla, will you?" She hung up quickly before he could ask anything else.

Next she tried Todd. Brad answered and drawled that he didn't know any Carlas, and Todd was at the Co-op Grocery with Jenny. Sheila gave Brad the same message she'd left with Jim and dialed Cal's number. She left a message on his machine.

"Strike three and I'm out," she told Aunt Mary, shrugging on her coat. "If anybody calls, ask if they know Quint's friend Carla and how to reach her. I'll be back in a couple of hours."

Before she could get out the door, however, the phone rang. The voice on the other end was none of those she'd expected, but that of David McLean. "You've been on the phone awhile."

"Without much success," she told him. "I'm trying to locate a girlfriend of Quint's. You don't happen to know someone named Carla, do you?"

"No," he dragged out the word, "I don't think I do." She was about to ask about Mrs. Parsons, but he spoke first. "Have you heard how Nick is doing?"

"I'm just on my way there now. The police think maybe he can tell me who pushed him—and I think it may have some connection with the murders. Oh, thanks for bringing back my car."

"Nae problem. I was just wondering if you'd meet me for a wee walk over by the lake. It's lovely there just now. Could you come before you visit Nick? It's a fine, brisk day."

She considered. "Maybe a short one. Shall I pick you up?"

"Och, no. I'll meet you on the beach nearest the Museum of Science and Industry. Think you can find it?"

David wasn't there when she arrived, and as she peered up and down the frozen lakefront, she wondered if this had been such a good idea. The wind swept across her as if she weren't there, chilling her through warm slacks and heavy coat. Few people were in sight—three intrepid joggers and a man throwing a stick to a dog. She recognized the dog before the man, and gave Yusuf a loud "halloo." He ran toward her bench, waved and shouted, then threw another stick a distance down the beach. Wolf bounded across the snow to fetch it. Pulling her coat tightly around her and burrowing her chin into her scarf, she settled onto the bench to wait.

She heard nothing, but suddenly the two ends of her scarf were grabbed and pulled tightly. Thinking David was playing a prank, she tried to turn. Her vision was going black. Frantically she clawed at the scarf.

She heard a sharp bark, a growl, and as suddenly as the scarf had tightened, it went slack. Her purse was roughly jerked from her shoulder, but she scarcely noticed. She clutched her throat and drew deep ragged breaths. Yusuf pounded up to her bench.

"Stay!" he yelled to Wolf. The shepherd was close to his prey, and his barks had already caused the man to drop the purse in terror. Obediently, Wolf stopped, picked the purse up in his mouth, and trotted back to his master.

"Are you all right?" Yusuf's dark eyes were full of concern.

. She took an unsteady breath. Swallowing was hard, but not impossible. "I think so. Did you get a good look at him?"

He shook his head. "No, Wolf was the one who saw him, and came to your rescue." He handed her the purse and ruffled the big dog's coat with affection. "He seems to like you."

"I like him, too." Sheila reached a tentative hand to pat the animal's back. "Why didn't you let him catch the man?"

"Many men carry guns." She couldn't argue with that, but wondered why a man with a gun would come close enough to strangle her.

"You didn't recognize him at all?" she persisted.

Again Yusuf shook his head. "He wore a ski mask and a hat."

Sheila stood a little shakily. "I think I've been here long enough. If you see David MacLean, tell him I've gone to the hospital to see Nick. Tell him to call me later."

Yusuf took her elbow. "Are you certain you should drive?"

She shook her head. "No, but I don't feel like facing my aunt, either, right now."

Yusuf's teeth flashed in his devastating smile. "At least you will be *walking* into the hospital, thanks to Wolf."

Somehow Sheila didn't feel like smiling back.

YUSUF INSISTED ON accompanying her to her car, for which she was grateful. Her knees were shaking and her legs felt like noodles. When he'd gone, she collapsed into the seat and let tears of rage and fear pour down her cheeks. Should she call Mike? What could he do? The man, whoever he was, was long gone by now. She had her purse back, and besides—she couldn't endure a lecture about sitting on park benches alone.

That was exactly the thought she needed. She blew her nose, started the car, and turned resolutely toward the hospital.

But one question hung just before her all the way, no matter how intently she tried to banish it. As she turned off the engine, she pounded the wheel in frustration. "It just couldn't have been David!" Why, then, deep inside her, did she fear it could?

Nick was pink and chipper in green-striped pajamas. "Good to see a familiar face beside Annette's," he greeted her huskily. "But you're looking peaky. You coming down with something?"

"Just worn out from doing your work as well as my own." She perched on a chair beside him so their faces were level. After inquiring after his health ("I've felt better—you don't have a cigarette, do you?") and reporting on the Community Dinner, she broached the subject of his fall.

"I didn't hear a thing," he insisted. "I was working on our taxes—getting ready for the auditors—and I'd spread them out in the conference room because it would be free for a couple of days. About nine I decided to knock off and go home, so I switched off the light and started down the stairs. That's all I remember.''

''Could someone have followed you—someone who came out of the stacks on the third floor?''

He started to shake his head, then checked himself. ''Do you know, I do remember hearing something—a door closing, I thought. I stopped to listen, turned, and went back a couple of steps, but I didn't hear anything else. I'd started down again when...''

''...somebody hit you on the head,'' she finished. ''I'm sure of it, Mr. Capeletti. But you don't have any idea who?''

He shook his head, and his husky voice was full of regret. ''None at all. Who would do such a thing?''

''Somebody who didn't want to be seen.'' She stood and gave him a smile. ''Well, you take care of yourself and rest up. We're all piling up the work for you to come home to.''

He gave a hoarse chuckle. ''Just as I expected. Thanks for coming, Sheila.''

As she returned to her car, she had one satisfying thought. David MacLean couldn't have pushed Nick. He'd been with her. But though she stayed near the phone all the rest of the day, he did not call.

Mike called about nine for a report on her visit with Capeletti, but he was so abrupt that she was distant and didn't say anything about the attempt on her own life. ''Get the word around Markham that Capeletti didn't see anything,'' he ordered, ''for his own protection. We're calling off the guard on his room.'' Just before he hung up, he growled, ''One more thing—don't accept any more rides until this thing is over. Hear me?''

"I hear you, Mike, but why? If you think you've got the right person—"

"Think? Hell, I know I've got the right guy for the Forbes murder. But I can't pin Evelyn Parsons on him just yet. Until I do, you take my advice, Sheila, and don't be alone with anybody from Markham."

TWENTY

SHEILA DREADED going to work on Monday. In spite of heroic efforts on the parts of the secretaries, the lecture was far from ready to mail. With Dehaviland and Capeletti both gone, she'd carry the entire weight of the institute for the first time. Her throat throbbed, and her heart ached for Mrs. Parsons and Quint.

To her surprise, she discovered that for once the Markham grapevine had failed to function. Yoshiko greeted her cheerily and leaned over her door to whisper, "I called Capeletti last night. He enjoyed your visit, and is doing fine."

Sheila waited for Yoshiko to mention Quint or Evelyn. Instead she bustled down to her desk looking almost happy. Mr. Rareby whispered a genial "Good morning!" as he headed toward the stairs. Even Mr. Southard gave her an almost respectful grunt as he came in for his mail. Not many students were about—Markham had no Monday-morning classes—but those few who did pass her door waved and greeted her normally.

No one mentioned Quint Barringer. No one mentioned Evelyn Parsons. No one mentioned murder at Markham.

Finally, nerves raw with worry about Quint and with waiting for the proverbial shoe to drop, Sheila left her desk and headed in search of a strong cup of coffee. As she entered the coffee room, she found a cozy scene. It could be entitled, she thought grimly, "Study of Suspects."

Morning sun streamed through one casement and poured over Cal Williams' shaggy head as he slouched across an overstuffed chair, listening intently. His fur hat had been tossed behind him. One boot dangled over the chair arm, swinging gently back and forth.

Across from him the sun touched Peter Lucas, setting his hair aflame against the dark leather sofa. His long fingers sketched his argument in the air. "If you compare our policy in Nicaragua with our policy in South Africa—"

"But Nicaragua is a war between people of the same race, not between whites and blacks," Todd objected. He straddled a ladder-back chair, resting his chin on the top rung.

"Whenever you talk like a racist, Todd..." Stan's reedy voice interrupted from the shadow of a wing-backed chair.

"What's the matter, Stan?" Brad drawled lazily from where he was braced on pillows on the floor in the midst of them. "He crowding your turf?" He turned his head a fraction and saw Sheila. "What do you think, Mrs. Tyler Travis?"

Sheila had not realized how much rage was bottled up inside her until her words came pouring out. "I think you are a bunch of insensitive clods. How can you go on with your interminable wrangles while Quint...Quint..." To her disgust her voice broke.

"What about Quint?" Cal spoke, but his question was reflected in four pairs of eyes. Even Brad had lifted his head and was regarding her with his full blue gaze.

"You really don't know?"

They continued to regard her blankly. "He should be here for this seminar," Cal said, "but we moved it from Wednesday to Monday, and when I tried to call him yesterday, no one answered his phone."

Sheila hesitated. Was she the one to tell them? Why not? It wouldn't be a secret very long. "Quint's in jail. He was arrested Saturday for the murder of Melanie Forbes."

Their reactions varied greatly. Todd's brown face filled with concern and disbelief. "No way, Sheila. Not Quint."

She nodded. "Yes, Quint."

Stan's eyes narrowed until his face became, if possible, even more weasely, and his thin mouth curved for an instant in what Sheila could only describe as a smile of pure malice. Then he raised one eyebrow and inquired, "Does Dr. Dehaviland know?"

She nodded. Brad turned his head slightly on his pillows. "Sorry, Stan. There seems to be something of which you were not informed." He turned back to Sheila. "Is Quint in Cook County?"

She nodded.

"What evidence do they have?" Peter demanded. His face was whiter than ever, and his eyes blazed.

Even as she considered what answer to give to him, she could not help noticing Cal Williams. His eyes were narrowed in disbelief or concern, but his whole frame slumped in relief.

"I can't tell you anything about evidence," she said to Peter, choosing her words carefully to tell the truth without conveying it, "but I was told he was arrested. I assumed you all knew, too."

As one man they shook their heads. Stan's voice filled the silence. "I don't think you should discuss this until Dr. Dehaviland makes a formal announcement."

Brad snorted. Todd chewed at his lower lip. Cal turned to Stan and demanded, "What are you made of, man? One of your friends is in jail, and you don't think you should discuss it?"

Peter alone seemed to comprehend Stan's point of view. "I don't think Quint himself would want us to talk about it until we have some facts. I wonder if he can have visitors."

Sheila nodded. "On Mondays. I thought I'd go at one."

His eyes burned into hers. "You got a car?" She nodded again. "I'm going with you. I'll be in the library. Call me when you're ready to leave."

It was a command, not a request, but Sheila didn't mind. In spite of Mike's orders, she'd be glad of Peter's company in that part of town. She didn't think he or anybody else would hurt her when everybody knew they were together. Also, she wanted to see his reaction to Quint, and Quint's to Peter. With a final nod she drew a cup of coffee and went back to her desk. The third lecturer was being unreasonable about travel and housing arrangements. Even with death tied to its tail, Markham staggered on.

She was putting down the phone from talking to their travel agent when Jim Lucas blazed into her office, looking as anguished as she felt. Again, in spite of the bitter cold outdoors, he wore only his thin gray jacket. He carried his mail—one lone electronics catalog.

His eyes were huge, his face very white. "Is it true what I just heard? Quint's in jail for killing Melanie?"

She nodded.

"What makes them think Quint did it? He wasn't even in town."

Sheila sighed. "Apparently he was, Jim."

He shook his head vehemently. "He was *not*. I drove him to the airport myself, Friday morning."

She jerked to full attention. "You did? Did you see him off?"

He shook his head slowly. "I just dropped him at the curb. It was Christmas, you know. The place was mobbed. Then I brought his car back. Would it help if I swore I took him to the airport?"

"I don't think so, Jim. Quint didn't fly home until Monday. And he won't say where he was. The police think he pretended to go home, then came back and killed Melanie. If you told them you took him to the airport, they'd only think that proved premeditation."

"But why should they think he killed Melanie?"

"From what I've heard," she said carefully, "Evelyn Parsons was in Melanie's apartment when someone called. She thought it was Quint."

"Oh, no!" His eyes widened with concern. "Was she sure?"

Sheila shook her head. "No, but the way Melanie acted after the call made Evelyn think it must have been him. Or so I understand," she added quickly.

Jim gnawed on one of his knuckles. "Quint wouldn't hurt anybody, Sheila," he raged. "He *couldn't*!"

She sighed. "It's hard for me to believe, too, Jim, but almost anybody can kill given the right circumstances."

"But they shouldn't take Evelyn's word if she wasn't sure."

Sheila shook her head sadly. "They have other evidence, as well. In fact, if Evelyn had lived, any *doubts* she had that it was Quint might have helped him. But now that she's dead . . ."

He stood absolutely still and the color drained from his face. "You didn't know?" she asked gently.

He seemed to come from far away. "What?"

"That Evelyn Parsons has been killed?"

His lower lip began to tremble, and he clutched it between his teeth. Without another word he turned toward the stairs.

"Jim," she called, not wanting him to leave like that. "Maybe your evidence might help after all."

He stopped, and half-turned. "How?"

"By proving that Quint didn't have his car. I heard that one piece of evidence was something recently found in his car."

"Two months later?" He obviously didn't believe her. "What?"

She wasn't prepared to tell him everything she knew. "You'd have to ask the police. But if you can testify that Quint didn't have his car..."

He leaned over the door, arms dangling and hands clasped, and thought about it. Finally, regretfully, he shook his head. "I can't. I parked behind Pres-Res. Peter and I thought about driving downtown, but parking's such a hassle, we rode the train. When we got home at midnight, the car was gone. Quint lets several guys use it, so I figured somebody besides me had a key. By the time I got up in the morning, it was back, and I forgot about it. But if I said it was gone..."

"...the police would be sure to think he'd come for it. No, Jim, that won't help at all."

He took a deep ragged breath and seemed to pull hope from the bottom of his lungs. "His dad can afford a good lawyer; we don't need to worry." He straightened his shoulders and headed across the reception hall. "Be seeing you."

TWENTY-ONE

YOSHIKO'S DOOR remained firmly shut all morning. Sheila did not know whether Dehaviland had called to tell her about Quint's arrest or not. At noon when Yoshiko passed on her way to lunch, however, her face looked haggard and old.

Sheila rose from her desk and spoke softly at her door. "I'm going to see Quint on my lunch hour. Do you want to come?"

Yoshiko's face grew worried. "Do you think that's wise? Dr. Dehaviland has said—"

"I'm going," Sheila said firmly. "Do you want to come?"

Yoshiko shook her head. "I don't dare." Before Sheila could reply, she hurried on. "It's different for you. You have a privileged position here. For me—jobs are hard to find when there are so many university wives. And with our son in college and our daughter in med school..." She shook her head and her black eyes were deep and anguished. "I dare not go, Sheila."

Sheila spoke on impulse. "Do you know anything that could help him, Yoshiko? Do you know where he went that Friday?"

Yoshiko's eyes became wary. "Dr. Dehaviland has asked me not to discuss this with anyone."

"We have to discuss it, Yoshiko!" Sheila spoke urgently. "I don't believe Quint killed that girl, and neither do you. But unless we can find out where he was, he's going to trial. You know, don't you?"

The president's secretary was silent as her love for Quint struggled with Dehaviland's commands. At last she nodded slightly. "I knew he didn't go home," she whispered. "His parents called here that Friday afternoon looking for him. Evelyn took the call, and came to ask if I knew where he was. They weren't expecting him home until Monday afternoon."

"Evelyn mentioned that call," Sheila recalled, frustrated that she hadn't thought of that earlier. "She said, 'But then that call came...' I thought she meant the call at Melanie's. Did you know where Quint was?"

Yoshiko shook her head. "I even asked him last week. He said he'd tell me someday, but he never did."

"Well, he's going to tell me *today*," Sheila said grimly.

As soon as Yoshiko returned, Sheila got her coat and went for Peter. They said very little until she swung onto the Dan Ryan Expressway. Then Peter finally asked the question she had been dreading all morning. "How come you know so much about this when nobody else does?"

Sheila kept her eyes carefully on the road. "In my job I get certain information, Peter." She wondered if he would leave it at that. He didn't.

"Which job?" he demanded. "Are you working for Markham or the police?"

"Markham, Peter. My involvement with the police is minimal." There, Mike Flannagan, she thought sourly. What do you think of that? She swung into a faster lane.

He probed deeper. "What else do you know that we don't?"

She expelled a deep breath. "Not much, Peter, and what I know I can't share. I can't even tell you why. But believe me when I tell you that while I don't love Markham as much as you do—"

"*Love* it?" he said in a voice of derision. "I don't love Markham. I loathe and detest the place."

Her mouth dropped in astonishment. "I thought you always wanted to come to Markham."

He laughed shortly. "Not me. All *I* ever wanted to do was play the piano—anywhere, anytime."

She drew her brows together, trying to understand. "Then why are you here?"

Out of the corner of her eye she could see that he was looking at her as if she were half-witted. "Because America needs me."

"Doesn't America also need pianists?" She swung around a slow driver and changed lanes again.

"You drive like a maniac," he said.

"That doesn't answer my question. Do you really think the world needs diplomacy more than it needs music, Peter?"

He shrugged one shoulder. "Sure. Don't you?"

She shook her head. "Not at all. But it isn't what I think that matters. It's your choice."

"Choice?" The word was a whisper, a cry of pain that choked him. "If you only *knew*! At Christmas..." He brought his clenched fists down hard on his thighs.

She nearly touched him then, but she didn't. He too closely resembled a wounded lion. "I know, Peter. Jim told me. He just didn't say why you made the decision you did."

He glared at her, breathing hard. "What decision? As the senator said when I barely *mentioned* that I might consider music over Markham, 'How can you compare the self-centered gratification of playing the piano with a call to serve your country?'"

She wanted to change the subject, but the agony in his voice forced her on. "Well, I happen to believe that different people are made to do different things. I think we serve our nation and possibly our Maker best by being and doing what *we* are made to do." She grinned. "And I sure get more out of your music than I ever did out of embassy functions."

He gave a low, bitter laugh. "But you're not a Lucas."

She was exasperated with him. "Surely there had to be a first Lucas, Peter, somebody who left farming or carpentering or something else to go into politics. Can't you be like him?"

He didn't smile, but even with her eyes firmly on the road she could feel his gaze. When he spoke his voice was so low she could hardly hear it. "Who takes care of Markham, Sheila?"

She laughed aloud. "Markham can make it, Peter. Leave it to the others."

He snorted. "What others?"

"Todd. Yusuf. Quint. Even Brad," she replied. His silence was total. "They do care about it, Peter," she argued, "just in a different way. They care about what Markham is now, and will be, not what it has always been. That's why they are so upset about the lectures—they want Markham to do better." Still he didn't speak. Desperately she pleaded, "Be yourself, Peter."

He said nothing, and as they had just arrived at the huge yellow jail, she concentrated on parking. As she stopped the car, he finally spoke, his voice almost a whisper. "Really, Sheila?"

She nodded. "Really, Peter."

Slowly tears began streaming down his cheeks, and he made no move to brush them off. At last he drew a deep, ragged breath and turned his gaze to meet hers. "Sorry, but you can't know how good this feels. I've been tighter than a spring since Christmas."

She nodded. "I kept expecting you to pop any day."

He rewarded her with a grin.

"Goodness, you're attractive when you smile!"

He gave a little laugh. "You haven't had much opportunity to notice, have you?" She shook her head. "Well, I still have some thinking to do, but you've let in some light. I'll try to remember to smile at you at least once a day."

"And send me a ticket to Carnegie Hall." She opened her door. "Now let's brave this system and see if we can find Quint."

After presenting proper identification and being frisked, they rode the elevator to the long visiting hall with its glass window to separate prisoners from visitors.

"I'd expected a little more privacy," Sheila admitted to Peter as she surveyed the short plastic partitions that formed booths isolating neither people nor noise. Each booth had a speaking circle cut in the plastic and a stool, but the circle was too high to reach if one sat on the stool, and too low to reach if one knelt. The only solution was to ignore the stool and straddle it, bending down to talk like two cranes.

"Everybody seems so young," she observed.

Peter nodded. "Just one big gang party." Perhaps, she reflected ruefully, visitation day was a sort of party. After all, it only came once a week.

Quint entered the prisoner's room and peered through the window to see who had come. Sheila let Peter go first to the speaking circle, but was close enough to hear what they said. There was no obvious constraint on either side. Still, she reminded herself, Peter Lucas was, above all, a performer.

"Thanks for coming." Quint looked pale, less sure of himself in khaki jail clothes than he had in a three-piece suit.

"How are you, brother?" Peter asked him.

"Oh, it's not much worse than the Pres-Res." Quint gave him a lopsided smile.

Sheila stopped listening, to give them what privacy she could, but after a very few remarks they ran out of conversation and Peter yielded her his place. "We want you out of there," she informed Quint as soon as she had greeted him.

"I'll vote for that," he agreed.

Desperation and the knowledge that they had less than a quarter of an hour made her blunt. "Then why don't you tell them where you were on the night of the murder?"

He stroked his cheekbone from ear to nose and back again. "I can't, Sheila. There's too much at stake."

"At stake? Your *life* is at stake."

He shook his head. "I don't think so. I spoke with my lawyer this morning. They don't have any evidence on me."

"Quint," she exclaimed, "you don't want to be let off just for lack of evidence!" She took a gamble. "Were you with Carla?"

He was clearly startled. "How'd you know about Carla?"

"Never mind that now. Does she know you're here?"

He shook his head. "I'm going to call her tonight. I only get one call a day, so Saturday I called my lawyer and last night I called my folks." He'd make a good diplomat, she thought sourly, the way he put duty before pleasure.

"May I call her this afternoon, just to say where you are?"

He hesitated, then nodded. "Sure. Just tell her I'll call after nine, and she's not to worry."

"Of course not." She made a face at him. "Why would she?" He grinned.

She memorized the number just as the guard stepped up to touch him on the shoulder. Whatever Quint had been up to on the weekend before Christmas, Carla must be persuaded to tell.

TWENTY-TWO

How long the girl had stood in the doorway Sheila could not have said. She felt a presence and looked up to confront a huge pair of eyes the color of semisweet chocolate. They were considering her uncertainly.

"Are . . . are you Mrs. Travis?"

It was Carla Alonso, all right. Two short phone conversations had imprinted that soft musical voice on Sheila's memory.

"I came as quickly as I could." The girl peered up and down the hall. "Can we talk?" Her accent was flawless, but there was something about the way she phrased her sentences that made Sheila wonder whether she had always spoken English.

Sheila indicated the big green chair and for the first time firmly shut the top of her door. Then she sat down in the smaller tapestry chair and waited.

For a time Carla sat silent, twining and untwining her fingers in her lap. They were long, gracefully tapered, suited to her height and delicate slenderness. She was not pretty, Sheila thought, but her features harmonized into a picture of gentle loveliness. Her forehead was wide, emphasized by the Alice-in-Wonderland band that held her straight black hair out of her face. Her eyes were fringed by long lashes and her skin was pale cream except for a stain of rose on each cheek. She wore no makeup, and needed none. Her wide mouth looked as if it usually tilted up in a smile, and tiny laugh wrinkles were beginning beside her eyes. But today no smile tilted her mouth.

"Is Quint really in jail?" Her lips trembled. Sheila nodded. "I haven't heard from him since the police . . ."

"Tell me about that," Sheila suggested.

Carla hesitated, looking into her lap. "I saw them out the window. I didn't know what to do, so I didn't answer the bell. Quint came down the sidewalk, and seemed to know one of them, a big man with blond hair. I thought it was all right, but I didn't want to be there when they came in, so I hid on the fire escape. When they left"—sudden sobs wracked her—"they took him with them! He's never called me since."

Sheila let her cry until the sobs lessened, then handed her a tissue. Carla wiped her eyes and blew her nose thoroughly. "Sorry. But I've been so worried, and I feel like such a coward. I should have stood by him. But I was so afraid! And afterward, I did not know what to do. Do you know why they took him?"

Sheila nodded, and spoke as gently as she could. "He's been accused of murdering a young woman."

"Quint?" her voice rose in disbelief. "But that's ridiculous."

"You know that and I know it. But you may be the only one who can convince the police."

"Me?" She was obviously bewildered.

"You can tell them where he was on the night of the murder."

"Why don't they just ask him? Quint tells the truth."

"They have asked him, Carla. He refuses to tell them."

"But why? Why shouldn't he tell them . . ." Her voice stopped. When she spoke again, it was very low. "This murder, when was it committed?"

"The Friday night before Christmas, they think."

Carla's body went rigid, as if some inaudible voice had screamed "Freeze!" She didn't speak again for some time.

Then she asked in a whisper, "It was done in Chicago?" Sheila nodded. If possible, Carla's face was paler than before. Even the faint rose of her cheeks had disappeared, making her look as if she had just stepped undecorated from Madame Tussaud's.

Finally she asked in a small voice, "If they knew where he was, they would definitely let him go?"

Sheila had to be honest. "I'm not positive, but I think so. Melanie Forbes was almost certainly killed that night."

Carla's voice was a lash of scorn. "Melanie Forbes? Is that who they think he killed?"

Sheila felt a smile hovering about her own lips. "You think it unlikely?"

Carla nodded emphatically. "Of course. Quint never saw her after May. And now..." She stopped.

"And now he's in love with you?" Sheila supplied.

Color rose in her cheeks, and her eyes grew soft. "Yes."

Sheila smiled. "Then I hope you can free him soon."

"If they knew Quint had no reason to see Melanie again because he loves someone else—would that be enough?"

Sheila bit her lips to keep them from smiling at the girl's naïveté. "I'm afraid not. That might give him a better motive than any they have come up with. Melanie might have been making trouble between you."

Carla was intelligent. Put bluntly, the argument made sense. But she did not respond as Sheila had hoped. Instead, gripped by some inner struggle, she now sat twisting and untwisting her hands. "They know he did not go home that weekend?" she finally asked.

Sheila nodded. "They know. And Quint won't say where he was."

"I see." She spoke so softly that if Sheila had not been beside her, she would not have heard. Then again Carla was silent for some time. Finally she raised her head. "Are you absolutely certain that if they know where he went, they will let him go?''

Sheila felt her temper rising. ''Considering what's at stake, don't you think it's worth the risk? Whatever you two were up to that weekend isn't worth forty years of a man's life. That's what he'll get if he's lucky.''

She emphasized the last three words. Carla recoiled as if physically struck, but her eyes flashed with scorn. ''You think we went away together for an affair? If only we had! I would gladly tell them that.'' She stopped, and her face was full of pain. ''But there is more at stake than you can know!'' Her hands knotted so tightly that the fingers looked as if they would snap.

To leave her privacy for her struggle, Sheila rose and went to the window. Sunlight streamed across a clear blue sky, making her yearn to fling on her coat and walk for miles, forgetting Markham and all its miseries. A whimper from across the room drew her attention. Would this gentle girl, so obviously in love with Quint Barringer, be willing to save him? What could be binding her so? An icicle, released by the sun, sped to earth.

Carla spoke. ''Mrs. Travis—Sheila? I don't know what to do. But I will tell you the problem. Perhaps you can help me decide.'' Tears hovered around her voice, but she held her head high.

As Sheila crossed the room to resume her seat, Carla began. ''Quint and I met last summer at his grandmother's place in Maine. I had been hired to care for his small nephews for two months, and Quint was up for the same time.''

''Are you in school?'' Sheila was surprised. She would have put the girl nearer twenty-five.

Her guess was vindicated. ''No, I teach kindergarten. But that gives me summers free.''

Sheila shuddered. "You are a better woman than I if you spend summers with small children after teaching them all winter."

Carla's mouth tilted in the first smile Sheila had seen since she arrived. "I like children." Then she grew grave again. "But this is not what I meant to tell you. We had a wonderful summer, and were glad to find we would both be in Chicago this fall. We've seen a lot of each other this year, and we"—she paused—"we want to be married. But there are complications."

"With his family?"

Her dark hair swung in negation. "No, with mine." She heaved a deep sigh. "You see, my parents were Mexicans. They came into this country illegally, three years before I was born. While they worked as migrant workers, nobody cared if they had papers or not. Or," and her voice grew bitter, "if we lived or died. My two sisters died before they were five. Then, when I was nine, Mama died too." Her voice trailed off, as if she relived that sorrow. Sheila had nothing to say, so she waited. This was far more complicated than she had imagined.

At last Carla resumed her story. "Daddy brought José and me to Chicago, to live with his sister. She is married to an American, so she is legal. We lived with her as her own children while Daddy worked from Michigan to Texas. José and I went to school for the first time in our lives." Her face softened. "He didn't like it much, but I knew right away I wanted to be a teacher." She paused for breath.

"And then," she continued, "when I was fourteen, Daddy was offered a job as gardener for a very rich man in Michigan."

"How could he take a job without a work permit?"

"The man didn't mind, as long as Daddy kept his estate looking nice. He even paid in cash, so Daddy didn't need a bank or a social security number. And," she added, forestalling Sheila's next question, "he paid very well. Daddy has been happy there."

"So what's the problem?" Sheila asked.

Carla bit her lip. "The police. When Daddy was on his way to the job, he came to get us. While he was here, the police found out about his being illegal, and came to get him. He escaped out the back door and went without us. But still the police watched our home, stopped me on the street and demanded to see my birth certificate. Carmelita and Joe were afraid, so we moved to another neighborhood. But we always live in fear. Daddy cannot come here, and we never write or call him from our own phone."

She looked into Sheila's eyes, and hers were pools of sorrow. "I love my daddy. I don't want him sent back to a country where he would have no work and no family. And I don't want Quint to lose good jobs because his father-in-law is..." Her voice broke. "If I tell the police where Quint was that weekend, what will happen?"

"You went to see him." It wasn't really a guess.

Carla nodded. "I wanted Daddy to meet Quint, and Quint to meet Daddy. They liked each other immensely."

"But why did Quint pretend to be going home? Why not just say he was going up to see his girlfriend's father?"

Carla chewed one fingertip. "I am always so afraid."

"But didn't I read somewhere that amnesty may be granted in these cases?"

"We are too afraid to ask," Carla said simply. "Quint thinks one of his uncles, a lawyer, may be able to help us. We are planning to talk with him in the spring. But for now, until Daddy is safe..."

Sheila looked at her gravely. "Carla, if you have to tell about your father or let Quint stand trial, which would you choose?"

She considered. "I'd choose Quint."

"Okay. First let me see what I can do. I have a..." she hesitated, because she wasn't sure it was still true, "...friend in the police department. Let me tell him your story without any names. Maybe he can verify Quint's whereabouts without bringing your dad into it at all. Did you see anyone else up there?"

"Yes." She brightened. "My father's employer is a friend of Quint's family. We went in one afternoon for tea."

"Great. Let's see if he could provide the alibi we need." She took the man's name and address, and went to call Mike.

He came on the line like a bull. "You see our man to-day?"

"Yes, but—"

"Did he give you anything?"

"No, but—"

"Well, he'd better. We've found evidence that Melanie was definitely in his car that evening. She had stepped in an oil slick. Some of it was on her shoes and some on his carpet."

Finally he paused. "Melanie may have been in the car that evening," Sheila told him somewhat tartly, "but Quint Barringer wasn't. Listen to me for a minute without interrupting."

He heard her story through without a word. Then he asked (sourly, she thought), "And this girl can prove they were in Michigan?"

"Yes, Mike, she can. But there's a complication." She told him.

He grudgingly agreed that the employer's word would be enough. "Now you've got me shielding illegal aliens," he growled, "but Michigan is a long way from Chicago jurisdiction."

"Mike, has anyone told you today you're a darling?"

"No," he grunted, "but when I look in the mirror tonight, somebody's going to tell me I'm a chump. Meanwhile, send the girl in to make a statement. You doing okay?"

She hesitated, rubbing her still-tender throat. But what could Mike do about it now? She couldn't identify the man—had no way of knowing if he was part of all this or merely an overzealous purse snatcher.

"Sheila, you still there?"

The growl on the other end decided her. Nothing was worth listening to what Mike was sure to say. "I'm here. Sorry, I was listening to somebody else for a minute." (No need to say it was her own conscience.) "And I'm fine."

"Okay. Maybe I'll come by tonight. And, Sheila?"

"Yes, Mike?"

"Before you start dancing in the streets, go look down the halls for another suspect."

TWENTY-THREE

As SHEILA STARTED work Wednesday morning, she reflected that this day had every opportunity to be, finally, a good one—even if forecasters *were* predicting the worst blizzard of the year. While the Henderson lecture hadn't gone out Tuesday afternoon, she had every hope that it would be printed before the day was over. Quint had been released Tuesday morning, and Mike had called last evening to say he'd be coming back to Markham today to "get on with it."

Only two shadows marred her morning: They were no closer to solving the case, and David MacLean hadn't called since Sunday. Strange to realize that she didn't know where he lived. Nick's records only showed the number of the university history department. Information had no listing. Even Bertha couldn't help—"lives somewhere nearby" was all she knew.

By ten o'clock it was so dark that passing cars had turned on headlights and automatic streetlights were beginning to flicker. Even the mailman seemed sped by a sense of urgency as he dropped his bag in the hall and waved a huge gloved hand.

Going in to check a detail of the next lecture with Yoshiko, Sheila was astonished to see on the secretary's desk a letter addressed to Dr. Dehaviland in a most familiar hand. What could Aunt Mary have to say to the president of Markham?

She worked steadily all morning. As the sky grew darker beyond her windows, she discovered, to her surprise, that

Markham began to seem a cheery fortress in a world of similar fortresses across the way. She felt brave enough to beard a particularly surly lion in his den.

She asked Yoshiko to take her calls for a minute and made her way to the basement. Cal sat alone in his office, staring pensively out the window.

"I still need to ask you one question, please."

He sighed heavily. "Well, out with it."

"You told Mr. Flannagan that you hadn't talked with Melanie since summer, but Evelyn Parsons said you spoke with her after the Christmas Community Dinner."

"Looks like Brad was right." He leaned back in his chair and regarded her quizzically. "You *are* detecting, not merely running this place in lieu of our illustrious but conspicuously absent president."

"What does Brad know about it?" She kept her voice cool as she took a chair near him. Mike might not approve, of course, but surely Cal wouldn't strangle her where somebody might come in at any minute. (She hoped.)

He laughed, a short bark. "Oh, his sister's husband is in the Japanese embassy. When he said you were here, she said you'd done a lot of detective work out there."

"Janice Albritten!" Sheila remembered that profile now—and the small, sly woman who bore it. "Did Brad also say his sister is prone to dramatics?" It was a far milder description than she was thinking.

"No." He said the word as if it concluded their conversation, but she still wanted an answer to her question.

"Well, I'm not precisely detecting," she evaded, "but I do want to know if your last conversation with Melanie— at the Christmas Community Dinner—might shed any light on her death."

He shook his head as if baffled. "Do you know I'd forgotten that conversation, Sheila? Honest. She was riding Winston Rareby about his leg, and it was more than I could stomach. I grabbed her afterward and told her to lay off. She pretended to agree."

"Pretended?"

"If you'd known Melanie, you'd know that any admission of fault was pretense with her. But who knows? Maybe she planned to repent. Anyway, that's all there was to it. I never saw her again."

She believed him. But did her own belief eliminate him as a possible suspect? Reluctantly, she had to admit she could be wrong.

She returned upstairs to find David MacLean standing by her door, looking around in a puzzled way. "So there you are!" he exclaimed as she crossed the reception hall.

She was surprised at how flustered she felt, and how relieved. After three days of planning what to say to him the next time they met, she could think of nothing. Questions flooded her mind, of course: Why did you invite me to the lakefront and not show up? Where have you been since Friday? Did you try to kill me Sunday afternoon? But now that they stood face to face, they all seemed irrelevant. Surely this man had not tried to kill her!

He seemed not to notice her silence, but stepped back, swung the lower half of her door open, and followed her into her office. "Sorry to be out of pocket for so long. I've been up with Mrs. Parsons much of the time, and out at the terminal."

His time with Mrs. Parsons had broadened his speech. "The tairminal?" she repeated blankly, sinking into her desk chair, with the broad expanse of mahogany between them.

"Aye. The Red Cross flew Jack Parsons home from Frankfurt, and flights got held up by bad weather in Europe. I was there most of Sunday; then he didn't get in until nearly dawn on the Monday."

"Most of Sunday?" All Sheila could seem to do was parrot his words—the important ones.

He settled into her big green chair and sucked on his pipe. "You've become a bloody echo since I last saw you," he commented between clouds of smoke.

She shook her head. "It's just that I'd wondered..."

"Ahhh," he said with a hint of a twinkle. "Well, I did try to call here Monday afternoon before seeking my bed, but Jim Lucas said you'd gone out."

She rubbed her forehead to clear her thoughts. "He didn't tell me," she murmured. "And yesterday?"

If David realized he was getting the third degree, he was unperturbed. "We had the service yesterday, just a quiet one, then this morning I put Jack on the plane back to Germany."

"You've spent a lot of time in airports."

"Och, it's been nae bother. Sunday I had a good book your aunt had lent me."

"A mystery, right?" she hazarded. His twinkle was as good as a nod. "But didn't you need my car?"

"Och, no, I used Evelyn's van. She wasn't needing it, poor lass. When a neighbor lad offered to drop yours off on his way to the university library Saturday morning, I let him do it. Did you get it, right enough?"

She nodded. "Sure. He parked it right near my door." She cupped her chin in one hand and considered him across the desk. Something he had said had rung a warning bell in her head, but what was it? Something about a book? A plane?

She narrowed her eyes. She had it now, and her mouth was set in a grim line. "I want you to do something for me, David." She told him what it was.

"And then?"

"Come by my place tonight. We need to have a council of war."

TWENTY-FOUR

JUST BEFORE LUNCH on Thursday afternoon the phone rang on Yoshiko's desk. Sheila heard the secretary answer, and transfer the call to the president. Then she tried to concentrate on the work on her desk. Aunt Mary's call had been the first step in their plan, and she could not afford to worry now whether or not they could carry it off.

She had not wanted to include Aunt Mary at all, but the little woman had insisted. "John Dehaviland needs to be in on the confrontation, Sheila, and I can get him there. I sent him a sizable donation earlier in the week. If your assessment of the man is correct, he will eat out of my hand."

"Aunt Mary!" Sheila had protested. "What a waste of money."

The wealthy old woman chuckled. "Money has many uses, Sheila. Sometimes it is the carrot needed on the stick to attract a particular kind of donkey. You handle Mike and the students, and I will deliver John Dehaviland when you need him." She smoothed her tweed skirt. "I have a few things to say to him myself."

But when she tripped up the steps of Markham from the cab a few minutes before the second anniversary lecture began, no one would have thought this dainty elderly woman had anything more serious on her mind than the charming effect she made. Her fur cape was draped over a suit of softest gray cashmere, and a fur cap perched over one eye. She flicked snow from her kid gloves and pulled them off, flashing diamonds and emeralds.

"Good afternoon, dear," she said formally at Yoshi-ko's door. "I called earlier, and Dr. Dehaviland kindly agreed to permit me to attend this afternoon's lecture. Will you direct me to it?"

Her husky voice was pitched slightly louder than usual, to swirl down the hall and under the president's door. He came to meet her. "Miss Beaufort? I am John Dehaviland and I've been expecting you. This way, please." He put out one arm to draw her toward him and ushered her into his office. When they emerged several minutes later, Sheila felt sorry for the lecturer with them. A few minutes earlier he had been the center of the president's attention; now he hovered on the fringe like a gaunt owl among peacocks, his gray wool suit eclipsed by the magnificence of Dehaviland's navy silk and Aunt Mary's cashmere.

Just before going to the lecture herself, Sheila phoned Mike. "I think something's going to be breaking here around four, Mike, and you'll probably want to be in on it. Can you come about three-thirty and wait in Wentworth—the big parlor downstairs?"

"What're you up to, Sheila?" If his growl was designed to intimidate, it almost achieved its purpose. She was glad he was half the Windy City away.

"I'll tell you then, Mike. Will you come?"

"Only because if anything happened to you, I'd have to answer to Miss Mary. I've half a mind to call her now and tell her to order you home. She told me this morning about how you nearly got your fool neck wrung Sunday—"

"I'm fine, Mike," she said hastily. "See you later." She rang off before he could say anything more.

Sheila scarcely heard a word of the lecture. As the students rose and filed out the door, she judged by their faces that this lecturer had outdone Dr. Henderson for bore-dom. No one spoke to the speaker except Stan, who hung on his arm like a sycophant until Dr. Dehaviland said, "Stan, would you like to join Dr. Whetlock, Miss Beaufort, and myself in my office for coffee?"

Sheila hurried down the hall to make sure there were enough cups. Stan came behind her, a flush of pleasure on his thin face.

Taking care to avoid meeting their party in the hall (running into Aunt Mary prematurely had no part in their plan), Sheila went back to check Wentworth, which was empty as she had predicted, then mounted the stairs.

The coffee room was almost as if the past seven days had never been. Todd and Yusuf sat in one corner deep in conversation with a circle of underclassmen. Brad sprawled on a sofa, eyes closed. On the floor beside him, Jim hugged his knees, while at the piano Peter played Beethoven's Fourth Piano Concerto. Usually Sheila loved that concerto—the despair of the orchestra pitted against the hope of the piano until finally they lifted together in one mighty swell of hope and delight. But while Peter was playing the hopeful part (a good sign?), Sheila's own heart supplied the despair. She did not anticipate any outcome of delight.

As she crossed the threshold the room fell silent. She filled her cup and pretended not to notice. Crossing to Brad's sofa, she asked, "May I share, Brad?" He grunted and moved his feet.

Cal and Quint entered just behind her. "Howdy, everybody," Cal said jovially. "We thought we'd have a cup of brew and see how this week's lecture is sitting on everybody else."

"Churning," Todd said shortly. "This really must stop."

"Agreed," Yusuf seconded him. "This wastes good time."

"Was last week's lecture this bad?" Quint asked. A clamor of voices assured him it was.

"I skipped it," Cal admitted. "Had just gotten back from out of town. But something needs to be done. This insults you, and folks outside won't like it, either." He seemed to see Sheila for the first time. "Has that first one gone out?"

She shook her head. "I've been otherwise occupied, you know. It should be ready by tomorrow."

He held up one hand. "Don't mail it until I can talk to the president and Rareby. In fact, if you've a transcript, let me read it tonight." She nodded, and he moved toward the door.

She was just wondering how to stop him when Brad's drawl did it for her. "Sit down, Cal, and let's ask our resident sleuth how her case is going."

Cal raised one eyebrow and looked at Sheila. She nodded. "I'd like to talk about the case," she agreed. "If we all put our heads together, I think we might come up with something."

Before anyone could speak, the door opened. Aunt Mary tripped in, followed by Dr. Dehaviland and Stan. "Don't let us bother you," she cried, fluttering her tiny hands. Her voice simply oozed magnolias. "Your de-ah president is just giving me a little tour of your lovely building." She beamed up at the president. "Could we just sit down for a few minutes and hear what your students have to say about that marvelous lecture? So much of it was incomprehensible to me, I'm afraid." She directed her last remark to the students. Most of them had the grace to look at the floor. Brad alone could not repress a snort. "And all those stairs have exhausted me. I could use a little rest."

Sheila had not heard Aunt Mary sound so Southern since an obnoxious woman from New Jersey remarked in her aunt's hearing that the only real difference between the North and the South was the terrible heat. She expected Dr. Dehaviland was finding it tedious, but instead he seemed to have fallen under Aunt Mary's spell. With a solicitous arm under her elbow he escorted her to the sofa. "I just learned, Sheila, that this charming woman is your aunt."

He strolled over to the fireplace and assumed what Sheila was coming to recognize as his favorite position, one arm nonchalantly resting on the mantelpiece. Stan took a chair next to Aunt Mary's end of the couch. She turned to Sheila.

"Stan has been so sweet to me, dear." If she'd had a fan, Sheila reflected, Aunt Mary would have tapped him with it. The underclassmen rose as one man, made hasty apologies, and left. Yusuf, too, rose. He crossed the room and bowed low over Aunt Mary's hand. "I am glad to meet you, but I must get back to my studies. Fatima enjoyed her visit very much. Will you do us the honor soon to return it?"

"Of course," Aunt Mary assured him.

Sheila considered those who remained. Could any of them be permitted to depart?

Peter crouched on the piano bench, drumming his fingers soundlessly on the keys. Cal, Brad, Todd, and Quint seemed willing to stick out Aunt Mary in order to discuss the murder. Or maybe they hoped to get back to strategy for dealing with the lectures. Stan looked as if he would like to leave, but did not dare. And Jim still sat on the floor, regarding the room like a child permitted to attend a grown-up party if he promised to be quiet.

Aunt Mary beamed at them all. "I didn't mean to break up your conversation. You all just go right ahead with what you were talking about." She leaned across the plump arm of the sofa and asked in a voice barely above a whisper, "Could I request a favor, Stan? I forgot my glasses, and I need to write down a phone number before I forget it." She rummaged in her purse as if it were a rat's nest instead of impeccably tidy, and eventually brought out a stub of a pencil and a scrap of paper.

Probably rummaged my desk for them before leaving home, Sheila thought with amusement. Aunt Mary was certainly playing a dithering old woman to perfection.

She handed the pencil and paper to Stan and began to dictate. "Three-one-two, eight-four-five, seven-six-oh-nine." When he had written it, she took it by one corner and held it far from her to read. "That's just fine, Stan. Sheila, please keep this for me."

Sheila took the scrap of paper and slid it into her skirt pocket. "When you arrived, Aunt Mary," she said, "we were just about to discuss Markham's murders."

Dehaviland stepped forward. "I don't think we need to discuss this matter during Miss Beaufort's stay."

"Oh, but we should, sir." Aunt Mary looked up at him with very wide brown eyes. "Why, an attack has been made on my niece's life. This has got to stop."

Every face in the room turned to Sheila in surprise. "No kidding?" Brad murmured. The others echoed it. Sheila nodded.

Dehaviland raised one hand. "But surely the police are the ones to deal with this. They do not appreciate amateur interference, and this is not really Markham's business."

Todd gave a short laugh. "I beg your pardon, sir, but when a body is found in somebody's basement wrapped in their rug, it's their business. Besides, most of us knew

Melanie, and all of us knew Evelyn. And Sheila, of course. I think it's past time we accepted this as Markham's business."

There was a general murmur of assent. Dehaviland considered, then nodded. "Very well, if anyone has something to say, say it. But I must stipulate that none of what is said here goes beyond this room unless absolutely necessary. Agreed?" Everyone nodded.

Sheila set her empty cup beside her feet and assembled what she had to say.

"It seems to me that we should start with the murder of Melanie Forbes. What we know so far is this: Somebody lured that young woman into the room below this one and persuaded her to try on a pair of earrings. He ripped one earring from her ear and strangled her with his bare hands. Then he rolled her in the carpet, dragged her downstairs, and deposited her in an unused basement storeroom."

"*We* know a great deal," Cal drawled.

Sheila ignored him. "Afterward, her bank account was systematically milked of nearly twelve thousand dollars by forged checks, all dated after her death. Was that to confuse the police, or for some other reason?"

She looked around the room. Todd, Quint, and Peter were looking at her. Brad's eyes were closed—if she hadn't known him, she'd have sworn he was asleep. Stan was tracing a circle on his thigh with one forefinger. Cal's head was sunk on his chest and he seemed to be studying the toe of one boot. Jim and the president were both looking around the room, as she was.

No one spoke.

Finally she said, "Why don't you tell us, Stan?"

He jerked his head in her direction. His eyes slid from side to side before meeting hers. "What do you mean?"

Her gaze held his. "I mean you forged Melanie's name to those checks in the three weeks after her death. Is that where the 'legacy' came from to buy your car?"

His thin cheeks flushed. "This is highly insulting! I did not murder Melanie Forbes. I didn't even know she was dead."

Aunt Mary leaned over and patted his arm. "Sheila never said you murdered the young woman, Stan. The murderer would have dated those checks before her death, to confuse the issue. But you dated them as you wrote them, didn't you?"

He shook off her hand and leapt to his feet. "I resent this very much. What proof do you have for these accusations?"

Sheila sighed. "A wad of paper, for one, that I found under the seat of your car. It was a scrap on which you had practiced Melanie's signature. At first that seemed to clear you, because it meant you had bought the car before anyone wrote the checks. But a call to your Volvo dealer revealed that the money you took would not have paid for your car without a down payment. That's what your uncle gave you, wasn't it, Stan?"

"Anyone could have put that paper there." Angry, Stan was even more unattractive than usual. His face had become a mottled red and his nose threatened to drip. He swiped at it and glared down at Sheila and her aunt.

Aunt Mary shook her head. "We have the phone number, too."

His eyes narrowed until they were mere slits. "What phone number?"

"The one you wrote for me. It contained all ten numbers. When police experts compare it with the numerals on the checks, won't they find they are the same? Even experienced forgers get careless about numbers. And you're not experienced yet, thank God.''

His face was a mask of fear, a weasel caught in a trap. "I didn't kill her!" he squealed. "And I didn't kill Evelyn, either. When I found her she was already dead!''

The room itself seemed to gasp and soak up all sound for several moments. No one moved. Then Sheila spoke to Stan in a voice of compassion. "So that's why you looked so ill at the Community Dinner. Not bad bacon at all. You hadn't called the police yet?''

He shook his head, his face a pasty white. "I didn't know what to do. I had gone out with some garbage, and there she was. In the dumpster. She looked..." he gulped, "...horrible. I didn't even recognize her until I saw her coat. I didn't know what to do," he repeated, appealing to Dehaviland.

The president inclined his head graciously. "You could have come to me, Stan. Although I find your conduct in the matter of the checks deplorable, I would certainly have stood by you in the matter of finding the body.''

Sheila noticed that even now he did not call Evelyn by name.

"But how did you get Melanie's checks if you didn't kill her?'' Todd asked.

Stan hung his head. "I borrowed Quint's car the Monday before Christmas for some errands. He'd said I could use it," he added defiantly with a quick look towards the car's owner. Quint nodded quiet confirmation. "I dropped my pen, and it rolled under the seat. When I bent to get it, I saw the checkbook. At first I assumed it had been there since spring." He gave Aunt Mary another defiant look. "I planned to return it," he insisted. She met his gaze levelly until his dropped. "But in that day's mail my great-uncle sent me a check for five thousand dollars and told me to get myself a new car. A car!'' he barked sarcastically. "Uncle Hugh hasn't driven for years. What kind of car could I get for five thousand dollars?'' His eyes scanned the room. "I thumbed through the checkbook and saw that Melanie had written checks that month. And she had fourteen thousand dollars left in that account. Fourteen *thousand* dollars!'' His voice was shrill.

"And you thought she'd suspect Quint of forging the checks?'' Jim raised huge dark eyes to him. "Oh, Stan, how could you, after all Quint's done for you?''

Stan whirled to glare at him. "What's Quint ever done for me except lend me a car now and then? Is that such a dent in the Barringer millions? And all the big corporations. Do they come after me? No, it's Quint they want, or Todd, or Brad. The kind of job I'm likely to get will be so far out of town, I'll *need* a car.'' He stopped and took a deep breath.

At last his fury had spent itself. Now he spoke with icy composure. "I never thought that anyone would be accused of stealing the checkbook—or forging the checks. I assumed that Melanie would not know where she dropped it, or, if she did remember, assume it had been stolen out of Quint's car. Either of them could have absorbed the loss and never felt it. But my savings? Six years I worked and scraped to get to Markham. And I was about to graduate with a couple of thousand dollars and no car. All I took was enough to almost pay for the car and the first quarter's insurance.''

Sheila and Aunt Mary exchanged glances. One mystery solved.

Everyone else in the room was looking at Stan in shock or distaste. He headed for the door, then turned, chin high. "That money made the difference to me between starting out with nothing and starting out with something. I took the money, and now you all know it. What you do with that knowledge is up to you. But I did not kill Melanie Forbes.'' He departed, slamming the door.

For a moment no one spoke. Then Todd's mild voice broke the silence. ''Well, I'm convinced Stan didn't kill Melanie. But if he didn't, who did?''

TWENTY-FIVE

"CAL?" SHEILA ASKED.

Every head in the room turned toward the astounded professor. "You were in the basement that night. Why didn't you come out when the lights went out?"

He gave an embarrassed laugh. "Don't scare me like that, Sheila. For a moment I thought you suspected me."

She sent him half a grin. "For a while I almost did. But only for a while. You may have had a motive," she ignored curious looks as she continued, "but a link with Markham would have been the last thing you wanted. Will you satisfy my curiosity and tell me why you didn't come out?"

He looked toward Aunt Mary, and back to Sheila. "I was sitting on the john, reading, if you must know. In Latin America you learn to just wait and the lights will come on. They did."

"What motive could you have had?" Brad asked lazily.

"The same one you had," Sheila told him. "A personal one."

"Oh?" he asked. "Thinkest thou that I killed the wench?"

She shook her head. "Not unless you did it in your sleep."

His lips flickered in a smile. "Glad to hear it," he murmured, dropping his chin closer to his chest.

Sheila turned to Todd. "Someone else will be glad, too."

He nodded. "Jenny didn't really think he'd done it, but, well...she couldn't help thinking he's been hiding something."

"Sweet kid," murmured Brad drowsily. "Jenny, not Melanie Forbes. Melanie Forbes was a bitch."

"She was not." A flush rose in Jim's bony face. "At times she could be real sweet."

"At times we can all be sweet," Brad replied. "Even you."

"Lay off him," Peter ordered, half-rising from the piano bench. Sheila was wondering how to break up this familiar argument and get on with the case when someone else did it for her.

The coffee-room door opened and a man stood on the threshold. "I say, am I intruding?"

She greeted him with a welcoming smile. "No. Come on in."

"We're unraveling our mysteries," Todd explained.

Dr. Dehaviland took a conspicuous look at his watch. "Could we conclude our discussions soon? I am rapidly running out of time."

"We're also rapidly running out of suspects," Brad muttered into his beard. "Welcome, David."

"Oh, dear." David took the seat beside Aunt Mary, the one Stan had vacated. "I find that juxtaposition most unfortunate, Brad. Have I arrived just in time to offer myself for a vacancy?"

Aunt Mary reached over the sofa arm to give him a pat. "I hope not, dear. But stay all the same." She turned to Sheila. "Why don't you just tell us, Sheila, and eliminate the suspense? Who was it who killed Melanie Forbes?"

Sheila looked at them all once more. At Peter, aflame on the piano bench. At Jim, his shadow, sitting quietly at her feet. At Todd and Quint, waiting. At Brad, feigning sleep. At Cal, who was enjoying this, she suspected. At Dehaviland, posing against the mantelpiece. At David, who was already reaching for his pipe and knocking it against his palm.

"Is it snowing out?" she asked him.

He nodded. "Lightly. But we got her moved before the worst."

"I'm glad." She turned to the others. "David's been very helpful to the Parsons family in their grief. He spent today helping Evelyn's mother move to her sister's. He spent all of Sunday at O'Hare, meeting her brother's plane."

She looked into a pair of startled eyes. "But you didn't know that, did you, Jim? You didn't know, when you called me and pretended to be him inviting me for a walk, then crept up behind my bench and tried to strangle me?" She gave him a sad smile. "I almost believed you. For three horrible days I feared it could have been David."

By her knees the translucent face was whiter than she had ever seen it, every bone standing out of the tightly stretched skin. As she stared into his eyes the whole room blackened until all she saw was that face, those huge spaniel eyes.

"Jim?" Peter yelped. He scraped back the piano bench and sprang to his feet, eyes blazing. Then he leaned across the piano and glared at her. "Jimmy couldn't have killed Melanie Forbes. He was with me that night!"

Jim didn't speak. His eyes flicked from Sheila's to Peter's and back, waiting for her reply. Sadly she shook her head. "You weren't, were you, Jim? What time did you leave the club?"

For a long moment his gaze held hers. Then his slid to his lap, where he was beginning to pick at a scab on the back of one hand. "About seven," he muttered. "It was easy. Once Peter is playing a piano, he doesn't see or hear anything. And they had given me a table in the far corner." He raised one thin shoulder and let it drop. "Who cares what happens to a shadow person?"

He looked back up at Sheila, and his eyes were pools of misery. "I didn't mean to kill her," he said softly. "I liked her. A lot," he added defiantly. "Most of the time. I just meant to frighten her, hurt her a little like she hurt others. I thought it might make her change." He stopped.

"It was you who called her about six?" Sheila asked.

He nodded. "I do impersonations too, you know?" His voice was bitter. "Not just Peter. So I called and pretended to be Quint. She wouldn't have come for me, but she'd come for Quint."

His eyes roamed the room. The others sat without a movement among them. "So I pretended to be Quint, and she fell for it. You should have heard," he said to Quint, "how eager she was. She really had a big thing for you, you know?"

Quint nodded. "I know, Jim," he said quietly.

Jim seemed to enjoy revealing his clever plot now that it had been uncovered. "I picked her up in Quint's car and told her he had sent me, that we would meet him at Markham. I had a key, you see, for practicing our program. All I planned to do was take her into Wentworth and leave her, saying that Quint would be along. Then I planned to pull the main switch and go back to Pete's club, leave her in the dark building. Melanie was terrified of the dark. I thought it would be good for her." He stopped. Then, his face gaunt with pain: "But I never meant to kill her."

Peter glided from the piano and slid to the floor beside his cousin. Tenderly he put his arm around his cousin's thin shoulders. "Hey, Jimmy, we believe you."

"What went wrong?" Sheila asked gently.

Jim chewed on his lower lip and picked at the scab. His voice was so low it scarcely rippled the silence in the coffee room. "I had bought some earrings. For Mom, for Christmas. When we got to Wentworth I showed them to Melanie. Asked what she thought of them. She took out those little harps she usually wore..." He looked up at Sheila and inserted apologetically, "I must have dropped them in my pocket. I found them later, and when you found her body, I didn't know what to do with them. I was scared the police might search our things. So I put them in your boot."

She winced at the memory. "I found them. What did Melanie do then, Jim?"

As he spoke, his words gathered momentum, as if he rushed downhill to despair. "She put Mom's earrings on and went over to look in the mirror. Then she—she laughed. She said they were so tacky that no woman would be caught dead in them. She said it was the sort of taste she would expect me to have. And then..." he gasped for air and cried, "...then she said she guessed a *cripple* wouldn't mind!" He rocked back and forth, face buried in his hands. "Oh, God!"

Peter held him so tightly that he, too, rocked. "And then you killed her, Jimmy?"

Jim shook his head. "No, I grabbed an earring and pulled it. It tore her ear. She screamed at me—horrible, awful things. I got so mad...so mad...it was like all the mads I ever held inside came pouring out all at once. I grabbed her by the throat to shut her up and I squeezed, I squeezed..." Tears rained onto his hands, clenched in his lap. While he fought for control, no one else said a word. At last he continued. "I didn't know what to do with her, but I couldn't stand to look at her. Her face was..." He broke off, swallowed, and went on. "I rolled her in the rug. Then I remembered that Jack once said the first storeroom down in the stacks was empty. I got Nick's keys and dragged her down there. Just until I could think what to do."

"What about that checkbook Stan found?" Cal demanded.

Jim shrugged, darted him a quick, nervous look. "It was in her purse, I guess. I took the purse to a dumpster up near Pete's club, but it got caught on the bottom of the seat when I picked it up off the floor of the car, and everything fell out. I guess I hurried too much and missed the checkbook."

"And your mother's earring," Sheila added.

He nodded. "But I never meant for you to be suspected," he said solemnly to Quint. "I thought you had gone away."

Quint nodded. "I shouldn't have lied to you, Jim." His lopsided smile was full of sadness.

The room was silent. Sheila felt tears clogging her throat, and heard a suspicious sniff from Todd. Brad had abandoned his customary languor and was leaning forward on the couch, hands clasped between his knees as if in prayer. Dehaviland coughed lightly, and when a log fell, shattering sparks, he took a quick, nervous step to the far side of the hearth.

Aunt Mary's husky voice filled the stillness. "But what happened then, Jim? Why didn't you just tell someone?"

"I didn't think anyone would believe it was an accident," he muttered.

"But surely," Sheila argued, "you had to know that her body would be found sooner or later. Weren't you worried?"

He shook his head. "I was at first. It was awful! But then when we got back from Christmas and it was so cold, I realized I was being saved again, just like staying at Peter's saved me from the accident. I've got something important to do, Sheila. Did you forget?"

"But, Jimmy..." Peter began.

Jim gave him an almost sunny smile. "It's going to be all right, Pete. Killing Melanie was an accident."

Aunt Mary spoke crisply. "But Evelyn's death could not have been an accident."

Jim whirled to meet her steady gaze, and his face flushed at what he saw. He leapt to his feet and backed toward the door. "I didn't want to kill Evelyn. I had to!" So complete was their paralysis that no one moved to stop him until he was almost out of the room. Then, with amazing agility, Brad flung himself against Jim in a tackle that sent them both crashing to the floor. David and Cal were there at once to help them up and shove Jim toward the chair Cal had just vacated.

Brad rubbed his left shoulder. "Haven't done that since high school," he muttered, dropping back into his seat.

Jim sat in Cal's chair, breathing heavily and glaring at Brad. "Someday I'm going to sock you," he said between clenched teeth. David rested a hand lightly on his shoulder.

"Tell us about Nick, lad," he suggested gently.

Jim's jaw trembled. "I didn't want to push Nick. I like Nick. But he was about to see me."

"What were you doing in the stacks?" David asked.

Jim dropped his gaze to his hands and began picking at his scab. "I'd gotten to thinking about how I put Melanie's earrings in my pocket. I wondered if I'd had Mom's in there, too, and dropped it when I was dragging Mel downstairs. Peter had seen them when I bought them, and I was afraid he'd tell the police if they found it. So when he went out that night—" He turned to Peter accusingly. "You were playing at the club again, weren't you?" He didn't wait for Peter's nod. "You should've told me!"

Peter shook his head. "It was just for a couple of hours. Filling in for the new guy. But if I'd told you, you'd have told them at home. You never could keep a—" His voice broke.

"What about Nick?" Sheila insisted.

Jim shrugged. "While I was in the stacks looking for the earring, Cal came down and started working in his office. Brad was in the library, so I had to come out on the top floor. Nick nearly saw me," he repeated.

"Is that why you pushed me into the coat closet?"

He nodded and buried his face in his hands. "I'm sorry." He sounded so thoroughly miserable that she reached over and touched him gently. "It's okay, Jim. No harm done."

Aunt Mary was made of sterner stuff. "But I ask you again, young man: What about Evelyn Parsons?"

Jim seemed to shrink into himself. "I *had* to kill her. She had it figured out—that somebody faked Quint's voice on the phone." He turned to Peter and said bitterly, "Except she thought it was you, of course. Everybody always does." He picked away at the scab on his hand. By now it was open, and bleeding. His voice was almost a mumble. "She called here, and I took the call because I thought it was the camera store. Remember?"

He was looking at Todd. Todd nodded. "Yeah, Jim. I remember."

Peter pulled himself to his feet and went to Jim's side. "You don't have to talk anymore, Jimmy. We need to call a lawyer." Gently he cupped a thin shoulder in one hand and squeezed it again and again, the long, strong fingers saying more than words ever could.

But Jim was struck by a sudden thought. He looked up at Peter and said in a wondering voice, "That was so lucky. What if she had gotten you, instead?"

Peter clutched him tighter. "Oh, Jimmy..."

Jim interrupted. "You couldn't have changed her mind." He spoke as if arguing against something Peter had not said. "She said you needed to tell, and if you didn't, she would. I knew if she told you, you'd figure it out. That's why I killed her, Pete. But I used my scarf. I couldn't bear to do it with my hands." He considered his bony fingers, clenching and unclenching in his lap. Sheila averted her eyes. "I had to do it. You can see that, can't you, Pete?"

"Oh, Jimmy," Peter repeated in a hoarse whisper. Tears flooded his cheeks, and he made no attempt to brush them away.

With one fingertip Jim reached up and wonderingly touched a teardrop. "Don't cry, Peter." His voice was gentle as a child's. "Please don't cry for me." Peter bent his head with a muffled sob.

Jim's own head was proudly high. "I have something important to do with my life. My life was saved so I could do it. Mother always said so. Evelyn was a nobody, and she was going to get in the way. I couldn't let her." He looked over at Sheila. "You're not a nobody, but I couldn't let you, either."

She remembered the scarf tightening around her throat, but she also remembered something else. "But you were sorry about Evelyn, weren't you?"

He nodded. "When you said she could have cleared Quint... I never wanted *you* to go to jail, Quint. I was so afraid, when Sheila told me Evelyn could have cleared you—I was afraid you'd be convicted. I didn't know *what* to do." He shuddered, then his head dropped. "When did you know it was me, Sheila?"

She sighed. "Not for sure until yesterday, when just by chance David said 'Nae bother.' That's what the Scots say, Jim. When you called, you said 'Nae problem.' The accent was so good, I thought it had to be David—or Peter. But when David insisted, Peter admitted he was at the club the night Nick was pushed."

She gave Jim a sad smile. "Actually you'd been trying to tell us all along, hadn't you? That day when Todd and Brad went to identify the body, you didn't ask who it was they found. At the Community Dinner, you told me you'd worked in the radio station with the mimic, too. You told me about Melanie's purse catching under the seat of Quint's car—'Volvos eat purses,' you said. I even knew you only got sick after that call Friday morning. But I so badly wanted it to be somebody else." She leaned forward in her seat and prepared to rise. "Mr. Flannagan is downstairs. Shall we call him?"

"Wait!" When Dehaviland spoke, she was startled. He'd been so quiet she had almost forgotten him, a shadow beside the fire. Now he held up one manicured hand to detain her. "I think we need further discussion before bringing in the police precipitately. Certain aspects of this case bear heavily on Markham. You should have thought of that, Jim, before acting so rashly. But while the deaths of those young women are, of course, unfortunate, Jim *is* a Lucas, and one of our own."

He paused for emphasis. Aunt Mary raised one eyebrow. "You aren't about to suggest, are you, sir, that we keep this little matter to ourselves?"

The president's eyes flickered, and a dull red rose in his cheeks. "Of course not," he denied hastily. "We cannot condone murder. But it is regrettable that a young man of Jim's promise should suffer forever for two impetuous acts."

Aunt Mary regarded him steadily. "Such as breaking and concealing a valuable clock?" He did not reply, so she drew herself to her full height on the couch. "You did break that clock, did you not, Dr. Dehaviland?"

Frosty blue eyes met brown. His were full of astonishment. "What has the breaking of a clock to do with this issue, Miss Beaufort?"

She slid off the sofa and stood facing him on the hearth. "It has everything to do with the issue, sir." When Aunt Mary called the president 'sir,' Sheila noticed, it connoted anything but respect. "As the leader of this institution you set its moral tone. You have led Markham as if leaders were above moral laws, and that pattern is contagious. Both Stan and Jim have excused their behavior by citing a higher good they serve."

The president raised his bushy brows. "Ethics, my dear Miss Beaufort, are relative. Surely you must know that."

"The answer to that, sir, is: 'Given that all things are relative, which of them are true?' You have acted, and set the example for others to act, as if the good of the moment were the only good. That is not and can never be truth. Your students are responsible for their own actions, of course, but yours was the lead they followed."

She tilted her head and shook it reprovingly at him. "We older folks have a responsibility to set a good example. So I ask you again, Dr. Dehaviland: You did break that clock, didn't you?"

Dehaviland paused. Cal's growl reached him. "I'd like to know, too, John. Did you break it?"

The president gave an impatient nod. "Yes, then, I did. It was an accident, of course. I was working late so I could leave town the next day. In replacing a cup on the mantelpiece, I swept the clock to the floor." He flicked one hand to show how insignificant this confession was.

"And what did you do with it then?" Cal's voice was deep, compelling.

Dehaviland had the grace to look at the floor. "I, ah, took it with me when I left the building, and tossed it in a dumpster on my way home." He raised his eyes and spoke to the students. "As leader of this institute, I have greater concerns than a mantelpiece clock. If Nick hadn't called the police, I should have replaced the clock and no harm would have been done. His, ah, impetuosity placed me in an awkward position."

"And," Aunt Mary also addressed the students, "Evelyn Parsons was first sacrificed to get someone out of an awkward position."

Dehaviland flinched. His eyes became blue stones. "Miss Beaufort, I greatly resent your implication that the minor incident of a clock is in any way related to these two murders."

The wrinkles around her eyes became more intense. "All things in life are connected, sir. Especially these events. When you shifted blame for the clock onto Evelyn's shoulders, she went to her friend Melanie Forbes for comfort. While there, she overheard a telephone conversation which led, ultimately, to her death."

The president's face became rigid. "If you will excuse me," he said with icy courtesy, "I have important matters to attend to. I am sure your niece will see you out." He inclined his head to all in the room and walked to the door. With one hand on the knob, he turned. "Perhaps you had better see Mr. Flannagan, Jim. You and he seem to have things to discuss." He departed with what remained of his dignity.

David MacLean stood. "I'm going downstairs, lad. Shall I walk you down?" Jim pulled himself to his feet.

Peter made a move to follow, but Cal pushed him into the chair Jim had just vacated. "I'll go with them. You come later."

When they had gone, Peter doubled with pain, and sobs shook his long frame. Sheila reached out and touched his arm. He turned and looked at her through eyes full of tears. "What will they do to him?"

"I don't know. But he's going to need you."

He nodded, but seemed unable to think or move. Todd spoke his name, and Quint went to stand by him, holding one shoulder, but nothing reached him until Aunt Mary's husky voice said crisply, "Peter?" He raised his eyes to meet hers. "There may be questions you want to ask Mr. Flannagan in an informal setting. I have invited him to our home this evening for coffee about eight. Would you care to join us? You'd be more than welcome."

He shook his head. "Not this evening, thanks."

"Then you can come to dinner on another evening. But don't be alone this evening, dear."

He nodded and pulled himself to his feet. Automatically he drifted to the piano and struck three long, somber chords. Then he looked toward the door. "I just can't believe it. Jimmy..." He stumbled out.

After an uneasy, heavy moment, Quint and Todd began a conversation in low voices, punctuated by an occasional grunt from Brad. Sheila looked quizzically at her aunt. "So you have invited Mr. Flannagan over for the evening?" she murmured. "Did you not hear me invite David last night?"

Aunt Mary tilted her chin. "Of course, dear. But Mike may have some things he wants to discuss, don't you think?" She gave her niece a look she remembered from her childhood, a look that meant: Not in front of all these people, dear.

Sheila stood, drained. "Well, we can cross that bridge when we get to it." She raised her voice. "For now, does anybody want to eat dinner with today's lecturer? I have a feeling Dr. Dehaviland is going to try to get out of it, and I'm not up to being charming."

The students conferred silently, then Brad gave a Gallic shrug. "Since none of us have volunteered..."

"...it's going to have to be all of us," Quint finished for him.

Todd sighed. "Okay, but only for Sheila. And in memory, ma'am"—he bowed to Aunt Mary with a flourish—"of the way you stood up to Dr. D. Maybe over pizza, fellows, we can introduce that man to modern political thought."

Aunt Mary shook her head. "After that embarrassing lecture? The poor man deserves a good dinner, eaten in peace. You'll have to manage without me this evening, Sheila. I shall be back in time for a last cup of coffee with your guests."

Sheila felt her eyes bulging. "*You* are going to invite that man to dinner? And pay for the meal?"

Aunt Mary flicked an imaginary speck of dust from one sleeve. "Of course not, dear. Abraham invited me, while we were having coffee in the president's office."

She gave the younger men a sunny smile and rose. As one man, they leapt to their feet. Todd hurried to open the door for her. In the doorway she paused, swept them all with a regal gaze. "Good day, gentlemen. Are you coming, Sheila?"

Sheila paused in the door. "Peter's going to be needing you guys." They nodded.

As she followed Aunt Mary, their voices rose in chorus behind her. "Be seeing you."

D · A · T · E

WITH A DEAD

D O C T O R

T O N I · B R I L L

Midge Cohen's mother has fixed her up again. What would it hurt to meet this nice Jewish doctor, a urologist even, and give him a try, she insists.

But all Dr. Leon Skripnik wants from Midge, an erstwhile Russian scholar, is a translation of a letter he's received from the old country. To get rid of him she agrees to his request. The next morning, he's found dead.

"An engaging first novel. A warm, observant, breezy talent is evident here."

—*Kirkus Reviews*

COFFIN
UNDERGROUND
Gwendoline Butler

First Time in Paperback

FOR THE TWISTED AND TALENTED, MURDER IS A GAME

Scotland Yard Chief Superintendent John Coffin is properly skeptical of
the evil reputation of the house at No. 22, Church Row. True, the house
has seen violent death over the centuries. None of it suspicious. Until
now. Malcolm Kincaid, student. Bill Egan, recidivist. Terry Place, villain.
Edward, Irene and Nona Pitt, victims. Phyllis Henley, policewoman.
Why have they died?

Coffin suspects something more than a haunted house. He sees a human,
complex web of relationships, interlocking and interacting in a way he
can't yet fathom, and in which people get caught up and destroyed—as
they play into the game of a very clever killer.

*"...appealing hero...a gripping tale of sinister fantasy role-
playing and bloody murder, sure to be relished."*   *—Booklist*

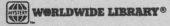